JASON FISCHER

VELOX
BOOKS

YOU'RE READING ANOTHER TERRIFYING COLLECTION FROM

**FOLLOW VELOX TO KEEP
THE NIGHTMARES COMING:**

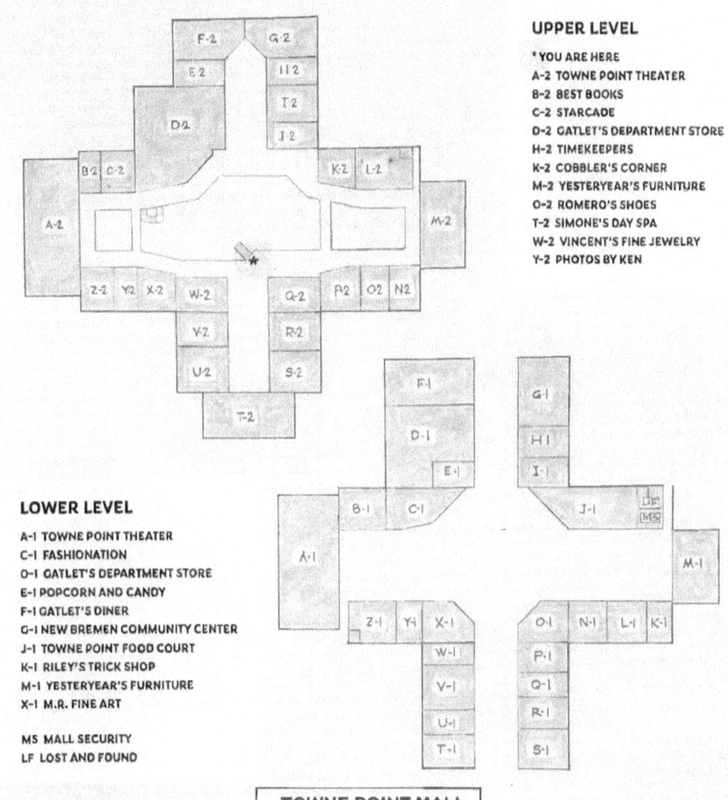

UPPER LEVEL

* YOU ARE HERE
A-2 TOWNE POINT THEATER
B-2 BEST BOOKS
C-2 STARCADE
D-2 GATLET'S DEPARTMENT STORE
H-2 TIMEKEEPERS
K-2 COBBLER'S CORNER
M-2 YESTERYEAR'S FURNITURE
O-2 ROMERO'S SHOES
T-2 SIMONE'S DAY SPA
W-2 VINCENT'S FINE JEWELRY
Y-2 PHOTOS BY KEN

LOWER LEVEL

A-1 TOWNE POINT THEATER
C-1 FASHIONATION
O-1 GATLET'S DEPARTMENT STORE
E-1 POPCORN AND CANDY
F-1 GATLET'S DINER
G-1 NEW BREMEN COMMUNITY CENTER
J-1 TOWNE POINT FOOD COURT
K-1 RILEY'S TRICK SHOP
M-1 YESTERYEAR'S FURNITURE
X-1 M.R. FINE ART

MS MALL SECURITY
LF LOST AND FOUND

TOWNE POINT MALL

CONTENTS

THE BIRTH

Nancy was terrified. Their baby had been born more than two hours ago, just a few rooms from the one they were locked in. Everything prior to the birth went well. The contractions began in the early morning, and they had a drama-free trip to the hospital without rushing. Though not painless, the labor was quick for a first child—or at least that was what the nurses kept reminding her as she dug in and pushed. But remembering how easy everything had been to this point did nothing to improve her state of mind.

"George, what do you think it is?" She stared desperately into her husband's eyes, searching for something hopeful. Shifting brought a sharp pain in her lower abdomen, the exhaustion dulling the intensity enough that she could ignore it.

Turning from the locked window, he looked at his wife. Over the sound of the pelting rain, he said, "I don't think it's anything." He folded his arms and looked over the top of his thick glasses.

"Then where's our baby? And why did it look... like that?" The high pitch of her voice betrayed her determination to stay in control. Rubbing her belly over the hospital gown, she longed to be near her child so she could close her eyes and finally relax. The void made her feel more alone than she ever had.

"You saw how many people were in the waiting room. They're swamped, that's all." He took a step closer to the bed.

The earnest look on his face irritated her. "But why did he look like that?!" Nancy demanded, cursing him under her breath. Ashamed of how quickly she could turn on the man she loved, she looked away from his questioning eyes to her toes, which were just visible through the edge of the sheet. They were painted the colors of the rainbow; the pedicure had been at her sister Patty's insistence. Her bohemian sibling had thought it would be cute to give the baby something nice to look at as he entered the world. When George saw Patty's work, he didn't hide his dislike. He called Patty a "hippy miscreant," asking why Nancy was always so willing to go along with everything her younger sister suggested. Nancy couldn't say for sure, but she felt their fight had induced the labor. It was hard to believe it all took place just this morning.

"I don't know. Maybe all babies look like that when they first come out, for certain people."

Taking a deep breath, the action bringing the same sharp hurt in her lower belly, she buried her anger, letting his ridiculous comment drop. She shifted in the bed, trying to relieve the pain that felt like someone was jabbing her insides with a sharp object. Patiently, she continued, "Why did she lock the door?"

Nancy knew the door was locked, but refused to let George try it. Not testing it made it somehow less real.

He smiled slowly, unconvincingly. "Let's wait ten more minutes. I'll go to the main desk and figure it out if nothing happens."

She nodded, trying to ignore the voice in her head. *What if you can't get out?* Quietly, they sat on the bed, watching the rain come down in sheets. It was nearly pitch-black outside. Within a minute, George was asleep, resting his head against her matted hair. He smelled like he usually did, of aftershave and the cheap strawberry shampoo they both used. Nancy gently eased her husband off her shoulder and lowered the bed slightly. Realizing this was her first quiet moment in the last few hours did not relieve the stress. Feeling the rhythm of George's breathing, she thought of all the words she wished she would have had the strength to say months ago when she could have changed everything. Remembering the look on his face when she had first told him about the pregnancy and asked if it was the right time for them. She swept away tears she had been holding in for far too long.

Twenty silent minutes later, the lock clicked, and the door opened. A very tall man who looked too old to still be practicing medicine entered. Groggily, Nancy peered around him, hoping to see her son looking normal in a bassinet. The door shut before she could see anything past his wrinkled lab coat. With a bright smile, he placed a manilla folder on the rolling feeding table at the end of the bed. "Good evening. I'm Dr. Cushing."

"Where's my baby?"

"He is in an observation room."

She did not like the way the man's eyes danced; the color seemed to change as he spoke. "Is he... okay?"

George awoke to squeeze her hand, and his concern added to her rapidly growing anxiety.

"He is in a... stable condition. We are just monitoring him because of something we saw in his bloodwork."

"I am telling you right now that if you don't stop beating around the bush, I will have a heart attack right here in this bed." She clutched the mattress with her free hand, making a fist.

"I perfectly understand. I have children of my own." He glanced at George, flashing a consoling smile, then pulled a chair near the bed. Seated, they were nearly at eye level. "Your son is safe, and his vitals are stable. We are still waiting for one more test." Not giving them a chance to interrupt, he continued, "We are very sorry to keep you waiting this long, but we were hoping to have confirmation one way or another before we approached you."

George interrupted, "You don't work here, do you? Where is our doctor?"

Glancing down at his badge, he said, "No, I was called in for my expertise in these matters."

The nurse entered at that moment. She was careful not to make eye contact with either of the parents. Walking across the room, she handed the doctor a round metallic object about eight inches in diameter. It had four equal pie-shaped components, each of a different color. The doctor took it, thanking her. She left quietly. The sound of the door latching shut pierced the awkward silence. Another click followed, almost too quiet to hear, as the deadbolt slid into place. George's eyes darted toward the door, but Nancy couldn't tell if he noticed this time or if his attention was drifting to something else.

The new parents sat on the bed, watching the doctor manipulate the apparatus. He arranged the components with dexterous fingers, forming them into two halves. Taking a vial from his lab coat, he placed it sideways into the round disk. Several seconds later, the components bubbled and changed into two distinct colors that neither George nor Nancy had ever seen before. By his expression, they immediately knew the result was negative.

Looking up, the doctor's face gave the impression that he had forgotten he wasn't alone. "Well, that was the last test." He stood, removing keys from his pocket. Unlocking the window and pushing it open, he turned absentmindedly and asked, "Do you mind if I smoke?"

Too anxious to speak, they both shook their heads.

Taking a strong drag, the man began. "You are right. I don't work here. To be accurate, I don't work here anymore. For many years, I have been called in on cases like this as a special consultant. Your son is a very rare child." A gust of wind tore through the room, splashing droplets of water onto the waxed floor. The man wiped the rain away with his coat sleeve, leaving a light flesh-colored stain on the thin material. "This will not be easy to hear, Mr. and Mrs. Carlson." He pushed the raindrops onto the vinyl floor with the tip of his finger before he continued. "Your son is shedding his skin."

Nancy let out a piercing laugh, drawing in the smoke she had craved for the last nine months. Quickly, she covered her mouth with both hands. Looking from her husband to the doctor, trying to hide the outburst, she mumbled, "What did you just say?"

"Your son is shedding his skin, and we had to place him in isolation to prevent infection."

"How?" Her insides ached. Feeling as if she could feel blood running through every vein, she hugged herself, wondering if something she had done had damaged her child.

Her husband spoke over her. "Is it a disease?"

"The actual truth is we don't know." He took a strong drag, inhaling half of the cigarette at once. "It may be genetic." He flicked the half-finished cigarette out the window, closing it tight. "Right now, there is no choice but to focus on his immediate health."

Nancy let out a sharp cry that filled the room. George hugged her tightly, as if he were trying to muffle the sound. Finally, when she was quiet, George looked at the elderly physician and asked, "So, what does this mean?" The new father chose his words carefully. "Long term?"

"Unfortunately, we are facing complete uncertainty here. I have only seen one case remotely similar to this in all my years."

Nancy said in a drowsy tone, "I want to see him." Her words were the opposite of her thoughts. All her fear and memories of time spent in hospitals with her dying mother were running through her mind, making it hard to think rationally. The memories were so strong she believed she could smell the disinfectant and her mother's body in the room where she had died. With her back tingling at the thought, she wanted to leave and somehow shake the overwhelming feeling that she didn't belong there. That the child was someone else's. Trying to fight the instinct, she let go of George's hand.

"I would strongly advise against that."

"You are going to let me see him now." Her voice was faint, but the panic just behind it scared her so deeply that she shivered.

She glanced at George, who was now standing, hoping for comfort, even if it was brief. His pleading look tried to silence her. She no longer cared about being a dutiful wife. Her timidness had got her here. She wasn't going to make the same mistake again.

"I will not decide for you, but believe me when I tell you this is a decision you will regret."

"Please take me to my child right now."

Dr. Cushing clicked the call button dangling from the bed. Almost instantly, the door opened, and he once again disappeared. Encouraged that he didn't lock it behind him, they strained to hear the instructions being given to the nurse. Moments later, she entered with a wheelchair and the doctor in tow. Although it wasn't necessary, they helped move Nancy from the bed to the padded chair. Once she was situated, he thanked the nurse, dismissing her. Before entering the hallway, he explained, "We have your boy in an incubator. With the condition of his... skin, we need to protect him from any foreign objects. I know you want to hold him, but for now, it is impossible."

The look on his face stopped Nancy from asking any questions. As the weary group slowly made its way out of the room, Nancy wanted to scream. But she knew this would halt their progress and that if she hesitated for even a second, she could never face her fear. She wrapped her arms around her midsection, doing her best to quiet her mind.

The ward was empty and oddly silent in the brightly lit hallway, except for the attending nurse and an overweight orderly she had not previously seen. Nancy gripped the arms of the chair, frightened and feeling very alone despite George being at her side. She focused on the room, trying to anchor her thoughts to something other than fear. The silence didn't slow her frantic mind. It was the middle of the night, but it seemed unlikely that there wouldn't be any noise on the floor that housed newborns. As she rolled past them, none of the hospital staff looked at her. They stared straight ahead into the nothingness of the blank wall. Their inattention made Nancy feel disconnected and ashamed, as if she had done something wrong.

It was a quick journey down the hallway. The rubber tires of the chair squeaked as they glided across the polished linoleum floor, the irritating rhythm playing on Nancy's already taut nerves. They finally stopped at the door labeled "Intensive"—there was a slot for other letters, but they were missing. Nancy expected a quick speech from the doctor. None was given. He walked to the door and looked through the small square glass panel, and his head of wild white hair obscured the view. Apparently satisfied that he was at the right place, the doctor typed a code into the pad, and they entered.

The room was so bright it almost glowed. Everything in the small space, including the ceiling, was illuminated in an intense shade of brilliant white. The room was nearly empty, apart from a gurney and a few formidable-looking machines covered in buttons, dials, and tubes that made slurping sounds as they pulsated. Plugged into the devices was the base of a medical bassinet, the top protected by a transparent dome so clean it was almost imperceptible. Before they were even through the threshold, a skeletal hand struck the dome. It slapped against the plastic, the fingers slightly probing in small arcs.

Once she saw the body the hand was attached to, Nancy immediately wished she had taken the doctor's advice. She pushed back onto the arms of the chair as if she were expecting a big drop on a roller coaster. Squirming, she looked at George. For the first time since they arrived, his stoic resolution had failed him. He stood slack-jawed, gaping.

Wondering how this could happen, she tried to focus on the machinery and keep her eyes off the child that she had just brought into this world. She tried to focus on the machinery surrounding them—anything was better than looking at what her love had created. Heaving, she brought both hands to her mouth, her flesh feeling like it was on fire. After two sharp breaths, she was confident she wasn't going to vomit. She jammed her hands onto the arms of the wheelchair, trying to slow down the sudden feeling everything was moving. There was a loud throbbing in her ears, making it difficult to hear George calling to her. Her eyes, as if possessed by something outside of her control, drifted back to the bassinet. Seeing the child, the sleep she had been holding off came over her, turning everything black.

A month later, the couple learned that all it takes to accept the impossible is experience. They had spoken to so many specialists that their words were becoming meaningless. Every meeting concluded with the admission that somehow, inexplicably, their child had developed into a living skeleton.

Nancy had been struggling to find excuses to avoid being in the same room with a child she found repulsive, to her own great shame. As soon as she could, she went back to work. Their need for money became the perfect excuse to hide. With George still in the final year of his architectural internship, she left him with no ammunition to argue with her about not being around.

They were currently sitting in a conference room in the hospital's administrative wing after listening to Dr. Graves from Baltimore make his passionate plea for why he was their best choice to be their son's caregiver. Nancy did not like the man. He had dyed hair and a long widow's peak, and the jet-black color created a severe contrast against his aging skin. She was instinctively distrustful of anyone who was not accepting of their own mortality.

Sitting at the conference table, Nancy adjusted the hem of her skirt. It was the first time since the birth that she had worn anything other than sweatpants or her work uniform. The dress made her feel whole, someone other than the woman to be pitied for her offspring. Over the last few weeks, it had felt like she had no history before her child was born. The entire experience was suffocating, causing her to question the choices that had led her here. As the self-examination intensified, the most significant question mark hovered over George. Even now, he was the same dull, quiet man, his expression and mood never changing. When they first met two years ago, his calm, intelligent demeanor had been intoxicating. His crooked smile always gave him the appearance of being in possession of some tremendous secret others would die to learn. She longed to be enveloped in that confidence once again. But with each passing day, she learned to hate the traits that first made her fall in love with him. Feeling frustrated and vulnerable, she turned to him. "What do you think?"

"I think they are trying to pressure us into making a decision that will only benefit them." He was writing notes on his pad. He didn't look up as he continued, "Not a single one of these people has any interest in doing anything other than getting a grant."

"Where does that leave us, then?" She may have been angry and hurt by him, but the doubts she had about his emotional support did not carry over to his intelligence.

Before he could respond, Dr. Cushing entered, holding a brown paper bag and a tray with coffee cups. He slid them across the table. "Thought you might need some fuel. You have been at it for, what?" He glanced at his watch. "Four hours now?"

Nancy smiled at the doctor. Growing up with no relatives other than her mother and younger sister, she was unaccustomed to having someone looking out for her. It was dangerous to feel that way toward a stranger, yet the usually cautious woman did not feel any apprehension. The man was neither charming nor charismatic, but she trusted him. She knew he felt the connection—she could see it in his smile.

She grabbed the coffee tray and responded. "It feels longer than that, but yes. Thank you for this."

"Don't mention it. By the look on your face, I'd guess you are no closer to a solution now than you were then?"

She took a sip from the hot coffee, shaking her head. She glanced at his hands and noticed that the tips of both index fingers were missing. She cringed, trying to hide her response. Ever since she had been very young, deformities of any kind always prompted an embarrassing irrational wave of fear in her. Amazed this was the first time she noticed this, she glanced at him, confident he didn't notice her reaction.

"I have met and compared notes with everyone as well. The hard truth here is that there is no scientific answer." He reached into his lab coat for a cigarette. Then, remembering where he was, he stared at the paper filter for a long second and placed it back into the pack. "Do you remember the first night when I told you I had only seen one case similar to this?"

George responded, "Yes." Slowly he lifted his head, pulling his focus from his notes for the first time.

"I have purposefully chosen not to share that case with you. Knowing what I know now, I feel it is time to explore other options."

"And what are those?" George grabbed his pen, ready to add to his already overflowing notebook.

"Before I get going, I must tell you that what I am about to say cannot leave this room. Are you both comfortable with that?"

The couple first looked at each other, then back at the doctor. Through a mouthful of bagel, she said, "Of course." George nodded.

"Thank you. I am sure you asked around about me, and I am sure you have heard I am what a lot of my more diplomatic peers would refer to as 'eccentric.' Early in my career, I took an interest in cases that baffled other doctors. My curiosity has not always been looked upon with favor by my colleagues. However, over a good deal of time, my reputation slowly grew, and I became accepted as the person to call if a case was... undefinable. It pains me to say it, but rarely did we come up with a solution in time. We learned a lot from them, and I like to believe that the knowledge helped others.

This kept me going to work long hours and facing the ridicule. I am giving you my brief history because I want you to believe me when I tell you that your son can live a long life with proper care."

Nancy opened her mouth, her eyes wide ovals.

He held up his hand in a kind gesture, asking for quiet. "There is a facility in the upper peninsula where patients are treated with unorthodox methods. It is a blending of psychology, metaphysics, and traditional care. I first met the facility's doctor when I was called in to consult on a newborn in Minnesota. The child was born with gills and scales. That was twenty years ago, and the boy is still alive today."

———

Eight months later, they made their way up winding hills through the densely wooded territory. They had to stop and consult two maps as they navigated the terrain to find the medical facility to which their son had been transferred. It had grown easy to ignore their son over the months since, but at his doctor's insistence, they had agreed to make the eight-hour trek. The longest discussion they had outside of their weekly calls with the doctor came when they finally agreed to name him. They settled on Chad, the decision equally joyless and utilitarian.

Silence had become the default between the couple. The long drive did nothing to change that. The scenery was at least breathtaking, making the situation slightly more tolerable. This was only the second time Nancy had ever left Illinois. The first was a road trip for her uncle's funeral, whom she had never met, during her final year of high school. As she watched the trees whip past her window, she wondered what living in a beautiful region would be like. It was a loaded thought. Why did she have to be born in such a dull place when beauty was so close? What force controlled such things as where and when you were born? Such thoughts felt meaningless and selfish as she was about to visit her son, but they consumed her.

Finally, the tiny sign that signaled the private road to Stratington Home appeared. The tree trunks were nearly close enough to touch, their many branches arching across the path, creating a natural tunnel. George slowed to a crawl. A branch scraped the vehicle every few seconds, letting out a high-pitched squeal. Nancy studied the trees, wishing she was the type who could identify what species they were. She knew that if she asked, George would know, but she didn't have the energy to do so, not after the first hour of their usual argument about Chad. George assumed that she, as his mother, should take sole responsibility for his care now that he was working. The car rose and fell, rocking along the uneven terrain, making her feel queasy.

They slowed almost to a stop as they approached a stream. Nancy thought she could hear the rushing of a waterfall in the distance. A makeshift bridge with no guardrails stood before them, and the narrow road grew tighter over the waterway. While her heart still pounded in her ears, George's reduction in speed at least steadied her stomach. The bridge creaked and popped as the tires inched along its length.

Once across, George put on the brights. The tree cover grew denser, obscuring the already waning light in a snarl of sticks like skeletal fingers. A massive stone structure stood in the clearing several hundred yards ahead. It had three floors and more windows than one could count. Nancy was struck by its similarity to the houses in the Hammer films she caught on late-night TV. They closed the distance, and the structure grew and grew, the sense of oppression it cast nearly palpable as it blotted out the sky. George rounded the circular drive and halted at the door.

The surrounding grounds were a collection of stone paths and moss-laden grass. It was much brighter in the clearing; Nancy welcomed the safety of the extra light. She took her husband's arm as they made their way up the stairs to the entrance. The door had an old-fashioned bell attached to a knotted rope. After pulling on it, they could hear the clanging on the other side of the massive door. It opened, and a slim woman in a cloth dress welcomed them. She moved the pile of papers from her right arm to her left, offering her hand to George. "You must be Mr. and Mrs. Carlson. I am Mrs. Iblis. Nice to finally meet you." She stepped aside, welcoming them in.

"I apologize for being late. We had a little trouble finding our way." George stepped back, allowing his wife through before he continued. "We called from the service station. I hope you received the message."

"No need to apologize. Nobody ever finds their way here on the first attempt. As these things happen, your unexpected delay accommodates the doctor's schedule. If you would follow me, I will take you to the office. Once we stop there, I can show you where you can freshen up."

They followed her through the expansive foyer, their footsteps echoing throughout the two-story room. The walls were covered floor to ceiling in a dark wood panel. There was no ornamentation of any kind except for a few wall sconces. By the look of them, they were electric, converted from gas, and oddly, they were the only illumination. Their soft glow was insufficient, creating awkward shadows. Nancy followed directly behind Mrs. Iblis. The woman smelled of bleach and flowery perfume. Somehow, the mixture was pleasing. They passed several dark rooms. Strangely, not all of them had windows, and the ones that did revealed furniture covered in sheets. The largest room had an enormous fish tank between two shutterless windows. Staring at the empty bubbling water was a fragile-looking girl in a dark dress. She turned and stared at Nancy. Her skin was gray, and she had a long nose with warts on it.

Finally, they entered what appeared to be the waiting room at the very end of the long hallway. Turning, their guide pointed at the couch. "Place your coats and purse over there. The restroom is just through that door."

Thanking her, Nancy took off her raincoat, grateful to remove it. The room was swelteringly warm. "When did you say the doctor would be available?"

"I would think it should be only a half hour."

Mrs. Iblis had a bright smile. Being in her office brought an unexpected, welcoming warmth.

The estimated half-hour became closer to an hour. The couple spent it drinking strong coffee and sitting on an uncomfortable couch. The nurse sat at her desk, pecking away at her typewriter, seemingly oblivious to her visitors. Staring at the clock, Nancy fought the urge to run. The images of her child's skeletal face danced in her mind to the point where she was becoming dizzy. George sat flipping through a magazine that was at least two years old, oblivious to the anxiety she was experiencing. Looking at Mrs. Iblis, she said, "How much longer do you think it will be?"

She kept typing, her heavily painted eyes never leaving the machine.

"Excuse me." Nancy's voice echoed loudly in the high-ceilinged room.

For the first time since she had sat down, Mrs. Iblis's eye and lip twitched in unison. "What is it?" Her tone was sharp, as if scolding a young child.

Nancy immediately wished she had remained silent. Just as she was about to speak, the doctor entered. He looked nothing like Nancy had expected. He was wearing a cheap dark suit that accentuated his athletic build. Curly blonde hair fell across his forehead, just touching his thick glasses. He removed them, placing them into his jacket pocket as he approached the couple. "My apologies for keeping you waiting. It is very nice to see you. I'm Dr. Ingram."

He leaned in much too close when he shook Nancy's hand. Feeling awkward, she slumped her shoulders, drawing into herself. The doctor didn't appear to notice her discomfort as he let her hand go and moved to George. Her husband, oblivious to such things, certainly didn't detect anything.

"Well then, let's step into my office." They followed the doctor, passing Mrs. Iblis, still hypnotically typing.

The room was large and disorderly. Haphazardly stacked books covered nearly every surface. Dr. Ingram sat at his desk and motioned for them to take a seat. He shuffled several stacks of paper around, settling on a wired notepad. "Thank you both for coming. As I mentioned on our last call, we have had some rather surprising results over the last few weeks, and I thought it would be best to share them with you face-to-face. Before I continue, I want to be sure that I am not giving you the wrong impression. Although we have had some possibly good news, this developmental treatment can take years."

"You have done your job, Doctor. We understand." George glanced at his wife.

"Well, let's get to it then. We have proven what we have suspected for some time now. Your son has no risk of infection, making it no longer necessary for him to live under a protective bubble."

"How can you be sure?" Nancy had a hard time making eye contact. She stared at his tie as she spoke.

"Once we were confident it was safe, we began slowly exposing him to multiple germs. It has gone so well that we feel he is ready to be removed from the plastic shell, hopefully permanently."

Nancy did not know how to absorb all of this. Dread enveloped the slight amount of joy she felt. After the first week at the hospital, the possibility of any normal relationship with her son no longer seemed conceivable. She felt humiliated, but she felt no maternal instinct. Any interaction now would be through a sense of obligation, which was the only reason she was sitting here. Filling the awkward silence, she timidly said, "Doctor, I don't know what to say."

"That is a perfectly normal reaction. I understand how disorienting this is, and I don't judge your reactions. You have been through more than any parent should ever be asked to endure."

George asked, "When do you plan to remove him?"

"With your permission, we could do it right now." The doctor leaned back in his chair, folding his arms. "I can give you some privacy if you want to discuss this alone."

George looked at his wife before responding, "I don't think that will be necessary. You handle his care, and if you feel it is safe, then you should proceed." He took out his notebook and continued, "What does this mean for his overall care?"

"We will continue the same path of introducing new stimuli and see how he reacts. If all goes as planned, we might send him home at some point."

Nancy did her best to contain her fear at the thought. Twitching slightly as she sat, listening to them talk, acting as if this was as simple as recovery from the flu, she wanted to scream. Was she the only one feeling terrorized by the baby made of bones locked away somewhere in this Gothic mansion? She turned to the doctor with glazed eyes as he described the comprehensive tests his staff was going to administer. Her face didn't show the faintest sign of the fear that was making her heart race.

Tugging roughly on her sleeve, George glared at her. "Nancy, are you ready?"

The doctor was standing at the end of the desk, smiling patiently. It was time to see her baby. Dr. Ingram led the way into a room filled with equipment that looked like it had come out of a science fiction movie. A bed was in the corner, next to a large window letting in moonlight. Sitting in the center was a long hose attached to what looked like a plastic doll dressed as a spaceman. Through the clear viewfinder where the face should be, Nancy saw the same eyes that had haunted her since their last meeting at the hospital. The tiny plastic suit swayed to organ music, reminding Nancy of the animatronic Christmas elves displayed in department store windows. Nancy clutched her stomach as waves of repulsion overcame her. Suddenly, she wanted to leave and never look back, but with George nudging her elbow, she edged closer to the display.

The doctor put on his glasses as he went to the bed. "Well, hello, Chad. You have some visitors to celebrate your big day." Dr. Ingram turned sideways and waved to the young couple, encouraging them to bend forward so they were at eye level. "Chad, this is your mother and father."

"He can't possibly understand any of this." She became aware her words were flittering and filled with anxious tension, although she fought to appear calm.

"We don't really know, Mrs. Carlson."

"I am sorry, really, I am. This is just so overwhelming." Nancy gave the fake smile that many years of waitressing in her youth had helped her to perfect. She looked around the room, feeling like the space was getting smaller. As her breathing became labored, she was aware of the smell of decay, conjuring memories of her mother's death room.

"It is absolutely fine. You don't have to apologize. If you two could please come closer, I will remove the protective covering." With nimble fingers, he removed the suit, undoing hidden fasteners. Within minutes, the doctor had the child free of the protective coating he had been in since birth.

Nancy stared at his tiny, gray, skeletal body, feeling like she was staring at some attraction in a carnival haunted house instead of a child born from her and George's love. Disgusted at herself, she found enough courage to hold his hand. The bony fingers were cold and sticky, slightly tugging as he stared forward, lightly swaying to the music, showing no recognition that anyone else was present.

After what felt like an hour, but in reality, was only a few minutes, the doctor completed his examination. Nancy was glad to let go of her son's hand. After scribbling notes onto a chart, the doctor said, "Nurse, please be sure to check his temperature every twenty minutes."

Nancy looked at the thermometer; it was room temperature. Following the doctor out of the room, they went back to the office.

"We are going to monitor him throughout the evening. If anything unexpected happens, we will contact you at the hotel."

In his calm way, George said, "Thank you, Doctor."

The doctor dug into his bottom desk drawer and brought out a patch of what looked like a shiny drop cloth and a glossy photo. The image was of a deflated suit that looked as if a man had shed his skin. It was flesh-colored and had cutouts for eyes, nostrils, and mouth. "With your permission, I intend to have Chad outfitted for a similar suit. There is no medical requirement for it other than to help him feel more comfortable in the real world as we begin slowly training him to take part in everyday activities."

George picked up the picture, making Nancy flinch. Handling the rubbery sample, she said, "And it would be made of this?"

"Yes. We will have hair woven into the scalp. We have several colors to choose from, and one is very close to Mrs. Carlson's."

Nancy just stared, trying to conjure a smile. After a brief conversation regarding care specifics, they returned to their hotel. That night in the cheap, unfamiliar room, she cried herself to sleep. She dreamed of running through the forest with her son chasing behind. His cold, skeletal fingers tried desperately to slow her down as he fought to keep up in his rubber suit.

***

Four years later, Nancy stood next to her sister in the foyer of their home in the woods, watching through the rain as the sedan made its way up the long driveway. The house belonged to George's employer, who was abroad for a year. As part of George's compensation for overseeing the design of the firm's most lucrative project at the time, Towne Point Mall, the largest mall in Illinois, they could live in the home.

Nancy wrapped her arms around herself against the chill of the summer rain. "You are sure you want to be here?"

"Please stop asking dumb questions."

"Patty, I am telling you, being around him is unsettling. I am just trying to prepare you for the shock. The suit is... hideous." Thinking of the permanent smile on the rubber face, her stomach tightened. She wished she'd had the strength to say no when Dr. Ingram suggested sending him home. George wouldn't back her up—not that it mattered to him. She wasn't surprised when he called that morning, saying he couldn't make it. It would've been easier to accept if she believed it was truly his work preventing him from being there, but she heard his secretary in the background of a restaurant.

Over the last year, he had taken to only coming home a few nights a week, spending his time in a hotel near the project to make the completion deadline.

Nancy no longer cared.

For her, it was just a matter of time before they had the talk. She knew she wouldn't initiate it, but would welcome it once it came. In her lonely moments, she practiced the conversation. She would picture George in his typical unchanging George way, calmly discussing the terms of their divorce as if describing the schematics of some building to an engineer. It was little consolation that she knew he would be fair and provide for both her and Chad. She would happily trade the security for a passionate argument.

Navigating the enormous car, Mrs. Iblis pulled into the open carport. Wearing an ill-fitting dress, she escorted Chad to the front entrance, her umbrella doing little to shield them from the driving rain. Nancy hurried them inside, hardly hiding her revulsion at the gleaming wet rubber child. He wore fitted slacks and a short-sleeved sweatshirt exposing his glossy arms. The matted hair on the top of his head matched the color of her hair. Drenched, the synthetic material allowed the captured rainwater to run down his latex mask, making the artificial skin glisten. Her son, showing no interest in his surroundings, stood staring forward, never looking up at his mother. Nancy was thankful for this; she had no desire to look into his eyes. Remembering her manners, she reached for the nurse's umbrella. The fabric spilled water across the marble floor. "So good to see you again, Mrs. Iblis. Let me get you a towel." The nurse smiled gratefully, adjusting the pin in her tightly bound hair.

Nancy glanced at her sister and saw the abject look of horror. She immediately felt selfish for subjecting her to their world. Nancy watched as her sister bent down, staring directly at her nephew.

"Hello, Chad. I am your aunt." She did not make physical contact with the rubber boy. Quickly standing straight again, she looked at the child's nurse curtly, saying, "It is nice to meet you. I'm Patricia."

"Hello. I'm Mrs. Iblis."

Nancy closed the oversized door. "How about we all settle down by the fire?"

Moments later, they were seated near the fireplace. They placed a blanket beneath Chad to protect the leather couch. Dispensing with the pleasantries of small talk, Mrs. Iblis reviewed the daily routine. Over the sound of rain pouring against the house, she explained that the boy only ate or slept once a week. However, they made it a point to keep him in the routine of lying down for eight hours at night. He spent his mornings listening to records. She had a box of his favorite albums in the trunk of her roadster. She knew they were his favorite because he would slowly rock to the sound of the organ music. In the afternoons, he learned different subjects as he listened to one of the staff read from encyclopedias. During the evenings, they encouraged him to roam the grounds, but if left unattended, he would not venture beyond his room.

When she finished her speech, she had a delighted look, as if she had just solved a great mystery. The rest of the time leading up to dinner was spent awkwardly showing their new guests around the home. Chad went willingly from room to room as long as he was pulled along, walking straight legged behind his family. As he walked, his suit slightly squeaked with each unnatural movement. Glancing back at her son, Nancy wondered if he wouldn't be better off without it.

That night, after Patricia went home, Nancy and the nurse put him to bed for his prescribed sleeping time. Afterward, over tea in the guest room made up for Mrs. Iblis, the women sat on the bed. Mrs. Iblis, in her slip, spoke in a more tender voice. "It is very good of you to do this."

"It is nice of you to say, but unnecessary. I *am* the boy's mother."

"Most would have nothing to do with the child if they were in the same situation."

"Well, everyone has a different sense of responsibility."

"It is remarkable that Chad has made it as far as he has. You really mustn't expect much from him."

"Honestly, I don't know what to expect or feel anymore."

"That's understandable, considering the circumstance."

She wanted to say so much more, feeling she finally had someone she could truly unburden herself to after all this time. Fighting the instinct, she asked, "How much time do you spend with him each day?"

"I am usually the one who reads to him in the afternoons and attends to his music sessions."

"Does he ever respond to you when you do?"

"No." Quickly, she added, "The only thing he responds to is music."

In a shaky voice, she asked what she had held in for so long. "How do you love someone who can never love you back?"

"You will learn to, over time."

The nurse's face was so sincere that Nancy could no longer hold in her tears. Mrs. Iblis hugged her. She felt vulnerable and foolish, gasping sobs that dampened the relative stranger's bare shoulder. "Please excuse me. I don't know what came over me."

"No need to apologize. Sometimes you just have to get it out."

With a sniffing nod, Nancy thanked the kind woman. As she made her way to the master bedroom, she stopped as she passed her son's door. It was open a crack, the hallway lighting illuminating a tiny sliver into the room. When she left Chad, per the nurse's instructions, he was lying in bed with a thin sheet covering him. The sheet was now on the floor, and her son sat at the edge of the bed, his rubber-encased feet not quite long enough to touch the shag carpeting. He sat deathly still, like a big ventriloquist dummy, staring at the wall with his permanently fixed bright red smile. Even in the near darkness, the painted face seemed to glow unnaturally. His eyes, the only natural part of his face, were dull and gray like a doll's. Nancy had decorated the room in a Western motif, with stenciled wallpaper displaying cowboys, wagon trains, horses, and teepees. She knew he was not staring at the decorations nor imagining shootouts with the wild cowboys, as she had hoped long ago. The thought grew more devastating when the realization came that he never would.

Their son's visits became more frequent as the seasons changed. Mrs. Iblis was no longer his only caretaker; Nancy would meet different staff members when she arrived to pick up her child. The drives were grueling, as she could no longer coax George away from his precious project to accompany her. Whatever sadness she had over their marriage ending was absorbed into her fear for their child.

The visits grew more complicated when she had several days with only her son in the enormous house surrounded by the woods. She would stare out of the wall of floor-to-ceiling windows, imagining that just behind the dense trees was a house half the size of hers. Inside the house, she lived out an alternate reality for her family, a reality in which their child had been born whole, and she and George were in love as she once believed they were. The fantasy was the only thing left to cling to. It was her sole motivation on those long days of positioning her son like a large doll in different rooms, hoping for some slight recognition that he wasn't the monster she believed him to be. The longing always brought guilt, but it never went away. On her darker days, the guilt became anger as she waited for some brief sign of life in him. Her desperate needs were never met. Except for his recognition of the awful organ music, she could not get him to look in her direction.

For today, she dressed him in slacks and a long-sleeved dress shirt; it was always easier when less of him was visible. They sat on the couch watching the *Clown Juggler*, a ridiculous cable access show that she, for no apparent reason, believed her son enjoyed. With the obnoxious "Happy, Happy, Trick or Treat, Trick or Treat" jingle playing, she saw the advertisement for Towne Point Mall. Her husband's project had finally opened last month and was now inviting shoppers to their indoor Halloween party. Touting free candy and games in each store, the jingle accompanied the announcer's rapid-fire delivery, summoning all the ghouls and goblins to come and celebrate this Saturday! Never in her life did Nancy believe in such things as precognition, but sitting there next to her rubber-encased child, she thought she had her first encounter. She moved closer to the foul-smelling rubber boy—most days she forgot to wash the suit, eager to avoid it—feeling that this weekend everything could change.

That early Saturday evening, her son wore two masks. With its cowling mouth and exaggerated eyebrows, the simple goblin mask covered his prosthetic face. The black hooded cloak concealed his rubber body. Under the anonymity of Halloween night, mother and son ventured out into the world beyond their home and into the mall of her husband's design.

Nancy clutched his gloved hand as they entered the glass vestibule. The activity of the mall overwhelmed her. The unexpected snow flurries had brought in all the frozen children from the neighboring streets. Surrounded by tiny witches, ghosts, and other ghoulies all clutching their multicolored sacks of candy, she pulled Chad down the tiled corridor, viewing the decorated stores that flanked them. At each entrance, tables overflowed with flyers and candy. Each trick-or-treat stand had the same decorative skirt advertising Mall Treats in black lettering curved around a bubbling cauldron. At each station, there were families standing in long lines, waiting to fill their treat bags. It was a madhouse; the children ran from store to store, their various intonations of "trick'r treat" echoing off the brick walls, temporarily displacing the organ music pumped through the speaker system. Behind each group trailed haggard-looking parents, desperately trying to keep up.

There was activity everywhere that Nancy looked. Compulsively, she glanced down at her son, worried about how he would react. He followed along wherever she pulled him, with no apparent interest in the kinetic world around him other than looking into the speakers in the ceiling, trying to find the source of the organ music. Fighting her disappointment, she continued, hoping tonight that all could change.

She came to the movie theater. Outside the ticket booth, below the enormous marquee, was a barrel filled with water and apples floating on the open surface. Nancy watched, somewhat concerned by the child in a witch's costume. Her head was submerged for a full minute, with no movement, as her group of friends whined about it being their turn. Looking around, all she saw were children with no parents. Nancy was just about to intervene when the child flung her head back, splashing water all over her friends, leaving a sizable puddle on the floor. The young witch removed the apple from her mouth, exposing a wide grin, holding her prize in the air.

Steering her son around the puddled water, she guided him to the candy table. At the end of the table, she grabbed one of the plastic treat bags, smiling at the young man tending to the candy. He was dressed in a plaid shirt with grayish paint all over his face to match the poster advertising a film about zombies in a hall behind him. Acting the part in exaggerated clumsy movements, he grabbed candy from the oversized bowl and handed it to Nancy. She tried to get Chad to hold the bag of treats with some effort. Pulling his arms forward, the plastic suit revealed itself from under the cloak. Quickly, she yanked it, looking from side to side to be sure that none of the other children had seen. After repeatedly letting the bag drop to the ground, she coaxed her son into holding the plastic bag at his side.

They made their way from store to store, collecting candy that would never be eaten. The displays that the mall put out in the interconnected corridors were impressive. Each vignette had its own unique theme. In front of the bookstore was a wicked display of a spider climbing down his web. For a second, Nancy thought Chad was interested until she brought him closer to the sign, and he just stood stock still as he always had.

Halfway through the mall, near the entrance to Gatlet's Department Store, she spotted a bench in a sunken section surrounded by cloth-covered benches. She took a seat, forcing Chad to sit beside her by tugging him down as she would a disobedient dog. Once he was in place, she thought she saw a flash of brightness in his eyes. With no one nearby, she raised his goblin mask. His head tilted slightly to the right, staring at her. Instinctively, she hugged him. As she pulled him tighter, she felt his thin arms wrapping fiercely around her small frame. It was so unexpected it almost made her jump. As they sat slowly swaying back and forth, she teared up, feeling what she had believed would always be impossible. Over her shoulder she heard, "That boy's costume is scary! He looks like a weirdo mannequin!"

It was a shout from a preteen girl passing by. The comment stopped her small group of friends, and they began to gawk and point. Nancy felt rage strong enough that she could have killed them. Staring daggers at them, her skin feeling as if it was on fire, they scurried away, giggling. Chad abruptly dropped his arms to his sides. Nancy eagerly clutched him, wrapping her arms around him tighter. Realizing he wouldn't hug her back, she pulled slowly away, the depression suppressing the anger. As she stared at his skeletal face, his look was once again vacant, like her heart. She wiped the running mascara beneath her eyes. Carefully, she put his goblin mask over his rubber face.

After composing herself, they made their way back down the long hallway. This side of the mall was a labyrinth of out-of-the-way stores in hidden corners. Everything smelled of popcorn as they passed a brightly decorated candy store. Near the counter was an odd man who looked as if he was wearing a wig. He was licking his finger as he stared at her. Over the organ music, she could hear him humming a strange tune. Swaying, his ridiculously round waistline thrust forward towards Nancy. She looked away, thinking she caught a glimpse of a pair of women's high-heeled shoes on his feet as she did so. Gripping Chad's bony hand, she quickly got out of his view, feeling as if she was going to be ill.

Walking further through the dark, meandering corridors, Nancy began questioning if coming to the mall had been the right choice. Considering leaving the fantasy that the mall would change him, she was surprised to see an escalator leading to the second floor. Until now, she was not even aware there was a second level. There were far fewer people on the west side, and there wasn't a single child in sight. The emptiness made the organ music echo across the corridors.

As she was about to turn back and leave, Chad began to enthusiastically pull her towards the mechanical stairway as they approached the escalator. Amazed by his interest, she followed quickly along. Having neither the experience nor dexterity to manage the moving contraption, he would have fallen if she wasn't holding his hand. She helped him mount the moving stairs. As they ascended upward, he braced himself, one arm on each rolling banister, his head looking straight down, staring at the metal grate. The organ music was noticeably louder the higher they got. When it was time to dismount, she put her hands under each arm and lifted him. Frantically, he wiggled in the air, pointing behind him, wanting to return. Nancy struggled to hold him in his slippery cloak. Wanting to keep him engaged, she turned, and they headed back down.

Somehow, as they made their way back to the first floor, it seemed darker. The shadows enveloped them. As the moving stairs got nearer to the ground level, Chad dove face first. Lying on the metal floor, he clutched at the grate. Nearly falling, she stepped over him to get to solid ground. Bending, she lifted him up. The instant she did, he threw a tantrum, flailing and twisting violently, his mask flying off. She could see the anger in his eyes. She put him down, and he immediately went back to the ground, his face inches away from where the stairs disappeared into the grated floor. He lay stock still as if mesmerized.

Nancy looked down the hallway, hoping no one was there to see Chad's exposed face. The dark corridor was empty, except for an exceptionally skinny man dressed as a cowboy in the distance. As soon as she looked his way, he tilted his large hat over his eyes and sauntered away.

She didn't want to interrupt her son, not when he was finally showing an interest in something, but as she saw how close he was to the moving stairs, she had to move him. Reluctantly, she wrapped her hands under his chest and lifted him. There was no protest. He simply went slack. As she placed him on his feet, he slowly turned and looked up at her, his mouth unmoving. Something inside her told her he was going to speak. As she waited, he lowered the hood from his cloak, revealing his prosthetic skin. The dim puck lights bounced off the fixed joyless smile glimmering in the reflected glow. Slowly, he raised his arms towards his mother, gesturing her to him. As she kneeled to embrace him, he pulled the treat bag over Nancy's head.

Shocked, she recoiled. Her movement only pulled him closer. As she tried to draw in a rapid breath, her mouth filled with plastic, gagging her, cutting off the air completely. Gasping, she frantically tried to stare through the thin material, making out only blurry shapes. Panicked, she struck her child, and the impact sent him reeling onto the moving escalator. Free of him, she ripped the bag from her head, gasping for air.

Immediately, she saw Chad's suit being chewed by the moving stairs. It drew him closer to its sharp jaws. The latex stretched as the metallic mouth mercilessly tore through his fake skin. Exposed fingertips desperately grasped out for his mother's help as the escalator's grate dragged him in.

Without hesitation, she grabbed him by the forearms, desperately pulling him. He dragged her closer in a tight embrace as she got a firm grip. Twisting, he fed Nancy to the metal teeth of the machine, forcing her hair between the jaws of unforgiving metal. Too shocked to scream, she stared up at her child's now exposed skeletal face as the stairway continued to churn, pulling her closer. Terror gripped her as she realized that all this time she had been right about her son. Feeling hundreds of pinpricks on her scalp, she grasped at her hair. Her wheezing tears stifled her scream.

"Please, no." She stared into the unblinking eye sockets of the now exposed skeletal face that appeared through the torn artificial flesh. Despite the pain, even as the machine devoured her long hair, then her flesh, ripping her scalp from her bone, she held him, hoping for some signs of life. As the darkness came over her, the realization that she would never have the warm moments she always dreamed of with her child stole her last bit of energy. Unable to hold on to him any longer, the mechanical teeth painfully gnawed away her humanity, leaving her to look like her son, who stood unmoving with his fixed stare.

———

It was hours before George was contacted about the gruesome death. He was told by a police officer—who looked as if he was barely out of high school—that the owner of a bookstore had found her minutes later as he was exiting after a long day's work. The metal grate had ripped her face from her skull, exposing it.

When he inquired about his son, the police did not know his child's whereabouts. For days, they searched every corner of the mall he had created and the surrounding area for the child in the rubber suit. After the cleanup, no one thought to look beneath the moving stairway. But if any mall patrons bothered to look at the bottom step, they would have seen his eyes staring up at them as he waited for next Halloween.

THE BOOKKEEPER

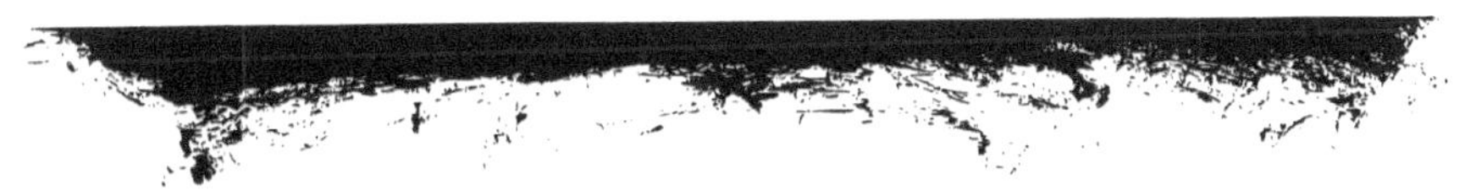

When Martin opened his used bookstore after leaving the world of trading and its narrow-minded ideology behind, he imagined he would be spending his days in intellectual conversations. Instead of arguing over the merits of finer literary works, however, he was currently negotiating the value of a twenty-year-old gardening book with Mrs. Johnson.

She was a regular of Best Books and Antiquities. Her weekly pilgrimage on the senior bus tour always brought a sale, but only after he made a healthy concession. Half listening as she pleaded her case, Martin found himself watching an odd man at the back of the hobby section. There was something about the man that Martin found disconcerting. As Mrs. Johnson's insistent tone increased, he tried to compose himself before speaking.

"I assure you, I appreciate your continued business, but you must understand there is very little markup on all of my merchandise."

"As I explained, I have a very limited budget."

Thinking of his grandmother, he stifled his chosen response and instead replied, "I will discount the book a dollar. That's the absolute best I can do."

The elderly woman, with a sly smile, pulled out her purse and started counting out change.

Martin wrote up the receipt and bagged *Gardening for Beginners*. Swiping the pile of change from the polished counter, Martin politely said, "I'll see you next week."

His insistent customer left with a brief nod, walking into the mall's main hallway. His attention turned to his only other patron. The man stood with his face inches away from the bookstand, slowly moving his head from left to right. Martin hadn't ever seen anyone so disproportionately configured in his life. All the man's significant girth was contained in his midsection, but his arms and legs were exceptionally gaunt. It gave him the appearance of a ballerina wearing a tutu. Wondering if his shape resulted from a medical condition or just unfortunate genetics, Martin exited the triangular counter behind which he spent most of his waking hours and approached him.

As he snaked through the mystery aisle filled with a healthy mixture of paperbacks and hardcovers that smelled of years gone by, his heart rate slowly increased. A reluctance to engage in confrontation was one of the main reasons he had taken the small fortune he had made in his previous life and opened the bookstore. Feeling the deeply buried emotions surface, Martin came to the hobby section, which was the largest mixture of books and peculiar antiques. "Can I help you, sir?"

"Perhaps you might. I was looking for a new hobby and found myself overwhelmed by the options before me." He let out a high-pitched laugh, staring with bulbous eyes at Martin. "Saying that out loud, it sounds ridiculous, doesn't it? How could you possibly know what hobby would capture my interest?" His smile revealed teeth so small they almost didn't seem real. "Are you the owner of this wonderful shop?"

The man's head reminded Martin of a giant softball. His skin was stretched so tightly it looked more like smooth rawhide than flesh. It didn't reveal a single blemish or pore. Accentuating an attempt to appear more youthful, the pear-shaped customer was wearing a small baseball cap exposing tufts of curly hair around the edges, the blonde locks looking clearly synthetic. Hiding his unease, Martin responded, "Yes, I am."

Not wanting to touch the man—Martin had the sense that if he did, it would lead to an odd infection—he neither offered him his hand nor gave his name.

"I love stores like this. The way you have everything displayed is so pleasant." Without taking his eyes off Martin, he grabbed a book off the shelf. Extending it inches from the bookkeeper's nose, he asked, "If I purchased this, would you happen to have a dummy amongst your antiques to go with it?"

The cover had an obnoxiously realistic ventriloquist dummy smiling beneath the title *Ventriloquism by Victor*. This close, he could smell the mustiness of the book, as well as his customer's fingers. The smell reminded him of the outhouse that used to be behind his uncle's fishing shack. Taking a step back, Martin quietly said, "No, I definitely do not."

"That's a shame. I think I would quite enjoy having a tiny wooden friend." The peculiar man parted his lips further, revealing more uneven, stained teeth.

Wanting the man out of his bookstore but not quite up to asking him to leave, Martin retreated. "Well, let me know if you have any other questions." Not waiting for a response, he walked back to his counter.

Over the next ten minutes, not a single customer entered the store. Such droughts were not uncommon at this time of day. Not only was the store empty, but as he looked down the mall concourse, he didn't see any activity in the other stores. Martin did his best to make himself look busy, rearranging the books behind his counter. Every time he would look back to the hobby section, his rotund customer would be squarely staring at Martin with his hand in his pocket. The silk material of his slacks was remarkably thin, making it easy to see that he was flexing his fingers in a rhythmic stroking motion. Quickly, the shopkeeper diverted his attention back to his made-up task.

With his back turned, he couldn't stop himself from imagining the man sneaking up behind and assaulting him. Although ridiculous, he couldn't shake the anxiety. With thoughts of the man's breath on the back of his neck, Martin contemplated calling mall security, as he was well past the concern of offending a customer. As he glanced at the phone, wondering how to say he wanted someone removed because he was giving Martin the creeps, the man, as if he could read Martin's thoughts, approached the counter. He held a thin book in his hand. Martin looked at the cover. It was a book on juggling. The softcover binding had netting attached to the bottom cover, with balls nestled inside. "Will that be cash or charge?"

With an almost lyrical tone, the odd man smiled and said, "Cash."

Martin watched the man removing his wallet. It was a child's wallet with a large cowboy leaning against a post stenciled into the fake leather cover. Ignoring the incongruence, he replied, "That will be eight dollars even, please."

The man removed the money. In a flash, Martin caught a glimpse of black-and-white photos inside the fold of the wallet. The images of the mannequin-like dolls made him sick to his stomach. As he grasped the bills, his customer purposely slid his index finger across the back of Martin's hand, making him flinch. Martin shoved the money into the register and wrote out the receipt. Refusing to make contact with the man again, he slid the bag across the counter.

The pear-shaped customer grabbed it. "Thank you. You have a lovely store. I'll be sure to tell my friends."

Martin watched the man leave the store and saunter along the mall's long hallway, his waist swaying in an exaggerated motion with each small step. Wanting to be sure he had exited the mall, the bookkeeper walked into the mall concourse. Standing in front of the storefront of Popcorn and Pop, he felt relief as the odd man disappeared through the glass doors of the west entrance. Feeling exhausted, Martin reentered his store, wishing it was time to go home to play with the kids and walk the dog.

That evening, after the chaos of getting the twins to bed, Martin kissed his wife, Margaret, and promised to help with the dishes as soon as he got back from his walk. They both knew his walk was an excuse for him to smoke his cigar, a replaced habit after he quit cigarettes, but neither spoiled the vice by discussing it. These shared understandings were the cornerstone of their marriage, each learning to take as much as they gave.

It was unbelievably hot, even for the middle of the summer in the Illinois suburb. As he made his way down the driveway, the humidity felt like walking through a wave of steam. Twilight was just settling over the neighborhood as he cut across his neighbor's prized lawn to the walking path. Smelling fertilizer and the dampness from the short rainstorm that had just swept through, Martin walked under the tree canopy and onto the asphalt trail.

Lighting his cigar, he heard the sounds of bullfrogs disrupting the steady cadence of crickets' rhythmic chirping. Martin imagined thousands of them just beyond the darkness. As he puffed vigorously, the smoke mixed with the already heavy air, creating a cloud that hung lazily around him. Lightheaded from the first drag, Martin saw a moving light off in the distance. It was hard to determine the source, as it was traveling in an erratic oblong circle several feet off the ground. Small beams arched, rose, and fell at a hypnotic pace. Slowly, Martin realized that the glowing lights were balls being juggled. Thinking of the man from the store brought a wave of panic.

Martin froze as he watched the balls rise higher. With only moonlight illuminating the path, the juggler appeared as a large, indistinguishable shape. After almost a full minute of watching the eerie light show, he heard a high-pitched giggling. The instinct to run shot adrenaline through him. He drew in a deep breath, trying to corral his wild thoughts. It felt like his mind was moving in a hundred directions. Finally, the need to know if this was the man from earlier won out. With trembling fingers, he reached for his lighter, quickly striking it. The flame did nothing to illuminate the darkened path beyond a few feet in front of him.

Realizing the spinning balls were getting closer, Martin, thinking of his family, walked briskly toward the shape. As he got nearer, the juggler's shadow appeared to be a long, skinny image. Suddenly, the juggling stopped, and the balls disappeared until only one was visible. The black shape thrust it to the ground and then stomped on it, mashing it into the path. Focusing on the afterglow of the juggler's ball, Martin did not see the shape saunter off into the woods.

Walking briskly, Martin stared at the glowing goo that was smeared on the ground. Standing over it, he rubbed it with the tip of his shoe. Squinting, he scanned the thick woods, trying to find the man. All he saw were the shadowy outlines of the forest. Slowly, he knelt and picked up the remnants of the ball. On the flattened end, he saw a crude drawing of a dog's face and, in marker beneath the picture, the word DOG. The lettering was childlike. Not knowing what to make of it, he suddenly felt it was important to keep the ruined toy.

Staring into the darkness, he thought of the odd man he encountered earlier. Quickly, dread filled him, feeling like liquid drowning his heart. He snubbed out his cigar and headed back down the path to his house with the overwhelming feeling that he needed to protect his family.

As he jogged back, the former accountant tried to calculate the odds that the night juggler he had just encountered was the same as the creep who had been in his store earlier. Thinking in his normal pragmatic way helped to somewhat calm his nerves, the focus being pulled from the physical sensations. Martin walked up the drive and entered through the back gate. Before he went in, he called Harry, feeling it would be best to let him sleep inside tonight. After several unanswered calls, he gave up, hoping the dog had just snuck off for his rendezvous with the neighbor's dachshund.

That night, after settling the chores, he double-checked every window and door. He knew he had to choose his words carefully. Telling Margaret what he witnessed felt like an overreaction, but as the night wore on and their dog still did not return, his anxiety was growing. Watching her slather lotion on her bare legs, he said, "Anything interesting happen today?"

"Well, if getting gum out of Tobi's hair is considered interesting, then yes?"

"Did he fall asleep with it in his mouth again?"

"Oh no. Your darling daughter put it there when he knocked down her kitchen fort." She looked up and grinned. "Remember when we thought having twins would be the best? Give the children constant entertainment?" She stuck her tongue out as she mimed choking herself. "Sometimes, I'd just like to ship them off to Grandma's for the day."

"Or month."

She let out a grunt of a laugh, tossing her hair scrunchy at him. "You're terrible!"

The way she smiled made her look like she did back when they were in high school. It was her full Margaret smile. Thinking of the days when mortgages, health care, and obtrusive customers didn't take up all his time, a wave of sadness came over him. "Just joking."

"Sure!"

"Has anyone been around lately?"

"Like who?!"

"Salespeople." He quickly filled in the thought, seeing the concern in her eyes. Her paranoia could be turned on much easier than it could be shut off. "When I pulled into the neighborhood, I saw some folks going door to door."

"No, nothing like that."

Watching her switch from lotion to inspecting her cuticles, he wanted to describe the man. He knew how she would react. Searching for a good way to do it, he finally saw no reason to get her riled up over something that might have just been a coincidence. From the bed, he glanced out the window. It was so dark he couldn't even see the doghouse. He fought the urge to go back outside, not wanting to give the anxiety room to grow.

Helping to decide, Margaret turned off the light and crawled into bed. As she had done every night since they were married eight years ago, she leaned over and pecked him on the forehead, saying, "I love you, darling."

With the lights off as he lay in bed, he was certain he saw a ventriloquist's dummy staring at him through the crack of the closet door.

He finally fell asleep.

The next morning, his children were watching their cartoons in the television nook. Martin, no longer being able to hold in the anxiety while sipping coffee, anxiously asked his wife, "Did you let Harry out?"

Margaret squinted at him as she worked over a bowl of meat and spices. "What're you talking about?"

"Harry. Did you let him out back?"

"Are you feeling all right?"

"Yes, why?"

"Because you are saying silly things." She looked up, flipping her hair back with a bemused half smile. "Who's... Harry?"

"Look, I'm in no mood for games!"

In unison, his golden-haired children looked at their father, annoyed by the interruption from the blue creatures that were hopping around mushroom houses. Looking from them and back to his wife, her expression had turned from amused interest into a focused stare. Glaring at her wrinkled forehead, Martin forced a smile as he said gently, "Sorry, guys." He walked up to Margaret. "I didn't sleep well last night. I'm sorry I yelled, but please come off it. Did you put the dog out this morning?"

Extracting her filthy hands from the mix, she stared directly at him and said, "Okay. You're really worrying me now. Why are you talking about a dog?"

"Why wouldn't I?"

"Because... we don't have a dog."

He cocked his head to the side, examining her. "Oh, sorry, I must have forgotten about that. Well, if we don't have a dog, why have we been buying so much food for him then?" He yanked open the pantry door. Pulling the boxes from the shelf, he frantically rifled through the various cans and other food, coming up empty. Quickly, he looked under the overhang of the counter. The feeding bowl was also missing. Trying to process why anyone would create such an elaborate practical joke, he looked back at her. Margaret stared at her husband, and Martin, for the first time in his life, thought she appeared authentically afraid of him.

"Honey, I think you should lie down. You don't look well."

Pointing his finger in the air for emphasis, he nearly shouted, "The doghouse!" He walked around the remnants of the blanket fort and went through the sliding glass door. Making his way to the side of the house, he quickly discovered that the doghouse was gone. He heard the swoosh of the back door, and Margret, wearing only her Stones T-shirt with big red lips, walked up to him. The wind was whipping her hair over her face.

"You're really scaring me."

"You think you're scared? Where the hell is our dog and his house?" He looked down at the grass in the exact area where he remembered the concrete pad having been located. With a shocked expression, he quickly patted down the grass with his sock, thinking of the weekend he had spent building it. The memory was so vivid his hand went to his back, remembering the soreness over the physical labor.

"We don't have a dog, Martin. We've never even talked about getting one." Margaret spoke slowly as if she was talking to their children.

"So, you're telling me that two months ago, I didn't bring home the stray that I found in the service corridor of the mall? We haven't been playing with him every night? Elizabeth didn't name him Harry after that dumb movie with the hairy monster we took them to?"

Exasperated, she responded, "No."

"Well, we'll see what the kids have to say about that, then!" As he spun to head back in, she grabbed the back of the shirt of his pajamas. Startled, he turned.

"I don't know what's going on with you, but I'll not allow you to bring the kids into this."

Martin saw the fear in her face. He finally felt that whatever was happening, Margaret had nothing to do with it. Suddenly, his clothes felt heavy, and it was becoming difficult to breathe. He leaned forward to hug her, and she took a step back. "I'm sorry, I must not be fully awake, but I really believed for a minute we had a dog." Feeling an overwhelming urge to take back the entire conversation, he quickly added, "It's okay, I'm better now." He wanted to believe the lie more than he had ever wanted to believe anything in his life. The image of the dog running and digging up the yard floated in his mind as if his memories were intentionally taunting him.

Margaret stepped closer and hugged Martin. Dripping her tears into his shoulder, she said, "I thought moments like this were over when you quit that horrible job. Do you promise you're better?" Margaret pulled her head back, staring at him with an almost childlike look of confusion. "Are you really just tired? You're truly okay?"

He caressed her back, feeling the silkiness of her long hair. "Yes, I promise." He immediately felt guilty for lying to her. As he squeezed her, he knew he had to get away from them. He felt he was at the center of whatever was happening, and the only way to keep them safe was to leave.

Later that day, with a store full of customers, Martin saw the juggler again in the mall hallway. In the sunken conversation area, the odd man sat alone on the bench. As soon as they made eye contact, the portly man reached slowly into his jacket pocket, pulled out the toys, and began juggling. The balls moved so slowly it was as if there was no gravity weighing them down.

There were several other mall patrons walking by, but none of them seemed to notice the macabre performance. Martin watched, ashamed of his hesitation to confront the man, as the corridor slowly cleared. Alone now, the man caught all the balls in one hand and reached for what appeared to be a white fabric bag. Expecting him to put the toys away, Martin was astonished to watch him pull the bag over his face. Painted in crude colors were lips and a nose, and surrounding the cutouts for eyes were large irregular circles. Through the burlap, he winked.

As he resumed juggling, the mask bobbed up and down, tracing the flight of the balls. Martin's throat was so dry it hurt to swallow. Frozen, he watched the balls fly in a perfectly repetitive circle. Moments later, with two young women approaching, the juggler caught the balls in one hand and pulled off the mask. The swift motion dislodged the curly wig, exposing erratic patches of hair amongst the baldness. As soon as the other shoppers were past him, he resumed his show, smiling in Martin's direction. Martin quickly realized this lunatic was putting on a special performance just for him. Finding strength, he ran out into the hallway to confront the juggler.

In an instant, the odd man was up, moving faster than should be possible for someone of his size, leaving the balls scattered about the floor. Martin was gaining ground as he ran toward the juggler when suddenly, a teenager on roller skates flew out of Popcorn and Pop, colliding with him. Athletically, he gripped the girl around the waist and twisted her, so he didn't fall directly on her, causing him to slam against the hard floor. He quickly disentangled himself and resumed his pursuit, running down the main corridor. It was too late. The man was no longer in sight. Dashing to the glass vestibule at the end of the long hallway, Martin peered out into the parking lot. There was no sign of him, just rows and rows of cars.

He walked back to the roller girl and asked, "Are you alright?"

"Fine." She looked down at her scraped elbow. "Why are you running around like that?"

"Why are you roller-skating in the mall?!"

She ignored the question with a shrug and an eye roll. "Hey, mister, are those yours?" She was pointing at the balls lying on the red carpeting of the sunken seating area. He walked parallel with the benches built into the waist-high brick walls and picked them up. Examining them, he found each one had a drawing in marker and captioned beneath Father, Mother, Son, Daughter, and Dog. The ball with the dog on it was slightly larger than the others, as if it wasn't part of the original set, and had a large black X through it.

His blood seemed to flow faster when he noticed the "daughter" ball was slightly dented, looking like a crescent moon. He pressed the ball carefully between his hands to reform its shape. Slowly, he walked back to his store, carefully handling the juggler's toys. Going down the classic section of the bookstore's long aisle, he entered his office. Not knowing what else to do, he locked them in his safe.

When he got back to the front desk, he immediately called Margaret. The call was answered with loud screaming in the background. Fighting panic, he said, "Honey, what's wrong?"

"Speak up, I can't hear you?"

"What's wrong with Elizabeth?"

"Oh... she climbed onto the back of the couch and then went straight down on her noggin. It was pretty scary for a second. I guess it was my panic, but when I first scooped her up, I could have sworn her head was caved in."

Martin could still feel the ball popping back in place in his palm, turning his stomach.

"Anyway, she's fine now. Just a slight bump. Isn't that right, pumpkin?" The sound of crying was slowly becoming convulsive sniffling—a telltale sign he'd learned that the injury wasn't serious.

Martin wanted to yell, "Don't leave the house," but quickly wondered what good that would do. Panic made its way through him as he thought of his daughter and how close she came to whatever fate Harry had experienced. "I'll let you take care of her then. I'm glad she's okay."

"Honey, why'd you call in the first place?"

"Just wanted to... check in. I really have to go now. Goodbye." He slammed the phone down, his legs feeling like they could no longer support him.

The rest of the afternoon was filled with tension as Martin tried to figure out a way to keep his family safe. He welcomed the intermittent thoughts that he was losing his grip on reality. It was the only explanation that his overtaxed mind could accept. All that he truly knew was that he was terrified and had an overwhelming feeling that if he left the store, something awful would happen.

Fatigue was making it hard to think. Checking his watch, he saw it was closing time. He walked to the front of the store and placed his key into the electronic lock that activated the metal rolling gate. As it slowly closed, he stared into the vast empty hallway of the mall, listening to the piped-in organ music. With a jolt, the gate contacted the tile floor. He slipped the locks into place, then went to the control panel behind the register and turned off the lights.

In the distance, he heard a high-pitched voice singing, "Which is next? Which is next?"

Looking down the rows of books, he saw the glowing balls rise and fall in their imperfect arc. The black shape behind them slowly bobbed down the middle of the display shelves, the large waistline swinging back and forth, nearly touching the books as he got closer to the front of the store. Martin walked backward with his heart pounding in his ears until he found himself pinned against the metal gate. He could feel the rigid, serrated slats pressed up against his back as he frantically tried to create more room between him and the man coming his way.

"Which is next? Which is next?" With each slow, meandering step, the light of the mall revealed more of the crudely painted cloth face. The crooked features distorted any humanity other than piercing eyes.

Martin watched the fixed fabric smile. The painted blood-red lips made it impossible to tell where they ended, and flesh began. Martin could imagine those lips caressing things they shouldn't. The thought nearly made him vomit.

He pushed with all his might against the unforgiving gate. "Help!" The word came out in a choked whisper, faintly echoing into the empty mall corridor.

The juggler slowly shook his head, saying, "No, no," stomping his foot mockingly against the hard floor.

"Please, leave me alone."

With a clown-like skip, the juggler caught all the balls in one hand, singing loudly. "Which is next? Which is next?" The mask danced along the shadows of the room, making it appear animated.

As if he was performing in a circus, he hummed a strange tune, twirling his free hand, and threw the balls higher into the air. Each glowing ball now nearly came into contact with the paneled ceiling. He slowed the balls as he tossed them, making the images on them perfectly visible.

Martin watched the crudely drawn faces of his children flash before his eyes. He wanted to run and tackle the man but couldn't find the strength. Instead, he stood frozen, wishing he could be anywhere but here.

Quickly, the juggler darted his feet out in a little dance. He giggled in a melodically humorless way. The noise echoed against the bookcases. "Which is next? Which is next? Time to take the test!" He skillfully plucked a single ball from the air and violently threw it against the vinyl floor. Letting the rest of them fall to the ground, the masked man cackled as he watched the single ball bounce in front of him. Raising his shoe slowly, he settled the ball onto the floor, and then, with a theatrical twist, crushed the obscene toy.

As blackness came over everything, Martin's last thought was what would become of his children.

The rickety bus made its stop in front of Towne Point Mall. Mrs. Johnson was the first to exit the aging vehicle. With a smile on her face, she entered the glass vestibule, welcoming a cool blast of air conditioning after the sweltering ride across town. As she made her way down the corridor, she passed several groups of teenagers milling about. She was wondering if her daughter let her grandchildren go out looking like streetwalkers. Mrs. Johnson considered herself progressive, but how did any of these girls expect to find a husband with their multicolored hair and clothes that were too tight? Thinking of her grandchildren reminded her that she was expecting to hear from her daughter—if she wasn't too cheap to make the long-distance call. It was, after all, her turn. Mrs. Johnson couldn't be expected to pay for all her calls, not with the tight budget she was on. If she did, she wouldn't be able to take her weekly shopping trips, and they were all she had to look forward to.

Turning the corner, she came to a day spa. She stood momentarily confused. She could have sworn that there used to be a bookstore in this very spot. Without giving it much thought, she looked into the waiting area and saw a portly gentleman sitting on a very modern-looking couch. Noticing her, he removed his ball cap and nodded, smiling. Something about his gaze made her shuffle away quickly.

FASHIONATION

Munir was inches from the closed-circuit television screen, squinting at the blurry image of his clothing store in disbelief. Rewinding for the fourth time, he watched the store he had just taken over go from empty to full in less than a second.

In disbelief, he walked back along the aisle, staring at merchandise he had not purchased, knowing something was wrong. Beyond the unexplainable appearance, the apparel was like nothing he had seen.

Grabbing the closest sweater, he rubbed his fingers against the dense fabric, inspecting the material. The quality was exceptional. There were no telltale signs that the sweater was mass-produced. Every stitch and pleat appeared to be hand sewn. Inside the collar was a private label, written in a foreign language, the umlaut making him think it was from Germany. All the lettering, including the price tags, was written in meticulous calligraphy.

He went to the phone on his makeshift desk, taking a deep breath to clear out the rising frustration. Dialing Lance Hill, the mall's manager, his eyes swept over the expansive space. The weight of the responsibility he had just taken on hit him hard. Thinking of his father and his many days selling clothing and other goods at flea markets to customers who treated him like a toy to be played with, he tried to understand what was happening. For the hundredth time since he entered the store this morning, Munir questioned his decision to move his tiny store to the mall. After several rings, the call went to voicemail.

"This is Munir Razen, your newest tenant in the upper atrium. I own Fashionation. Can you please call me?" He hesitated, then added, "I believe one of the other store's merchandise was delivered to me in error."

He paused, wanting to add, *I would really like to know how a mall with rent this high could not have prevented this.* Instead, he hit end. Conflict was not in his nature. Pleasing others always won out against any such urges. A lifetime of feeling like he owed someone for being in this country always suppressed any righteous outrage that might be nascent.

Behind him, he heard the chime of the service door opening. Looking down the long aisles, he saw his wife and his other reason for living walking past the wall of mirrors.

Claire, his six-year-old daughter, was dragging her backpack full of toys behind her. Her pigtails bounced with each step. When she saw him, her eyes lit up as she ran down the threadbare carpet.

She almost tripped just before she made it to him. Gripping her under her arms as he lifted her, he said, "Claire Bear, please be careful when you run."

"Okay, Daddy."

Wendy caught up, stopping a few feet short of him. "When did you order all of this?" She didn't even glance in his direction. Instead, she was thumbing through the new merchandise, inspecting it. "I thought we would use the inventory from your old store first. This had to cost a fortune!"

"I didn't." Grunting, he shifted his daughter to his side as he began walking toward the back of the store. "I don't know what to say, but somehow, this delivery company made their way here last night." He left out what he saw on the surveillance tape. His mind was moving too fast, making him unwilling to worry his wife over something he couldn't understand. Reasoning that he was protecting her somewhat relieved the guilt he felt for lying.

"You're kidding! What a riot!"

"I wouldn't say delaying the grand opening is a riot, dear."

"Why'd you think that would happen?"

"Where are we going to put our clothes now? We have nowhere to store this stuff. If we don't find out who this belongs to today and get it out, we're sunk."

"Well then, we'll have to do just that."

As they entered the back storage room, Munir put Claire down. She ran to the table and chairs that held the closed-circuit television and the video equipment and instantly began turning dials.

Staring at the static screen, he fought the impulse to pull her away. Watching the video had twisted his nerves. He knew what he saw had to be an odd glitch, yet he couldn't dismiss the anxiety when he thought of the video and the clothing appearing from thin air. "Hey, don't do that."

"Come on, Daddy, it's fun!"

"Claire, I said no."

Wendy dumped the contents of her daughter's backpack onto the table, spilling dolls, and coloring books out. "So, what are we going to do?"

"Do you have the number of the former owner? What was her name, Francis?"

"Yes, somewhere." She dug through her purse for close to a minute, finally producing a crumpled piece of paper. "Here you go."

Munir walked to the phone and punched in the number. In between the bell, he heard a faint scratching noise. Watching his daughter turn on the TV monitor, he was surprised by her giggling as she put her tiny hand over her mouth. Claire said loudly in the background, "Look at those funny guys!"

Wendy leaned her head to the side, staring at the screen. "What're you talking about?"

"The little guys in the store."

Munir looked at the tabletop, searching for the surveillance tape. The video he had watched earlier was missing. Hanging up, he walked to the table. Claire had started the video last night. The timestamp displayed four minutes before the merchandise appeared. It was exactly where he had rewound it to. "What are you talking about, honey?"

She pointed with her chubby finger in the center aisle on the screen. "Those funny little guys. They are working hard."

"What are you seeing exac—"

Wendy spoke loudly over him. "Honey! Let's do some coloring now."

Munir stared questioningly with arched eyebrows.

Wendy flicked off the TV and put a coloring book in front of her. With a fake whine, Claire grabbed her crayon and started furiously filling in the page, humming the tune to the Battle Hymn of the Republic as she worked.

She had been humming the song for several weeks after saying she had met a soldier in her room who taught it to her. Her increasingly overactive imagination frightened his wife more than it did Munir. Wendy insisted on stopping the behavior immediately. She was not willing to indulge in the fantasy anymore. The make-believe stories had become so elaborate that she had a growing community of friends, all with backstories that he couldn't believe such a young child could conceive. They were usually discussed when she was misbehaving, using them as culprits to avoid punishment.

Wendy stepped beside Munir and whispered apologetically, "You know what the doctor said about this. We need to move her focus."

"Yes, right." Leaning forward, he ejected the tape and put it into its sleeve. Claire watched as he put the plastic cassette in his messenger bag. She then looked from the screen to the air vent on the back wall of the room. Her eyebrows scrunched together as if she was in deep thought.

Staring at the air vent, Munir saw one of the screws was missing, and the cover was slightly askew. Knowing he was exhausted from the last few days, he used the excuse to move on. His work always anchored him, giving his actions a sense of purpose. Taking a deep cleansing breath, he said, "Wendy, we need to decide if we can move all this merchandise toward the back and make enough space for our clothes in the front. If we do, we need to begin immediately."

"We don't have any other choice, do we?"

"If I can get hold of her, I could force Mrs. Francis to get her stuff out of here. I don't have a lot of confidence that she will. Honestly, I don't think she is all there." He pointed to his head, circling his finger, emphasizing his point.

"We can certainly keep trying her. But I agree we should make as much space as possible. Even if you get her, there is no guarantee arrangements can be made to pick everything up in two days." She pulled a rubber band from her wrist and pulled her hair into a bun. "Maybe we are the ones who need our heads examined, trying to open on Thanksgiving week!" She gave a fake smile, biting her tongue, trying to defuse the thought they had both been avoiding. "This seemed so easy to do when we thought about a grand opening on Black Friday. Uggghhh! It will look like poop having everything jammed into the back of the store." She extracted her fingers from the rubber band and added, "Maybe we can sell her stuff and leave ours in storage."

"That would solve the immediate issue, but I don't feel right selling something I didn't pay for."

"Well, how about we put the money we make aside, and when we sell enough to catch up on our many bills, we can repay her?"

Munir looked at his daughter, watching her color the entire page, regardless of the lines. He knew he had little other choice: with the other store closed, he needed the money. He said, "I would prefer to bring at least some of our clothing in and put it in the front of the store. That way, we can try to sell both. I believe that would be the only sensible choice." Tension set into his shoulders, sending a tingling down his back.

Wendy grabbed a pen and pad of paper. "Okay. Try her again. I'll start inventorying women's apparel in case you can't get through." She walked back to the store.

Munir dialed the number again, staring at the TV screen. After what felt like a half-hour, he heard a recording of an elderly voice prompting him to leave a message. As he gave his name and number, he thought of the old woman who owned the previous store and how anxious she had been that day.

Replacing the receiver, Munir went to the vent, squatting down. As if expecting it to be hot, he carefully removed the metal plate with his fingertips. Staring into the dark metal box, all he could see was fading darkness. Turning his head to the side, he held his breath, trying to listen. There was a humming noise, and he thought he heard bells jingling. He wanted to ask his daughter what she thought she had seen, but couldn't bring himself to say anything. Putting the vent back on, he fastened two screws using his Swiss Army Knife.

Standing, he said, "Claire, why don't you come up front with us?"

"I want to stay here," she replied, not looking up from her coloring.

"Come on. You can color out there."

"You let me color by myself yesterday."

Munir stared at the vent. Trying to stay calm, he said, "I know. Please come now." With a look of annoyance, she rolled her eyes, grabbing a handful of crayons and her book. As they left the storage room, Munir hoped he could forget the foolish thoughts and find the strength to do everything needed.

After an hour of inventorying the clothing, the phone rang. Hopeful it was Mrs. Francis, Munir ran to the receiver.

"Son, son, are you there?"

"Hello, Pappa."

"Munir! The nurse you hired is trying to kill me again."

"I doubt that. Where are you?"

"In bed. Where else would I be?"

"Is Mrs. Long there with you?" He glanced back at Claire. She was sitting under a rack of dresses, playing with her doll.

In a near whisper, his father responded, "Yes."

"Give her the phone, please." Munir turned, looking down at the worn floor. He pressed the corner of the peeling vinyl tile with the tip of his shoe, hoping to reactivate the glue.

"No."

"Father, do it now."

Nurses came in four hours daily to ensure his father was eating and taking his medication. Frustrated he couldn't be there, Munir asked, "Hello?"

"Hello, I'm sorry."

"No reason to apologize, Mrs. Long. Were you giving him his I.V.?"

"Yes, he certainly hates the needle. If he would stop ripping out the port, we wouldn't have to go through this daily."

Munir looked across the floor racks at Wendy. Patiently, he asked the nurse, "Can you please hold the phone up?"

"Yes." There was a click followed by white noise.

"Father, Mrs. Long is going to give you your medicine right now, you must let her. I promise you she is not there to hurt you." Munir struggled to ignore the pangs of guilt he felt as he imagined his constantly shrinking father lying in his bed. His confusion seemed to have worsened over the last few weeks. "Mrs. Long, if you are ready, please proceed."

"Yes, I'm ready."

Munir listened as the nurse, in a sweet voice, described every step of what she was doing. As she did, his father, speaking his native tongue, brutally chastised her. It was very rare for him to not use English. It was always a point of pride that he spoke the self-taught language with only a hint of an accent. After hearing a long grunt, Munir assumed the I.V. was in place. In a reassuring voice, he said, "See, that wasn't so bad, Pappa."

In an echo, he heard, "I guess not."

"Mrs. Long, thank you for your patience. If you are settled, please put my father back on?"

"Of course."

"When will you be home, Munir?"

Not bothering to correct him, he sighed deeply. Munir hadn't lived with his father for almost a decade. He said, "I told you, not until Thursday." Somewhere in the back of his mind, he calculated the rising bills of the nursing staff. He or Wendy had been sharing duty with the nurses until the last few days, cutting the expenses in half. But with the added responsibility of the new store, they had no choice but to increase the shifts of the caregivers.

"Okay."

Even close to the end, his father's accepting nature came through. Being raised by someone who came to this country with nothing but a pregnant wife and hope had taught Munir many lessons. He had spent most of his free time watching his father being degraded by haggling customers as he tried to sell his clothing in every flea market in the state. Munir always looked at his experiences as an education on ignoring the ignorant, which had paid off as he tried to build his own life.

"I have to go now." Without a response, the line went dead. Suddenly, he felt something clutch his leg. Looking down, he saw Claire smiling up at him as she hugged him.

"Was that Grandpapa?"

"Yes."

"Did you tell him I said hello?"

"No, not this time."

"Can you do it next time?" Not waiting for a response, she squeaked, "I'm hungry!"

Glancing at his watch, he saw it was nearly noon. Feeling bad for keeping her cooped up in the store for the last few days, he asked, "How about some pizza?"

"Can we make it Frizza?"

Her favorite meal was laying French fries across the cheese. The nickname had stuck. "Okay." Munir took a step forward, with Claire clinging to him, making him walk like a zombie. "Wendy, we are going to get some pizza."

Hidden somewhere amongst the clothing, her voice came as if from thin air. "I'm going to keep working."

"Okay." Munir wiggled himself free and grabbed the key from the sales counter. Holding Claire's hand, they made their way through the service door. When they reached the main corridor, he asked the question he knew his wife would not like. "What did you see earlier when you were looking at that video?"

"Elves."

Watching her squint as she focused on the soaped-up windows of a space across from the theater, he sighed deeply. "What elves, honey?"

"The ones on the screen."

"They were in the store, huh?" He felt her grip strengthen as they approached the storefront with the remnants of an arcade sign in the faded brick. "Claire, how many elves did you see on screen?"

"The store was filled with them." She was concentrating hard on stepping on the tiles, avoiding the grout lines.

"Why can't I see them?"

"Everyone knows that grown-ups can't see elves!"

An elderly lady holding a bag labeled "Simone's Spa" made a production of going around them.

Claire said, much too loudly, "That lady's shadow is trying to get away from her daddy."

He gave a polite smile as he brought Claire down two steps to a conversation pit with benches projecting out of the brick walls. Holding his daughter's hand, he felt a constant tingling like electricity.

"Why did you say that?"

She shrugged. "I dunno."

Letting the talk of the woman go for now, he asked, "Earlier at the store, why did you keep staring at the heating vent?"

"Because that's where the elves live."

"How... do you know this?"

"Because the leader elf told me... " Humming the Battle Hymn quietly, Claire swung her legs back and forth as if on a swing. She stopped to say, "You know, I'm *really* hungry, Daddy." She gripped her belly and looked at him wide-eyed, smiling, exposing the gap between her front teeth.

"We will eat soon. First, let's finish talking, okay? When did they tell you?"

"Yesterday."

"Where?"

"In the back room, when they came out of the vent in your new office."

Munir blinked, feeling dizzy again. Placing both hands on the wooden bench, he gripped tight. "Claire, you must stop with this kind of talk. You're going to upset your mother."

"You asked me, Daddy."

Munir's stomach churned, making it whine. Nothing felt right since he moved out of the store he had taken over from his father. What he had assumed were nerves began to feel like a warning that the greed to earn more here was a mistake.

Claire put her tiny hand on his midsection. "See, you're hungry too!"

"Yes, honey. I am."

She hopped off the bench, holding her hand out for him. He took it, knowing he needed to keep busy, or his mind would stop him from getting anything done.

"Are you okay, Daddy?"

"I'm fine, Claire Bear. Are you okay?"

"Yes. Just real hungry." They made their way to Tony's Pizza place. Claire was humming a tune from a video game he had played in his youth but couldn't quite remember. As they entered, Munir wondered if there was a way out of his lease. Nothing about what had happened over the last few days felt right.

———

At noon on Black Friday, Munir's fingers ached from working the register. Since the grand opening, there had been a nonstop barrage of customers. He hadn't had a moment to stop as he logged each item. Looking at the day's total, he hoped to keep even a portion of the money. The receipts for the day equaled half a month's billing at his last store. But so far, nothing he had brought in had sold. The shoppers walked past his clothing and right to the other merchandise. Wendy stood beside him, smiling as she took in the next customer in line.

In his peripheral vision, he saw the flashing line on the phone under the register. He grabbed it and answered, "Fashionation." A loud scratching noise made him pull the receiver further from his ear. The rhythmic sound made his head ache. "Hello?"

"This is Mrs. Francis. Is this Munir?"

"Yes." The next words were hard to hear. The crowd around him seemed to get louder. Apologetically, he said, "Can you please hold on?" He hit the hold button and went toward the back room. "Wendy, I'll be back in a minute. I have to take a call." She gave him an exaggerated, frightened look, biting her lower lip. She tapped him slightly on the behind as he made his way to the back room. With a surprised smile, he looked back at her as he dodged around Claire. She had made a little fort behind the counter where she was playing with her toys.

Entering the back room, he eyed the vent. He had replaced all the screws, yet he glanced at it involuntarily every time he entered, making sure the metal cover was still secure. Grabbing the phone, he kicked the door closed, shutting out some of the noise of the busy store.

———

He clicked the hold button on the square plastic device and placed the receiver against his ear. "Mrs. Francis? This is Munir Razen. I took over the space you used to operate."

A high-pitched voice replied, "I know. I listened to your message. I was expecting you to call, eventually."

He bit his lower lip hard enough to draw blood. Something in her voice made her sound like she knew something he would never be able to comprehend. "W-Why?"

"Thought you might have some questions. What can I do for you?"

Munir cleared his throat, loosening his collar. "I walked into an unexpected delivery the other day. The entire store was filled with new merchandise. I assume that you possibly forgot to cancel your last order?"

"Oh no, that's yours.... It's a gift."

"What... why would you do that?"

"Didn't say it was from me..."

He thought he heard fear in her voice as her words trailed off. Munir tightened his grip on the phone. The room felt like the heat was turned on high. Sweat formed on his forehead. Nervously, he swiped at it. "From whom, then?" There was a long pause, the silence filling with an odd scratching noise.

"You will possibly find out... very soon."

"I need to know. I can't accept this." He contemplated telling her they were selling everything but putting the money aside. The admission got stuck in his throat.

"Oh, but you must."

"I don't understand?"

"Nothing to understand. The merchandise belongs to the store. You run the store, so it's yours to do with it as you wish. Just always remember this." There was a long pause. "Treat your customers fairly, and the merchandise with respect, and it will keep paying off."

"No, that's not what I meant. I understand how to run the store. I'm confused about why I'm getting something for nothing."

"Have you sold anything yet?"

"Yes."

"It has begun, and it will never stop... Never. It's yours to deal with now."

"Mrs. Francis. Wha—"

The line went dead. As the constant tone buzzed in Munir's ear, the scratching noise in the background grew louder, as if whatever was causing it was getting closer. Above him, the fluorescent lights flickered. His stomach turned. The all-too-familiar dizziness was back. Hitting the phone's switch hook, he punched in the number again. After ten unanswered rings, he finally hung up, knowing she must have disconnected her answering machine.

Wendy entered the room. She was standing with her hands on her hips. Seeing her brought some sense of calm. Ever since they had met, her smile had a soothing effect.

"Well...?"

"Well, I guess we have been given a gift."

"What are you talking about?"

"That was Mrs. Francis. She said all the clothing was a gift."

Laughing, she clapped her hands, putting her fingertips to her nose. "Wait, are you serious?"

The conversation ran through his head, feeling like the remnants of a distant dream. "Yeah."

"How can that be?"

"I don't know. She told me the merchandise was all ours now." *To do with as we wish.* Munir looked away from her, staring at the vent.

"Well, I need you upfront. The register tape stopped working, and the line is getting longer and longer. We can deal with the... ah... *gift* after we close."

Munir looked at the television screen. In the top right corner was a woman trying on a jacket. She was leering toward the register Wendy should be at as she pulled off the price tag. The woman then pulled another tag from her pocket and replaced it on the jacket's sleeve. "We have a customer who is trying to cheat us."

"Which one?" Wendy spun her head, looking back towards the store.

Knowing she would overreact, he said, "I'll handle it. Let's get back up there."

Munir watched her turn, heading back to the hectic room. As he followed, he began wringing his hands together, trying to process all that had happened in the last few days. The only thing he was certain of was that nothing in this world was ever free, making him more nervous than he thought he could handle. The last time he'd felt this way was when Claire was born. Wondering what penance he would pay for the gift, he worked his way back to the store, trying to smile at the line of eager customers. Off to his right, the woman trying on the jacket screamed out.

He jogged toward her. She was clutching her throat, and her face was beet red. Munir grabbed at her as she dropped to her knees.

"Ma'am, what is it?!" He feared it was her heart. She was now clutching near the zipper at her chest.

"The jacket... " She shoved both hands around the collar, digging in, pulling it from her neck. "It's too tight... It's choking me."

He wondered if she was now trying to pull an insurance scam, so he grabbed the zipper. It wouldn't budge. The woman's eyes fluttered, now looking more blue than red. Frantic, he tugged so hard that she rose with the force. Not knowing what else to do, he jammed his fingers into the fabric around her throat. Trying to pull the jacket from her skin, the circulation was cut off in his fingertips. He tried to extract them but couldn't. Claustrophobia seized him as he tugged.

Wendy knelt next to him. "What's wrong with her?"

"She is choking... from the jacket." His voice was so high it sounded like it came from someone else. He watched the woman staring pleadingly at Wendy, her breaths coming in empty gasps. "We must help her! Now!"

"How?" Wendy tugged at the zipper. The woman's eyes looked as if they were going to bulge from her head. Digging her hand in his back pocket, she withdrew his pocketknife and flicked open the longest blade. Carefully, she began to cut the material open.

With his fingertips feeling like they were going to explode, Munir whispered, "Don't... "

Working downward, Wendy made a long, diagonal cut. The customer gasped loudly, gulping in a sharp intake of air. She sat up, coughing, with drool running down her chin.

Wendy asked, "Ma'am, are you okay?"

The woman stared directly into Munir's eyes. Without warning, she suddenly stood up, tore the jacket off, and tossed it to the floor. "I'm... I'm sorry." She looked once more at Munir, then strode from the store.

He sat staring at the remnants of the jacket. The room seemed to be closing in around him as Mrs. Francis' words of caution echoed in his head. Closing his eyes, he said a silent prayer, hoping for guidance to help him understand what was happening.

Wendy knelt beside him, whispering. "Munir, we need to get back to work."

"We need to close. Something is wrong here. Very wrong, Wendy." He bit off, adding, "I wish you didn't cut that jacket, Wendy."

She placed her hand on his shoulder. "You can't let one crazy customer and a stuck zipper shake you."

He turned his head, staring directly into her eyes. "It's not just that. This place is—"

"Munir. You feel guilty about selling this merchandise. People are looking at us. We have bills to pay. Please, let's get back to work, and we can discuss this later."

He looked at an elderly woman standing behind Wendy. She had the prettiest eyes he had ever seen. Moving his focus for a second, he felt slightly calmer. With a sigh, he stood. "Okay." He walked back to the register, eyeing all the clothing around him, feeling like it would hop off the racks and bury him. Wendy grabbed his hand, tugging him along.

When they were both back to the register, Wendy said to the line, "Okay, who's next?"

Claire wrapped her arms around Munir's legs. When he looked down, she was smiling. "Are you okay, Daddy?"

He placed his hand on top of her head. "Yes, I'm fine." The lie stung.

The next morning, he entered the store and froze, staring at the clothing racks. They were full. Every missing jacket, purse, and dress had been replaced with identical products. Munir made his way to the back room. The black-and-white screen displayed an empty store. The recording light below it was glowing. Adjusting the dial, he pressed rewind. The squiggly lines filled the screen.

Watching the time stamp, he stopped at four minutes after two in the morning—the time the clothing had appeared the other day.

Frozen, he watched the screen flicker for a second, and the racks were all replenished. He held down the rewind button once again, getting the same result. Whatever was happening no longer felt like an explainable phenomenon. He looked at the vent on the back wall. Again, only a single screw was left, the others lying on the vinyl tile floor. Still staring at it, he pressed stop, slapping at the controls until he heard the tape eject.

He walked to the vent. He put his hand against the slotted metal and straightened it. The shock freed a spider web, which drifted to the floor. Smelling dust and what he thought was oil from the furnace, he felt a pulsating hum. The metal opening wasn't more than eight inches by eight inches. He laughed as he imagined a man trying to climb through such a tight space. His phone echoed in the small room, making him jump.

He walked to the table and lifted the receiver. Raising it to his ear, he feared that he would hear Mrs. Francis's harsh voice.

"Mr. Razen?"

The voice was unfamiliar, bringing relief. "This is he."

"This is Mrs. Shelton, the acting director of Always Their Care. I am calling today with some rather unpleasant news."

There was a long pause. He knew this call could come at any time, but the slight mental preparation was little solace for him. "Well, what is it?" His voice cracked on the last word.

"Mrs. Long called in sick, and now your father is refusing to let her replacement enter his room. He has been belligerent, and with it being the weekend, I have no one else to send out on such short notice."

Relief swept over Munir. He placed his hand on his chest and sighed deeply. "How long is it until he has to take his next dose?"

"I don't have his chart in front of me, but if I remember correctly, his medicine is administered at nine a.m. and then again at nine p.m."

"Is someone with him still right now?"

"Yes."

His father lived in an apartment that was over a half-hour away in the next town. Munir had tried repeatedly to have him move into his home, but never succeeded in overcoming his stubbornness. Countless times, the superstitious man had explained to his son that he would die in his apartment, as this was where he felt the strongest connection to his wife. So many times, Munir had talked himself into believing he had done right by his father, the whole time knowing the truth. He had been far too busy with his work to do any more than care for his father's most basic needs. The apartment held far too many connections to a past that Munir struggled to forget. "I'll have my wife come by within the hour."

"Thank you. Sorry to inconvenience you like this. I can assure you Mrs. Iblis has tried all she can to calm him. She's one of our best nurses."

"I must go now. Thank you for the call."

Munir called Wendy and asked her to go to his father's house before coming to the store. When he hung up, he rewound the tape and watched the clothing appear as if from nowhere again. Struggling to find a logical explanation, he wanted to scream out all the frustration that had been building over the last week. It took all his strength to ignore the thoughts that this was not explainable. That he was possibly dealing with unnatural forces. He was not typically one to come to such a conclusion. When he was a child, his father would tell him stories of such happenings, men blessed or doomed by otherworldly spirits, but Munir dismissed the cautionary tales as the folly of the uneducated. The only distinguishable thought that held him close to reality now was that Mrs. Francis was somehow orchestrating all of this for a reason he could not begin to understand.

He sat down and calculated the cost of closing down for a few days. Not only would his store default, but he would not be able to pay for his father's care through the end of the week. Grabbing the keys, he made his way to the front of the store to open the gate, hoping today could be different. As he walked down the aisle, the clothing around him felt as if it had doubled, reaching out to grab him like it had the woman yesterday. Trying to force the thought from his head, Munir said a silent prayer, trying to find the strength to get through another day.

The activity in the store finally slowed down around eight. With a little more than two hours before closing, Wendy convinced Munir to stop by his father's. Initially, He was reluctant, but the day had gone well—so well, his early thoughts of supernatural occurrences were pushed so far in the back of his mind that he felt some sense of happiness for the first time in days. He wanted to bring Claire with him, but she was asleep in her new favorite place behind the counter.

The drive over had helped him regain focus. Being away from the store and its many pressures lifted a weight off his chest.

When he arrived at the apartment complex, Munir let himself in with his key. Passing the dining area, he could almost smell the combination of wax and sugar, the remnants of all the birthdays he celebrated in the cramped, windowless room. His father always overcompensated for the grueling schedule he put his son through by giving him lavish parties and gifts. Going down the hallway, he was pleased to see all the photos they had sent of his daughter adorning the walls. Coming out of the bathroom holding a plastic water pitcher was an older woman with a pleasantly oval face wearing very plain faded scrubs. Her eyes were wide, matching her mouth as she breathed, "What?"

Finishing her question, he said, "Sorry I didn't ring. I didn't want to disturb my father. I'm Munir." He extended his hand.

"Hello, I'm Mrs. Iblis. Please excuse me for not shaking your hand. I just sanitized everything." She raised the pitcher and inclined her head in its direction.

"Perfectly alright. Is he still awake?"

"Yes, why don't you come in?"

He followed her to the bedroom in the cramped hallway. The room was oppressively warm. There was a steaming bowl of onion soup on the nightstand table, mixing in with the distinct smell of the elderly. A sea of pillows propped up his father with two layers of sheets pulled to his neck. Intensely, the tiny man stared at the blank wall. Munir made a production of removing his coat and hat, turning his back to the nurse and his father. He needed a moment to compose himself. The shock of seeing his father's gaunt face and frail body was overwhelming. He had always been rail thin, but he looked even lighter than the last time Munir had seen him. Veins and sores lined the few patches of his exposed skin, which looked so dry it reminded Munir of the texture of raisins.

A glance around the aging room provided a stark reminder of how little the man received for all his efforts. Munir's thoughts drifted to his store, reminding him why he worked so hard. He took a damp towel and placed it over his father's forehead. "Pappa. The nurse is going to give you your medicine now."

"Yes, son. Yes." He nodded, the loose skin on his neck jiggling.

Thinking of the half-hour drive, Munir sighed deeply, wishing his father would have just allowed the nurse to do her job when he called earlier.

As she worked, Munir switched on the television, looking for the weather report, hoping the prediction of snow had changed. He came across the evening news. It confirmed that the snowstorm was not only coming, but much earlier than first expected. He flipped to an old black-and-white movie. After the nurse had finished, Munir kissed his father on the forehead.

His father gripped him with hands that were covered in liver spots. "Did you bring Claire?"

"No, not this time. Remember, you saw her this morning, though."

His eyes showed he wasn't quite following. "Can we call her?"

Munir hoped he would drift off to sleep. "Perhaps in a little while."

His father's grip tightened. "Please! Now."

Extracting himself, he nodded. After eight rings, he heard Claire's voice. "Daddy?"

"Claire Bear, you're finally up."

"We're still working, Daddy."

He smiled, thinking of her at the register. "Are you bagging the clothes with your mother?"

"No, I'm in the back room."

"Why?" Munir thought of the vent. He snapped at her, "Please go back up front by your mother, Claire!"

"Why? I'm watching the TV."

"Claire. Please listen to me."

Ignoring him, she said, "The little men are back."

"Claire, put your mother on the phone."

Munir heard shuffling. Moments later, there was a knocking noise and his daughter's voice. "She's busy."

"Are you still in the backroom?"

"Yes."

"Can you please leave the room?" It was taking an effort to hide the fear and anger in his voice.

"I tried... I even knocked on the door, but it was locked."

"Honey, why is the door locked?"

"I dunno. Maybe the elves did it."

"Claire, can you see her on the television?"

There was a brief silence. "Yes, I can see her."

"What is she doing?"

"Walking to the front to close up."

"Honey, I'm going to hang up now and call the store phone again. Please do not answer. I want your mother to."

"Okay!"

The connection ended immediately. Munir, with shaking fingers, dialed. The phone rang and rang...

Munir waited five minutes before calling again, by which time his father had fallen fast asleep. He picked up the receiver. After a full minute of listening to the steady ringtone, he hung up. Wringing his hands, he left the room, trying to slow down the rising anxiety. Telling himself this was all from his daughter's growing overactive imagination, he made his way to his car, feeling like something dreadful was about to take place.

On the drive over, he stopped at the gas station and called the store. There was no answer. When he called the security station at the mall, it went to a recorded message. Munir pulled into the parking lot, trying to come up with an excuse for his wife not answering to slow down his racing thoughts. Entering through the loading dock, he sprinted down the service corridor. The back door to his store was locked. Jamming the key in, he had the sense that something was wrong.

As the door flung open, the space was silent. Noticing the lights were still on, he felt a tinge of hope. In his mind, nothing tragic would happen with the lights on. His eyes searched the sea of clothing aisles. He called out, "Wendy!"

No answer.

In a much more resigned voice. "Claire?"

Again, silence.

He took a few steps forward and noticed the racks had been replenished. Listening to the dead silence, his guilt reminded him that this moment would come. It was finally time for his growing debt to be paid. Desperately, he shrieked, "Where are you!"

Walking to his right, toward the check-out desk in the distance, he saw Wendy lying on the floor near the entrance. Munir sprinted up the aisle and kneeled beside her. She lay amongst hundreds of tiny black rocks. Her exposed skin was a collection of cuts and bruises. Someone had covered her eyes with carefully arranged X's. Munir put his finger on her bloody wrist. She moaned at his touch.

The dread turned to panic, making him shiver. "Honey, what happened? Are you okay?"

She moved her head to the side. The coal fell to the floor. "Claire. Go find Claire."

"Let's get you up."

"Find Claire!" She gripped his forearm so hard it stung.

Pulling free, he dashed to the back storeroom. Removing his key, he fumbled to open the lock and finally opened the door. Munir's stomach ached as he looked around the empty room. The only thing that appeared out of place was the heating vent lying on the floor, exposing the large rectangular hole it had covered. Munir took a few tentative steps into the room. As he got closer to his desk, he saw Claire's feet poking out from underneath it.

He knew she was dead, taken in return for the wealth that came from his merchandise. It was the only possible conclusion to this arrangement. Holding in the anxiety that made him feel like he was going to pass out, he found it hard to catch his breath. The thought of her being taken from him would not penetrate. Slowly, he shuffled forward. Feeling too weak to lift his feet from the floor, he inched closer to a reality that was ripping his heart in half. Somewhere in the distance, he heard bells jingling. Slumping forward, he began to kneel when he saw Claire's colorful gym shoes move slightly.

Munir leaped forward, calling out, "Claire... baby!"

"Daddy?!" Claire fled the safety of her cocoon under the desk and threw her arms around him, nearly toppling them both over. "Don't ever leave me again, Daddy!"

She dug her chin painfully into his shoulder. He hugged her tightly, trying to catch his labored breath. "I was so, so scared."

He lifted her, trying to see her face more clearly. She trembled in his arms as she squirmed tighter against him. He flexed, trying to squeeze away her fear. "Never, I promise never again." Absorbing her convulsive sobs against his chest, he quietly asked, "What happened here, Claire?"

Her words were muffled as she spoke into his jacket. "I was watching her on the screen, then the elves attacked her."

"What elves, Claire?" Munir looked at the small television set on the desk and saw that it was recording. He took a step forward.

"Don't put me down!"

"I won't." She clutched him so tightly that he almost dropped her. He felt numb and cold as he fought to get a better grip.

Wendy limped into the room, her pupils dilated, slamming the door behind her. "We have to go." She leaned against the door, breathing heavily. There was a thudding noise that jerked her forward. She spun, putting both hands against the door. "Munir, we must go now!"

Munir felt his daughter tense up. He lifted one finger, placing it against his lips. There was another loud thud against the door. They looked at one another, asking an unspoken question. He asked softly, "What happened out there?"

Wendy's hand went to her quivering lip. "I don't know. All of a sudden, I started to get... I don't know... attacked by pieces of coal."

The door began shaking. This time, hundreds of banging noises sounded like rain pelting glass.

Munir's thoughts ran together, and he fought to work out what to do. Wendy grabbed a chair and braced it against the door. "Munir, what's going on?"

His eyes traced the room, stopping at the vent. "Call the police."

He motioned her over with a nod as he stroked the back of Claire's hair with his free hand. With her head buried in his chest, he sat in the office chair and looked at the monitor. In the top right, he saw the spot where Wendy's body had been. Munir hit rewind.

The videotape made a whirling noise, and two squiggly white hazy lines danced across the screen. Wendy came and sat on the desk, placing her hand on Munir's shoulder. She looked too exhausted to speak, but took the phone and dialed.

As she gave details, he was glued to the screen. After a few seconds in reverse, he saw Wendy roll to her side and jerkily go from laying on the floor to kneeling to standing. The entire time, it looked like she was trying to fend off some unseen threat. It made him think of a bee attack the way she spun and swatted around herself. When Wendy was calmly walking backward, he hit the play button and watched in horror as she fended off the phantom attack.

Munir asked, "Claire."

The response was a muffled cry.

"Claire, what happened?"

She shook her head violently, her forehead smacking Munir's chin with enough force to make his teeth click together. "No!"

The chair's metal leg made a loud noise as the door moved. It was still closed, but that brought no relief. Trying to stay calm, he said, "Please tell me who attacked your mother."

Wendy' hung up the phone. Her eyes exploded into tears, yet she sat silently staring.

"We have to go before they get us too!" Claire squirmed.

"Who?" With effort, he pulled Claire away from his chest and stared at her red-rimmed eyes.

"Please, the elves, Daddy, the elves! There's two of them right there, going back into the hole in the wall." She pointed with trembling fingers.

The look of complete terror on her precious face was more than he could take. He looked at the floor, seeing nothing but the bare tile. There was a solid thud at the door. Quickly, he looked at the chair. He knew it wouldn't hold out much longer, not against whatever was out there.

Wendy leaned in and wrapped her arms around them.

"Wendy, how long will they take to get here?"

"I don't know."

"You—" He stopped himself from yelling. "Okay, everything's going to be okay. They are going to call the security office, and someone will be here any minute." The door shook, the thudding noise so loud he could picture the metal denting. He stroked her arm, trying to believe his lie.

"Wendy, can you please call the security office?"

She did as requested. After a few seconds, she said, "It just keeps ringing."

"Keep trying. The guards might be walking their rounds."

Wendy was rocking back and forth, pressing the receiver tightly to her ear. Her eyes were glued to the front door. "Okay, Munir."

———

Overwhelmed by the knowledge that the penance was coming due, Munir let out all that he had been holding in for so very long. Pulling Claire to his chest, he wept, his tears streaming into her hair. After a few seconds, he realized Claire was no longer crying. Instead, she was silently hugging him, patting the back of his head with her tiny hand in the same caring way he would when she would awaken in the middle of the night after a bad dream.

He grabbed her hand and said, "Honey, show me what happened?"

She nodded and hit rewind on the tape.

The timestamp of the video showed November twenty-fourth.

He sat watching Wendy replace the price tags. Munir looked at her. "What did you do?"

"I was raising the prices. Everything was selling so quickly that I figured we could make a little more. Then, I don't know what happened..." Her eyes were glued to the door. "It was like something invisible was attacking me."

"No—" Munir watched the screen. What seemed like a hundred tiny elves started running up and down the aisles.

Wendy began twitching and swatting at the air. As she passed the elevated display, she grabbed the ski pole from the male model and held it like a club.

With each step she took, the tiny elfin workers scurried to avoid being crushed, their faces terrified as they ran. The elves watched as Wendy haphazardly grabbed the sweaters they had spent so many hours creating. Pressing herself against the mirrored wall, she used the items as a shield, and the tiny elves climbing them were flung across the room, plummeting to their deaths.

Finally, after witnessing the carnage inflicted upon his workers, the elf Munir assumed to be the leader, threw down his blueprints and pulled a wooden horn from his belt. With incredible agility, the elves scurried to the center of the store. After a few seconds of yelling, they ran down the vinyl pathways in groups of three in separate directions. The agitated elves moved harmoniously, leapfrogging over one another in perfect V-shaped patterns. As they converged upon Wendy, they catapulted over one another, creating a growing ladder of alternating elves, each supporting the other. Skillfully, they positioned themselves around her. Standing at the top of the highest elfin ladder, the leader in the red hat once again blew his horn. As it echoed, the towers of elves began throwing coal. The attack started at the highest point, each elf launching their weapon, then cascading to the floor, rolling away to safety.

Wendy tried desperately to shield herself from her unseen assailants, frantically swatting into the air. Still, the tiny rocks pelted her so relentlessly and from every direction that she eventually succumbed to the attack, falling to her knees and screaming in pain. Wriggling on the ground, she was covered by the tiny pellets. Coal was now embedded in her skin, leaving hundreds of tracks of blood on her damaged flesh. Looking as if she had just been pushed through a thousand tiny razor blades, she curled up on the floor.

Munir let go of Claire's hand.

She looked as if she was going to fall asleep. "Is Santa... in there." He looked at the vent. "With these elves?"

"No."

"Why not?"

"Because he's mad at them. They did a bad thing."

"What did they do wrong?"

"They wouldn't listen when Santa told them not to punish others. That's why they keep coming here now, because they're banished." She struggled with the last word; it sounded like 'a band shed.'

"What do they do here?"

"They give gifts."

"Why?" She stared off into space as if she didn't hear him. Calmly, he gently pushed her bangs from her face. "Claire, honey. Why?"

"Because they think if they're good, Santa will let them return to the North Pole."

Looking up at Wendy, he didn't know what to say. All he could think about was wishing he was anywhere but here. The door banged again, the echo filling the room. Claire jabbed her head into his chest, squirming tightly against him. He knew no one was coming for them. The store and its secrets would swallow them whole. A devastating emptiness settled into his bones. Slowly, he stood. Wendy cradled next to him as they walked toward the door.

Claire yelled, "It's too late now!"

Her words made his eardrums ring as the door flung open. Munir gripped Wendy's hand. Everywhere he looked, the elves surrounded them. When the first piece struck him, it felt like a wicked paper cut drawing blood. Instinctively, he turned, trying to use his body as a shield for his daughter, but he knew there was no escape. He wept as the horn blew, and the coal came hurtling from all around them.

THE GAME OF LOVE

S tanding in the dim vestibule of the aging Towne Point Mall, Sarah, wearing heels and a tight dress, wondered where she'd taken the wrong turn in life. Considering backing out again, she held the phone tight to her ear, shivering. Her acting coach, who also served as her landlady, was trying to prepare her for her first paid date as the signal went in and out.

"Many of my students do this. It's not a big deal. Remember, all you have to do is get in there and pretend it's a performance. It really isn't much different. Just be a character for a few hours."

"It's not the same as stage acting!" she yelled into the phone and instantly felt guilty. Janet had been so kind to her since her fiancée had left her after he got a series of TV commercials. Sarah tried to focus as her mind replayed the last few months and the benchmarks of her downward spiral that led her to this job.

"It's not like you have to sleep with them or anything like that. These are just lonely guys looking for someone to talk to. If it was any more, do you really think I would have suggested you do it?"

Sarah couldn't stand talking anymore or listening to Janet's rationalizations. Feeling more vulnerable than she ever had, she said, "Thank you for calming me down. I must get in there now." Without waiting for a response, she hung up and walked into the mall, feeling exposed and ashamed.

The aging movie theater was playing a retro horror slasher *A Valentine's Day*. Looking at the faded poster of a masked man holding a pickaxe, it dawned on her for the first time that today was the fourteenth. She had been too busy between acting calls, work, and classes to think of such frivolous things as a lover's holiday. If everything had gone as planned, she knew she would be eating a nice dinner with her fiancée instead of meeting a stranger for money. The thought weighed her down, her heart still aching for something she thought she couldn't live without.

She walked past the gloomy stores in the nearly deserted mall, each just a shell of the once happy beacons they used to be. Most had rolling gates covering the entrances, reminding her of skeletal remains. She pulled up the text from her client.

The shuttered storefront she was meeting him at had no sign, but the dusty outline of the word *Starcade* and a picture of a spaceship was etched into the brick above the closed gate. Following the directions given in the text, she entered the dark hallway on the right. A steel door without a handle that was labeled "Employees Only" barred her path.

Sarah examined an antiquated intercom system before pressing the button. After what felt like forever, a gruff voice barked, "Yes?"

"Hi. I'm Sarah Highsmith. Here to meet with Harry Palmer." When she let go of the button, she heard labored breathing.

Depressing the button again, she lowered her voice, feeling very self-conscious. "I'm with the, um... gentlemen's agency." There was the sound of what she assumed was a push bar clicking.

She opened the door and peered into the darkness. The intercom chirped again. "Please come in. Follow the hallway to the main arcade. I will be with you in a few minutes."

Opening the door fully, seeing only darkness, her chest felt like a weight had been placed upon it, stealing her breath. Instinctively, she adjusted her short dress. Then, getting into character, she decided to think of it as only a costume. Remembering her stage training, she took a deep cleansing breath, whispering aloud, "Focus."

Somewhere in the distance, she heard the digitized sound of games. The hallway was dark, dusty, and haunted by the phantom aromas of a concession stand. Smelling popcorn and onions reminded her of being with her father at a ballgame. As her heels clicked along the hard floor, she wondered what he would think of her now if he was still alive.

Each step brought her closer to the distant glowing light until she came to the main room. In the center of the vast space were eight identical video games, their screens displaying demos and scrolling through lists of high scores. Squinting at the intermittent flashing lights, Sarah noticed that each machine played the same menacing tune at different intervals. The sounds irritated her as they spiked in high-pitched electric crescendos. She approached the nearest stand-up console, which had a stencil of an asteroid across the top. "Mr. Palmer?" she shouted.

Someone tapped on her shoulder. Sarah nearly jumped out of her skin as she spun, seeing a middle-aged man wearing a tight T-shirt and jeans that were rolled up at the bottom. His short hair was gelled into a mini mohawk. Her heart beat rapidly as she tried to decide if it was too late to leave—not only the mall but also her dream of acting and all it was taking from her. Suddenly, rural Iowa didn't feel as repulsive as it once did.

"Hello, Sarah." He extended his hand slowly.

Out of habit, she awkwardly shook it. "Hi."

"My apologies for startling you. I've never done anything like this before." He let the sentence drop as his eyes traveled up and down her body, tracing her curves.

Bashfully, she slumped forward, crossing her arms in front of her chest. "I didn't know there were arcades like this still open." She tried not to stare at his hair and his vain attempt to look younger. Shifting her eyes back to the machine, she could still feel his stare.

"There aren't. I had these games brought in. Sadly, this was an empty room before I began leasing it a few months ago."

"Oh. Do you plan on opening soon?"

"No. This is, for now, an expensive nostalgic hobby." He looked away for the first time and caressed the console to his right. "Frankly, at times, I don't know what I'm doing. Have you ever started down a path only to find you might not want to be on it?"

Shifting in her heels, she wanted to scream, *"Yes, right now!"* Instead, she watched him stare lovingly at the control board before his mouth slackened, and he looked genuinely frightened.

"I bought the first machine and before I knew it," he waved with an open palm, presenting the long row of games, "I had acquired all of these. They are very old, and I need to cannibalize parts from each to keep them going." With a heavy sigh, he quickly continued. "You must think I'm quite odd. I contemplated telling you how I planned on spending the evening. But honestly, I was concerned you wouldn't show. My... eccentricities aren't always so well received. Especially by women."

"I don't know what to say." Sarah let out a nervous laugh. The games played around them, creating peculiar shadows from the demo screens, and the electronic squeaking continued.

"Well, the simplest thing to say is that you'd like to stay. I can promise you a unique evening, if nothing else."

"As we... um, discussed over the phone, I'm available until midnight." The second the words came out of her mouth, she wished she could pull them back. It was more than feeling like she was selling herself. It was deeper, something more alarming than shame. Although the room was massive, she felt trapped, like she was in a very tiny space, trying to find a way out. Sweat beaded beneath her hair before sliding down the back of her neck.

"Very well then." He stepped to his right and put his hand on the console. "I do this because this was a favorite of ours."

Sarah glanced around, expecting someone else to come out of the shadows. But it was just the two of them in the dark room.

He motioned toward two joysticks and round tracking balls below the screen. "If you don't mind indulging me, would you play?"

"I'm afraid I'm not very good at these types of things."

"Oh, don't let that bother you. I'm not very good either."

"Really? You have so many."

"I guess I'm kind of like the golfer who has every club but can't hit the ball straight." He jabbed his hand into his front pocket and pulled out a fistful of coins. Placing them on the console, he nodded to her to come closer before he turned, grabbing the joystick.

Sarah moved closer. She stared at the side of his face, realizing he was older than she had originally thought. The light from the screen exposed deep creases. "So, what do I do?"

"The joystick moves your ship." With a flick of the wrist, he spun the ball. It spun loudly, like a cue ball on a pool table that was halfway trapped. "This will spin the ship. The red button on the top shoots lasers. It's all pretty silly, but I believe you will enjoy the game."

"Okay."

"Good. Very good." He grabbed two coins, placed them to his lips, and whispered what sounded like a short prayer before placing them in the slots. They disappeared with a metallic clang. "Here we go then."

Sarah gripped the joystick and watched as geometric figures floated across the curved screen towards her ship. The stilted movement felt like it was putting her into a trance. Slightly dizzy, she put her hand on the tracking ball. She instantly felt something come alive inside her. It was as if a trigger had been pulled, releasing a new sensation she had never felt before. Anxious, she tried to let go, but couldn't. Desperately, she attempted to pull away from the console, but felt as if her fingers were glued on. Suddenly, a small hot current of electricity from the tracking ball ran up her arm through her torso and back down to her other arm through the joystick in a continuous arc. Panicked, she tugged, making her flesh feel as if it was separating from the bone.

When she opened her mouth to scream, her teeth stung as if they were being infused with electricity.

The man to her left blasted the advancing asteroids with ease, the tracking ball and joystick making rhythmic clicking noises as he flexed and manipulated them. "I know you must be very scared right now. You'll feel nothing if you follow my instructions exactly."

Sarah tried to speak again, but no sound came out. Nearly hyperventilating, her lips moved, but only the thoughts of the words were there. She leaned back with all her weight; still her hands would not come free.

"Better use your lasers before they get you!"

Sarah couldn't think straight. She gasped for breath as her eyes moved around the kinetic lights flashing on the console.

Tiny dotted lines of light shot across the screen from his spaceship. "I'm aware that you can't speak. The shock will pass soon. Please start playing. If your ship explodes three times, it'll be... game over for you."

Sarah mouthed, "What?" Frantically, she fought to speak, but only panting breath escaped.

"I'm very sorry to do this. Please believe that. I just don't have a choice anymore." He swayed, miming his ship to safety. "Time is running out."

Her ship was surrounded by sinister geometric shapes. Some instinct forced her to hit the button at the top of the joystick, shooting dotted lines and destroying them. The ability to expertly navigate the game came from somewhere inside her that she couldn't understand. Everything seemed to slow down on the screen as she saw each move long before she had to make it. Weaving through the chaos, a calm descended as her fingers seemed to act on their own, manipulating the control panel.

"Oh, Barbara!" the man gasped, a mixture of relief and excitement in his voice. "Thank heavens it's you."

Thinking thoughts that weren't her own, Sarah felt love for the man standing next to her, filling the void of her fiancée. She became disoriented as she watched with detached confusion as her hands twisted, maneuvering the controls. She desperately wanted to run, yell, or smash the game. Instead, she stood rooted in the same spot.

"Sarah, don't resist. Just let Barbara take over. I know how this must feel, but you have no choice now."

Closing her eyes, she strained to speak. The words came out sounding like digital programming. "What's happening... to me?" Hearing her new voice, her computer voice, pushed her nerves beyond endurance, pulling her from the trance that had overtaken her. She jerked her body forward and back, tugging against the invisible restraints that held her to the game.

"This is the place where I first fell in love with my wife, playing this exact game. I can't explain it, but the love from that moment somehow got transferred into this machine, leaving a path back to her. Now, every Valentine's Day, I can access it. But I needed someone to help bring her back."

In the corner of the screen, Sarah saw a glowing image form. It was the shape of a very small woman. The image grew in tiny, frenetic movements, appearing to walk slowly toward the screen, looking more and more like a person. Her eyes darted among the ships that flew around the screen. As digital fragments sheared off the attacking ships, she used her hands to shield her head.

Sarah tried to scream, but her tongue felt as if it was affixed to the roof of her mouth. As the image became larger, a face began to form, the digital face of a terrified woman. In a jittery motion, the growing image pushed against the screen as if she was struggling to make it through an unseen barrier. Her intense eyes burned through Sarah.

"Since she passed, something has called me to this machine. I have spent the last ten years trying to bring her back each Valentine's Day. It's the only day I can see her like this." He kept the game going. "Finally, everything is in place. I have the machine, this room, and a *willing participant*. Now I just need the game to keep going until the transference takes place." His eyes never lost focus as he blasted through the growing numbers of enemy ships. "Barbie, we are so close. Hang on!"

Sarah shook with all her strength. The digital woman's hand suddenly came out of the screen and grabbed Sarah's wrist. Her fingers were like jolts of electricity burrowing into Sarah's nerves. Watching the shimmering light that was an electric woman, Sarah felt the fingers penetrate beneath her skin, taking her over completely.

A digital voice called, "Harry, come to me."

Sarah's entire body shook as her vision blurred, watching the loving eyes of the stranger next to her.

"I promise you, you will not be harmed. Please keep the game going. This will be over very soon."

Sarah watched as an asteroid destroyed his spaceship.

"There is only one life left. Please keep us together." He leaned forward, pausing inches from Sarah's lips, which were quickly becoming glowing energy.

Sarah could see the flashing reflection of the game in his tearful eyes as he leaned in. His lips touched hers, tasting like copper. She was powerless to pull free, and his energy made her legs feel as if they were going to give out. With the hair in her nostrils singeing, he disappeared into a digital vapor, floating into her mouth, and then appearing in the game.

Sarah's hands suddenly became her own again. She quickly let go of the machine, shaking her aching fingers as she watched the couple get nearer to one another. As an asteroid got closer, they both looked up at her, terrified. Every instinct pushed her to run, yet she couldn't stop staring at the screen. Thinking of her lost love, she quickly grabbed the joystick, hit the button, and saved the ship. The two digital figures finally touched, hugging. They were both growing smaller, looking less human and more like part of the game.

Sarah tentatively backed away, watching them become one giant, brilliant light. They shimmered brightly as the remnants of their digital arms lovingly caressed each other. Love like she had never known swelled inside her. Hearing their thoughts, Sarah cried, thinking of them reuniting in a forever place, living in their private digital world. Feeling very alone, Sarah turned, running from the arcade and into the darkness of the hallway.

TANGLED WEB

A knock on the door made Robert's heart drop. Quickly, he dumped the paper towels he had been using to clear the web into the trash. Through the thick steel door that separated him from the department store, he could hear the familiar organ music and the voice of the only person who, to the best of his knowledge, knew he still worked there.

"You going to let me in?"

Robert pressed his ear tightly against the cold metal. "Is anyone else around?"

"Open the door... weirdo."

With a sigh, he opened the lock. Anne entered wearing her Gatlet's badge. She'd pinned her hair on top of her head using an oversized decorative Christmas pin that had a glowing light. "Greetings and salutations. How are things in the office of doom?"

Robert quickly slammed the door shut. The second it closed, he felt slightly more at ease. "Why are you here?"

"Good to see you as well. Yes, I'm doing great, so kind of you to ask." She stopped in the middle of the room, looking at the waste receptacle next to his desk. Her voice dropped an octave. "Ohhh. Is the spider back?"

The tension attacked his shoulders at the mention of the creature that had been torturing him for the last few weeks. "Yeah."

"Did it have that same thick web?" She stepped forward and stuck her fingertip into the discarded towels. She extracted a portion with her pinky. It stuck on contact, leaving a long trail as she stood up straight. "Yuck! This can't be real. It's like a friggin' cord." She shivered, shaking the web off her finger, and letting it fall to the linoleum floor. "Did you call maintenance?"

"Why're you here?"

"Why do you get so weird every time I venture down here?" Her eyes narrowed.

Having no one else to confide in, Robert wanted to tell her, but found he couldn't. The words were stuck, held back by either instinct or fear.

Saving him the trouble of fumbling through an excuse, she went to his desk, grabbing his pencil drawings. "These are really good. Like really good." She turned, smiling, exposing lipstick that was half chewed off. He couldn't remember having seen her with her lipstick not half gone, making him wonder how she sold cosmetics. Being half made up somehow seemed to suit her boundless energy, but he couldn't see anyone trusting her for advice, looking disheveled as she did. She was holding a pencil sketch of a kitchen from the late sixties at eye level, examining it with her head tilted sideways. He'd copied it from an old brochure he found in the files of the warranty department that he spent most of his time in.

"Thanks."

"How long have you been drawing?"

"Not sure. I guess I started about eight weeks ago." He knew it was very close to that. The spider web that had been taking most of his attention appeared the next day, making it easier to remember.

She spun her head in his direction with wide eyes. "And you're this good already?!"

Robert shrugged his shoulders. Compliments always made him want to crawl deeper into himself than he already was. "It's quiet down here. So, I've had plenty of time to practice."

"I could practice until I die and not do anything half as good."

Into his chest he mumbled, "Thanks." Looking down at the floor, he saw the discarded web. He imagined hairy legs crawling up his pants. He shuddered, trying to hide it from the girl he wished he could find the courage to ask out.

"Ha! Look at you, all turning red." After a quick antagonizing smile, she moved to his next drawing. "Are you working through lunch again?"

He reached into the filing cabinet on his right and grabbed his bag lunch, presenting it with a quick flip of the hand. "Yeah. Got a tight budget." He placed it back just above the pneumatic tubes that were installed when the store first opened in the seventies. They were there to transfer mail to the various departments. He squinted, searching the area around the paneled ceiling where the tubes protruded for gaps large enough for a spider to squeeze through.

"Okay."

He thought he saw disappointment, but was never good at these things. Finding courage, his lips parted to ask if she wanted to come down and join him, but the ringing of the phone interrupted him. Her head jerked back from the obnoxiously loud noise. The mechanical bell went off again, echoing in the small office. The phone was as old as everything else in the room.

"That sounds like a friggin' air raid bell! Aren't you going to answer it?"

"It's some kinda glitch. No one will be there. I've been getting calls like that for a few weeks."

"How do you know it isn't a customer needing service?"

I haven't had a service call in over a year. With a sigh, he walked past her and smelled her perfume. Every time he inhaled the flowery aroma, he felt weak in a way that frightened and exhilarated him. He picked up the receiver, and his chest tightened. "Gatlet's Warranty." There was a slight hum and the persistent scratching noise that had been there on the last few calls. The noise reminded him of a fingernail rhythmically scratching the inside of a plastic cup. He hung up, placing the receiver back in the cradle, canceling out the rhythmic echo. "Nobody there."

"Maybe it needs tuning? Is that the word?" She looked at the trash once again, her forehead wrinkling as she stared at the discarded pieces of the web. "Why this place doesn't catch up to the nineties is beyond me. Do you want me to tell maintenance? The office is near the cosmetics counter."

"No!" He cringed for shouting. "Um, I mean, no thanks. I'll take care of it."

"Again, why are you so worried about people coming in here?"

"I don't have time to get into it right now." He glanced up at the clock, hoping she would have to leave, as the store was opening in less than a minute. "Just promise me you won't say anything."

"Okay, suit yourself." Following his eyes, she glanced at her watch. "Anyhow, I got to get upstairs before they send out a search party for me. Doors opening in a few." Flashing a bright smile, she added, "Duh! I nearly forgot the reason I came down here. I wanted to make sure you didn't forget about us going out to eat tonight... trivia night at Cozy Corner? Tonight's the qualifying round."

"Oh, of course. I'll be there." The chance at a hundred-dollar gift certificate to the mall was the only way he could explain someone like her paying any attention to someone like him. He met her there by chance last month, impressing her with his knowledge of obscure facts, and they teamed up, and since then, they'd been meeting every Tuesday.

"Okay, partner, see you then." She opened the door, fumbling with the lock.

Peering around her, Robert struggled to see down the long brick hallway. "Please don't forget your promise."

"Huh?"

"To not talk to maintenance."

"Yeah, whatever."

The second she left, Robert locked the door. Alone again, the hum of the fluorescent lights was the only noise in the office that was feeling more and more like a tomb. Knowing he had over eight hours to kill, he returned to the filing cabinets to find something to draw. Skipping several folders of past kitchen renovations, he stopped at one labeled Hedren. In it was a picture of a kitchen dated October nineteen seventy-eight. He remembered that was around the time the mall opened. When he saw the woman in the photo, he knew it would be his next drawing. Her gaze seemed to speak to him.

Sitting down and putting pencil to paper, Robert felt like he was in the room in the picture. So much so that even the lighting seemed different. The hum was gone, replaced with the soft laughter of the woman in high heels that matched her auburn hair. In a trance, he studied her, trying to figure out how to sketch her.

The shrill ring of the phone pulled him from his concentration. He lifted the receiver and replaced it, quickly severing the connection and glancing at the clock. An hour had gone by since Anne left. He stared at the hands of the clock, waiting for them to speed up as if in a cartoon. There was no way that much time could have gone by. He let out a grunt of a laugh. "As if the spider hunt isn't enough, now I got to figure out how to fix a clock." Resuming with his pencil, he got lost in his sketch.

With each stroke, the model became more real to him. He swore he could feel her presence in the room, her warmth and energy fueling him to continue. Leaning closer to the sketch, he smelled an intoxicating perfume. As he filled in the details of the model, he was filled with a sensation that he was creating what had been missing in his life: a silent, unjudging companion. As he filled in the outline of her dress, he imagined what underthings she wore. The thought made him tingle with excitement. Lightly shading in the curves, he was picturing sexy garters and stockings, like he used to see in the catalogs he would sneak into his room when he was a kid. With each line he drew, without effort or planning, his mind and hand, as if they were guided by an unseen force, created a nearly flawless drawing. Moving downward on his sketch, he completed the hem of the dress, and then, for the first time, it was as if his muse had disappeared. He struggled to get the proper arch on the high heels, so much so the tip of the pencil dug deep into the paper, leaving a tiny hole.

Ignoring the frustration, he moved on, taking a moment to close his eyes, visualizing every line and curve of her face. The mental scan took in every contour of her pretty nose and even her slight imperfections. Having read somewhere that symmetry was the most attractive feature of the human face, he decided he would correct hers. In a flourish, he perfected her beauty, brushing and shading with the tip of his finger. With every pencil stroke, he felt more confident that he belonged on Earth to be in this room to create this woman. The hours and hours of free time that the job created were there for this reason.

Carefully, he completed her hair, smudging the drawing to add depth. Robert's tracing movement no longer felt like graphite on paper but human hair, momentarily lifting the loneliness that he always carried around. For the first time in months, he allowed himself to think that all the time he had wasted alone wasn't for nothing.

His fingers ached. Massaging them, he glanced at the clock. His heart skipped a beat. If it was right, the store closed ten minutes ago. When he stood, his leg muscles were stiff. He stretched as he walked across the room and placed his ear against the door. The organ music was off. Knowing the only way that could be possible was if the clock was accurate, he whispered, "What the fu—" Slowly, he turned the knob. Peering down the hallway, half the lights were off. Management always did that to encourage the retail workers to get out as quickly as possible to avoid paying extra.

He put the back of his hand to his forehead, wondering if perhaps he was coming down with something and had unwittingly fallen asleep. His temperature felt normal. Assuming he had most likely dozed off, healthy or not—it wasn't the first time in the lonely space—he grabbed his jacket. Glancing at the photo, he didn't want to leave it there. Something deep down told him to bring it with him. With a quick shake of his head, he turned off the light.

Robert clicked the lock to the office, hoping there wouldn't be any new creatures in the room tomorrow. He was determined to leave the growing anxiety inside the room. His office, with its crooked warranty sign, seemed more and more like a tomb over the last few weeks, but the thought of not coming back brought equal parts of fear and relief.

As he walked down the long brick-lined hallway, tension grew, returning to his shoulders. The closer he got to the first-floor concourse, so did the desire not to return, the feeling inspired by the plastic holiday decorations that had hung on its walls since the late seventies. Reminders of so many past Christmases alone weighed him down.

The management of the mall's last anchor store seemed intent on keeping the space a time capsule. He passed the animated North Pole elves surrounding the replica of Santa's workshop. He hated the way the glass eyes of the motion figures seemed to follow him on his way to the escalator. Their jerky movement spoiled the illusion that they were from a magical realm and not just plastic animatronics.

Reaching the second floor, he hurried past the door of the manager's office, nearly sprinting. He paused momentarily at the oversized display of the two-tiered model train tracks. The toy trains were running so fast he could smell the heated motor, making him wonder if they ever turned them off. As Robert made his way to the main exit, he weaved his way behind the shoppers, wondering how the ridiculous displays still drew such decent crowds.

Exiting the double glass vestibule, the chill of the ferocious late December air attacked his bare skin. He pulled his collar up tight and strode through the parking lot. It was Tuesday, and tonight was half-price night at Cozy Corner, the small restaurant nestled in the corner of the mall's parking lot. He entered to the nearly deafening noise of a crowd. The lure of chicken wings had proved irresistible to the residents of the Illinois suburb. Peeking through a mob of heavy winter jackets, Anne's waving hand was barely visible. Glad to see his coworker got a premium spot at the bar, he joined her, hopping onto the leather barstool.

"Good to see you, stranger!"

Robert sat swiveling on the bar stool. Seeing the cloudiness in her gaze, he suspected she was at least two beers in. "Hey." They were practically screaming over the crowd noise. Robert took off his heavily padded jacket, sweltering in the packed room. Every time he was here, he wondered if the heating system was faulty or if the management kept it warm to encourage drink sales.

The waitress, wearing an ill-fitting uniform, brought over two mugs of beer in heavily scratched plastic replica steins. She looked out of place behind the bar, like she would be more comfortable teaching grade school children than dispensing beer. With a demure smile, she left them to their drinks.

"Hope you don't mind. I took the liberty." With a quick wave, Anne gestured to the beer.

His fear was slowly letting go as he stared at her. He felt more and more as if she could solve all his anxiety with her smile.

"Thank you." He grabbed the beer and took a sip. It tasted bitter, as if they hadn't cleaned the tap in some time. Robert looked at the blurred image from the large mirror running the length of the bar. Most thought it was there to make the room look bigger, but he knew it allowed everyone to leer at others anonymously. The room was filled with younger people playing verbal chess, trying to become better acquainted. Looking at a group of young women in short skirts behind them, he cringed, feeling that always invited trouble in a bar.

Anne gently tapped his elbow. "See anything you like?"

Feeling embarrassed, his face heated, feeling like sunburn. "No, really no." She smiled her wide smile, revealing her half-painted lips. He wanted to ask her if she painted them that way purposefully but couldn't find the courage.

"Okay then. So, are you ready for the big event?" She stared at him. After a few seconds in which he did not respond, she said, "You know, the quiz?"

"Oh, yeah, sure. Ready as I'll ever be." He took another strong sip, his head getting a little lighter, reminding him he hadn't eaten lunch. Thinking of the day disappearing as it had brought a ringing to his ears. He couldn't remember drawing the picture, yet the model's face now floated through his memory. He tried to ignore the increasingly loud buzzing noise. He clenched his fist around the beer, hoping the coldness would give him something to concentrate on.

"Why are you so weird at work?"

He couldn't tell if her bluntness was endearing or annoying, but it was hard to have any negative feelings towards her. Not knowing what to say, he took another sip. She kept staring. His stomach rumbled as if the beer was trying to escape. "I don't really understand what you mean?"

"It's like you're hiding."

He took a deep breath, closed his eyes, and said what he had been concealing for so long. "It's because I'm..." The simple words felt like a weight was lifted from him. He straightened up, staring deeply into her eyes. "I think I'm collecting a check because everyone forgot about me."

"What's that?"

Finally uncorked, he blurted, "I used to report to a manager who was let go. He was, ah, a little disgruntled. I asked him who I would report to, and he said he didn't care. Well, a few days went by, and nobody came. I just kept showing up."

"You keep getting your checks, right?"

"Yes."

"Well then, you're being paranoid. Companies don't just pay people without keeping track of it. You still have a job."

"Or... they just forgot to tell HR to cut me off."

"You're working, aren't you? So, what's the big deal?"

"That's the thing. I show up every day. But there hasn't been a service call in nearly a year."

"Wait! You've been showing up like this for that long!"

Robert closed his eyes and spoke into his chest. "Yeah." He fought the urge to leave. As he was searching for the right thing to say, he felt her hand on his arm. He couldn't remember the last time someone touched him. "I don't know how I let it go for this long. It just kinda... happened this way."

"So, what do you do all day?!" She leaned to the side and curled her leg under herself as she stared with arched eyebrows.

Try to catch a spider that I suspect is hunting me. His back tensed, picturing the last thick web. "I read, draw, and hope for a way out of the situation. This is my fault for not acting immediately. It's not that I'm lazy, but change isn't easy for me." He leaned back, wanting to leave. Anne closed the distance, leaning in, and held his forearm.

"I'm so sorry you have to deal with that. It has to be awful sitting there alone."

"You don't think I'm a... jerk for showing up so long?"

"No! You need your check, just like all of us. I mean, maybe you should have said something earlier, but I know how easy it is to slip into something you didn't intend to."

His heart fluttered as he thought of leaning in and kissing her. "Thank you for saying that."

"What're you going to do?"

"Right now? Hope to get through the holiday and then after maybe find the courage to possibly fess up."

"I could go with you if it helps."

Her fingertips massaged his arm gently, sending a tingling sensation that seemed to travel directly to his heart. "Yeah. I think it would."

"Tell you what, I'm heading out to visit my dad tomorrow afternoon. I'll be back on Monday. I know you said you want to wait, but if you're up to it when I come back, how about we go to the office together?"

No, I can't! Ignoring the screaming inside his head, he placed his fingers over Anne's hand. Her warmth gave him strength. "Yeah, I would like that." As if she could read his earlier thought, she leaned in and kissed him lightly on the lips. Tasting the barely there lipstick, he brought his hand to the back of her neck. She withdrew her lips and placed her forehead against his momentarily before pulling back with a bright smile. Sighing deeply, he hoped he would always remember the taste of her breath.

The lights flickered, and the waitress announced it was time to begin the quiz. Robert, relieved he didn't have to say anything that could spoil the best moment of his life, sipped his beer.

Politely, he smiled and nodded toward the screen above that displayed the first question. As the night went on, he drank precisely four beers and ate twenty mild wings, as he had done on their last visit. It was a perfect night.

***

As he entered the office the next morning, he took a deep breath, remembering his hope for a clean office. When he flipped on the light, the largest web yet greeted him. Staring at the well-constructed strands that spanned from the ceiling to the table just behind his chair, he grunted into the room, "Come on! Take one day off."

The constant hum of the fluorescent bulbs swallowed up his words. By some trick of the light, the intricately patterned web appeared of multiple shades of gray. As he examined the handiwork of the creature that was disrupting his routine, the unnaturally thick strands disgusted him. The spider's newest lair looked more like an item purchased in a novelty store than a trap for insects. As his stomach churned, he realized how uncomfortably close the web was to his desk, making him wince.

Wrapping his hands in paper towels, he pulled at the web from the top where it was attached to the dusty ceiling tiles. The spider's handiwork sprung free, piece by piece floating through the air. Working in very slow movements to avoid the web contacting the bare flesh of his arms, he was able to pull it loose. Imagining a tarantula with the circumference of a drink coaster crawling in and out of his mouth made him clench his teeth.

After a minute of quick swipes, he was satisfied with his work. As he had done every day for the last two weeks, he went over every crack and crevice along the walls and baseboard of the small room, finding no obvious entry point.

Looking for something to force his concentration from the spider, he grabbed his drawing from yesterday. In the brochure, as he compared the sketch, he realized he had somehow drawn the kitchen in mirror image.

Grabbing his thermos, he poured the rest of his coffee into the cup, admiring his work. Taking deep cleansing breaths for a few seconds, he examined his dream girl when the phone rang, piercing the silence. The mechanical bell in the relic startled Robert, causing him to spill all over the drawing. Simultaneously, he threw napkins on the paper and picked up the plastic receiver. He barked into the plastic contraption, "Gatlet's Warranty!"

"Hello, my name is Kim Hedren." There was a pause, and in the background, there was a loud scratching noise. "I am calling because my refrigerator keeps turning on and off. We purchased it some time ago. However, the tag on the back says it has an extended warranty and to call this number."

Holding the phone between his shoulder and ear, he mopped the coffee off the drawing. It distorted half the pretty face he had just completed. Looking at it, he tensed, leaning forward. Holding in the obscenity he wanted to yell, he asked, "When did you purchase it, ma'am?"

"Well. Let's see. It was before Charlotte was born, so it had to be at least ten years ago."

"If it's that old, the only thing that would still be covered is the motor. Is it still cold inside?" He had removed as much of the spill as possible. Fortunately, the damage was contained to only the right side of the model.

"Yes, I think it is."

"Might not be the motor, then. Can you please give me your address, and we can schedule an appointment?"

"Eight forty-two Terrace Drive in Orland."

The address she gave him was just under an hour away. He cringed at the thought of having to leave his cocoon, making his hand shake enough that the address he was writing looked blurred.

Before she spoke, the scratching noise was growing louder, making it hard to hear. "Would you be available this afternoon?"

Taking a deep breath at the thought of putting off redrawing his dream woman, he asked, "Could we possibly schedule it tomorrow?"

"No, I have a previous obligation." There was a long silence. In the background, he heard a faint tapping noise. It was louder, overtaking the scratching. "Will you be the one coming to perform the work?"

"Yes."

"Will you be able to accommodate me?"

Clenching the receiver tightly, he replied, "Yes."

"Very well, thank you, Robert."

Before he could respond, the line went dead. Pulling the receiver free from his ear, he stared at the plastic and sarcastically said, "You're welcome. See you then." He punched the desk with the side of his fist. Although pleased to have a legitimate reason to be employed, the intrusion into his insulated world was frustrating.

Realizing there was nothing else to be done with his drawing until it dried, he stuck it to the corkboard with a thumbtack, picture side down. He grabbed his tool bag from beneath the desk and shook it before unzipping it, thinking of the spider. After opening it, he performed a quick inspection, realizing he only had about half of what he needed. As he got up to open the closet where he stored his tools, he couldn't shake the feeling it was going to be a very long afternoon.

Pulling open the louvered door, Robert saw the newest web spanning across the closet. His stomach churned as he stood frozen, looking at the sinewy, almost transparent net it made. Agitated terror overcame him as he thought of how the spider had been working so close to him for who knows how long. He dropped his bag and kicked the closet door. Watching the offensive web flitter in the air, he imagined thick legs scurrying over the cordlike net.

Robert grabbed some paper towels and glass cleaner. He stabbed at the web. The long strands clung to the back of his hand, sticking to the fine hair. Repulsed, he frantically wiped the residue off using a flinching motion, his ears ringing loudly as he worked. Swatting at his forearms, he felt as if hundreds of tiny insects were crawling up his arms, looking for retribution against the giant destroying the trap they had so skillfully crafted.

He thoroughly inspected the chair, desk and surrounding area, seeing nothing. With only a few minutes to spare, he filled his tool bag, imagining phantom legs crawling up his socks the whole time. As he passed the corkboard and his sketch, he noticed the paper had rippled in the spot that was stained by the coffee. Besides half the model's face being distorted, it was in decent shape. Feeling a little optimism amidst the panic, he grabbed the address off his desk and headed to the office door to get the service van from the garage.

As he always did, he placed his head against the door, listening for anyone there. Every day, he was sure he was going to walk into a passing manager, and they would remove him from his haven and his much-needed income. Holding his breath, all he heard was a light scratching, reminding him of the phone call.

Faintly, he thought he heard a female voice say, "Yes, soon." He paused for nearly a full minute, pressing his ear against the cold metal. Confident the hall was clear, he opened the door slowly. It revealed a very dark foyer, obscuring the shape of the squeaky voice at the end of the narrow passage.

"Please come in."

Robert squinted, looking ahead through the shadows.

The hidden voice said through the darkness, "The kitchen is just this way. Please close the door behind you."

He stepped backward into the office and dropped the tool bag. Staring down the narrow hallway, he thought he could see the shape of a woman. Panicked, he slammed the door shut. With labored breaths, he whispered into the empty space, "What?"

The word seemed to anchor him, bringing back a tiny amount of strength and reason. He gripped the handle to the door and turned it slowly. Inching the door open, he leaned against the wall and stared down the same foyer, taking a half step back as if the extra couple of inches would provide some safety. The shadow advanced toward him in fragmented movements.

"Are you coming?"

The words echoed in a deep bass like they were penetrating him through his skin.

Quickly, he slammed it closed again, shouting, "Please, if this is a dream, let me wake up right now!" He closed his eyes and leaned against the wall, his head spinning and his stomach rumbling. Deep down he knew the wish was useless. He was not asleep, but he clung to the thought. Turning, he leaned against the wall and slid down, sitting on the dirty linoleum. Straining to hear, there was only the same dull hum.

After a few minutes, he slowly made his way to the desk. Finally, he grabbed the phone and brought it to his ear. The line rang without him dialing a number. Hitting the transfer switch did nothing. The phone kept ringing. In a flash of panic, he slammed the receiver down. As he sat in the chair staring at the door, he wished he had locked it.

After twenty minutes of his mind stretching his nerves, he found the strength to go back to the door, knowing if he didn't get control soon, he might never do so. He jerked the door open. As he peered into the dim light, he saw that nothing had changed. Taking small tentative steps, he walked down the narrow hallway, ready to end whatever distorted delusion his mind was conjuring. Standing in front of him was a woman wearing a formal dress. As she ascended two small steps, he noticed she had a slight limp.

Robert looked back at his office. The door was slowly swinging closed. With a yelp, he reached for the handle, missing it by inches. It closed completely, locking shut. Instinctively, he reached for his belt clip, realizing the keys were back on his desk.

With no other option, he slowly turned, directed his attention forward, and began walking. Each step echoed through the darkness. Guided by the dim light, he shuffled along, feeling like a thick band was being tightened around his chest.

Once through the hallway, he saw the outline of the woman turn, taking a small step down. Following, he came to the kitchen. It was laid out exactly as the sketch he had drawn earlier. Robert took in the oddly familiar surroundings, his eyes tracing every inch, hoping the hallucination would end soon. He slipped the strap of his tool bag off his shoulder as if in a trance. Muscle memory was now guiding him. The fridge was on the right side of the L-shaped design of the room where Kim now stood. She turned and Robert took her in.

Her clothing and figure were a near duplicate of the model from the photograph he had drawn. The dress was a different color, but the design was identical, with the squared neckline and matching hem. Tracing every inch, he discovered the material was tight enough to leave very little to the imagination.

From the dress up, the only similarity was her hair color. She wore her auburn locks down with severe bangs and a wave that obscured a good portion of her face. From what he could see, she was very alluring—so much so that, despite the fear, he longed to be near her.

Kim turned her head, her hair waving back and forth. Placing one hand on her hip, she pointed at the fridge. "Since I called you earlier, it has been staying off for longer periods." She flipped the side-by-side door open. Placing her hand inside, she said, "Now it's barely cold."

Taking a step towards her, he looked at her left hand. She quickly balled it into a fist as if she were concealing something. "What's happening?"

With a sarcastic tone, she replied, "That is what you are here to find out, Robert."

"How'd you know my name?" He searched for a way out of the claustrophobic space but found nothing but ordinary objects that were haunting his thoughts.

"Whatever do you mean?" She let out a brief chuckle. "How could I not?"

Robert looked at the back door of the kitchen. It had two deadbolts, neither of which was a key. He thought of dashing to the door but knew that he would be pinned in with nowhere to go if it was locked. Directly to the right, he saw another door. Assuming it was to the basement, the urge to run to it was overwhelming. "Miss, I don't know what's happening... but I have to go. I have other appointments scheduled for today." His voice was shaky, not sounding like himself, adding to the growing panic. Somewhere nearby, the familiar scratching noise was growing louder.

"I can't let you leave... just yet." The teeth glistened in the dull light. "Not after waiting this long."

He thought of running back down the hallway. The idea of getting caught in the darkness, with her behind him and no exit, made him freeze. "Please ma'am, please. We can reschedule for tomorrow, okay?" Each word made his heart rate increase. "I... I don't even have the equipment I need to fix your refrigerator."

"How could you know that without even inspecting it?" She stepped to the side, making room for him to come closer. "After coming all this way, you might as well look, don't you think?"

Ignoring instinct, his legs moved as if he were in a trance. He took a step toward her, trying to buy time until he could figure out a way to escape. Grabbing the door of the olive-colored appliance, her perfume was intoxicating. He reached inside the fridge and put his hand against the back wall, feeling for the vibration of the motor. Trying to buy time until he could think up a plan, he closed the door and said, "Let me look at what's going on." She took a small step back as he shuffled the appliance forward. Their bodies came into slight contact with one another. Feeling her hip against his forearm brought a wave of disgusted passion.

He quickly turned sideways into the narrow opening behind the appliance, urgently needing to be free from her touch. Knowing she was watching his every move, he played out the part, trying to look as if he was focused on repairing the machine. Pinned between the enormous fridge and the dirty wall, he could barely lift his arm to unplug the cord and replace it with the voltage tester. The meter did not move. Robert, in a voice much too loud, said, "Well, I think I might have discovered the problem."

She stepped behind him, pinning him tightly in the enclosed space.

Over his shoulder, he made up the first excuse that came to him. "Looks like you have a bad outlet or a loose wire." Relief washed over him, believing he had found an excuse to get her to leave the room and whatever madness he had slipped into. "The, ah, the good news is that's an easy fix—and cheaper than a new fridge." Out of the corner of his eye, he could see the edges of her hair inches from his face. He wanted to look away from her piercing stare but couldn't.

"Can you fix it?" She shifted her head slightly, the shadow covering her profile almost disappearing. "Is there nothing you can do? If it is a matter of money, I can pay you."

The thought rushed to him, making it seem like he could breathe normally for the first time. "I'm not supposed to, but if it is a loose wire, I can fix it. Do you know where your electric box is?" He did his best to say calmly, "You have to turn off the power first."

Taking a step back, she said, "The power is in the basement, but I'm not sure where."

"Should be easy enough to find. If you can run down there and flip the switch, I can get this fixed up."

"I'm not exactly dressed for that." She looked down at her dated dress. "Could you possibly do it for me?"

He hid the disappointment that she didn't bite. Hoping there was a window downstairs, he quickly said, "Of course. I may have to turn off the main circuit, so the power will go off everywhere. You might want to warn anyone else who is home." He held her gaze, anxiously waiting to see if she'd reveal if anyone else was in the house.

"It's just me and my daughter, Charlotte. She is most likely taking a nap. That girl does little else." She gave a knowing smile as she pointed to a door at the back of the room. Beside the door was a large corkboard that was a collage of flyers and coupons from various stores in the mall. "The basement is right through there. Thank you again for being so kind."

Grabbing his flashlight, he attempted to smile. His lips felt as if they were made of concrete, weighing them down into a permanent frown. Trying to hide the feeling of uneasiness, he turned his head away. As he walked to the door, he remembered something she had said earlier about the fridge being as old as her daughter. He found himself relieved to know that, even if he encountered another member of her family, at least a child would be easy to get away from. Quickly, he walked toward the basement. The door didn't want to open. Both deadbolts were still latched. It took some effort to spring the locks. They groaned against the pressure of his shaking fingers.

Somewhere in the distance, he heard a scraping noise. So close to the back door, he thought again of running. He gauged the distance from Kim, realizing that she would be on him in seconds if the deadbolts didn't cooperate. He opened the door to the basement. If it had a window, it was his best chance. If it didn't, it would at least buy him a few minutes to think.

Making his way down the stairs, he groped for a light switch, his head spinning. Finally finding it, he flipped on the light. The basement was damp, very dark, and mostly unfinished except for two half-painted walls. In the dead center of the room was a series of boxes creating a makeshift hallway. Navigating through with the beam of his flashlight, he saw the electric box in the far corner. As he walked toward it, he fluttered his hand frantically before him, removing thick cobwebs.

Moving around a wall of boxes, he came across the spider. The hideous shadow slowly revealed itself. Scampering on hairy legs, it was nearly the size of a German shepherd. Robert froze. His brain was trying to make some sort of sense of what he clearly saw, thinking it had to be a left-over Halloween decoration. Watching its deliberate stalking movement, he bit his tongue hard enough to draw blood.

Suddenly, the eight-legged mass scurried sideways and pounced on him. He was in no condition to even try to defend himself as the weight of its leathery body clung to him, wrapping its many hairy legs around him. Falling backward, the back of his skull contacted the concrete floor. As his vision faded out, he could see a phantom vision of the model from the brochure smiling.

The room was nearly black, with only a small stream of light filtering through, making it impossible to discern anything other than shapes. The clearest was that of an enormous spider. It clung to the same web as Robert. The creature was lightly bouncing up and down, using its legs to absorb the shock of the moving web. Its thick torso remained perfectly still, the head pointing directly at him.

Robert tried to shield his face at the sight of the creature, quickly realizing he couldn't move. His lungs burned as he took sharp breaths, the panic making him warm all over. Straining, he wiggled, but his arms were tightly pinned inches from his body, feeling like they were swaddled by an unseen thin cloth. His frantic efforts to move only caused the web to sway faster, the vibration now making the spider appear to dance in the darkness. It scurried towards him. As each hairy leg lifted from the web, Robert cringed, hearing a sickening, sticky slapping noise.

Shaking every muscle, desperate for freedom, the spider was now inches from his face. He strained against the impenetrable web until he thought his heart was going to explode. Hoping to get one part, any part of his body free, the only movement he could muster was the slight nodding of his head. Just as he felt bristled hair against his cheek, he screamed. Seconds later, blackness seemed to pull his eyelids down as consciousness slipped away once again.

Coming out of a fitful sleep, he felt so warm he imagined the sun beating down upon him. When he opened his eyes, there were only dark shadows, reminding him of where he was. From somewhere above, he heard the sticky noise once again. Glancing up, the spider's shadow came slowly into view, dangling on a single strand, stopping directly in front of his face. He closed his eyes so tight he felt a stabbing pain in his eyelid. He prayed silently as the monster caressed his face with legs that felt like carpeting rubbing against the stubble of his beard. Skillfully, he felt the spider disentangle itself, each leg slowly adhering to the tight web surrounding his body. Robert tried to wish the creature away. If it was going to eat him, he hoped it would do it right now. Anything would be better than being trapped like this.

The spider began nuzzling its face against his, making a gurgling noise, which was quickly followed by chunky discharge being spit onto his face. He closed his mouth and tried to eject the substance from his nostrils with a strong breath. As he quickly inhaled the needed air, he nearly choked. Using the tip of his tongue to flick the thick liquid from his lips, his tongue brushed against something that felt like a straw.

He cried out in disgust. The noise caused the leathery body to pounce, shaking the whole web. Each upward thrust of the dangling web caused Robert to come into contact with the monster's thick torso. It felt like a sack of bundled rags bouncing against his own motionless upper body.

For what seemed like hours, the spider lay across Robert, its body heat making him sweat. He licked the sweat from his upper lip. The salty liquid made him gag, but he swallowed it, needing relief from his thirst. Robert, tired from fighting, helpless, and vulnerable, slept with the creature lying against him.

Suddenly, there was a dim light in the room. Through puffy, sleep-filled eyes, he saw Kim standing a few feet before him. She smiled as they made eye contact. He knew what she was going to look like even before she turned her head.

The right side of her lips and chin drooped almost to her neck, the entire side of her face nearly erased, matching the drawing hanging back at his office.

The spider came crawling from behind the mountain of boxes. Slowly, it caressed Kim's nyloned legs, nuzzling itself against her. She spoke softly as she stroked the hairy body. The spider rose, welcoming her massaging hand.

Her voice came to him in a soothing, near whisper. "I know, Charlotte, it is okay. Your friend will eventually eat when he gets hungry enough."

"Please just kill me and get this over with!"

"Oh, we aren't going to kill you, Robert. You're here as a companion for my daughter. She's very lonely. Just like you were when you brought us to life."

The hairy monster seemed to sense his stare as it turned, and for the first time, Robert got a good look in the added light of the multi-eyed, childlike face. With a bright smile, it sauntered to him. Trying to recoil, he violently fought the sticky web, gaining nothing as the spider quickly scurried up his tangled web.

Back at the department store, Anne finally got to a manager on her lunch. She was growing more frantic with every passing minute. Robert hadn't opened the basement office when she returned yesterday morning. When she came down at noon, she pounded and even tried calling the warranty number. Worried that she was going to expose him as she promised she wouldn't, she slept on it. When she returned today, and he still wasn't there, she could wait no longer.

When she found Mr. Gatlet's son and explained her concerns, he looked up Robert's file, and she could tell by his expression that he had no idea who he was. After nearly begging, they made their way downstairs. With Mr. Gatlet at her shoulder, she flipped the light switch to the warranty department.

As the fluorescent lights slowly flickered to life, they were both shocked by the massive spider web that covered the entire length of the back wall of the office. Nestled in the exact center of the web was Robert's pencil drawing of a beautiful woman standing in a dated kitchen, holding a very hairy child's hand. The child held a black and white doll. Beneath tufts of artificial hair, the worn cloth of its face matched Robert's. His eyes were wide, and his lips stretched, giving him a fixed look of terror.

THE EXPANDING ROOM

"Something is wrong here." Richard stammered. "The number of people... it doesn't add up." He anxiously watched the face of Joe, his fellow volunteer, for a reaction. Richard's heart plummeted when Joe reacted with a look of shock, followed by anger. The rejection stung badly. Richard had waited so long to open up, and Joe was the one person he thought he could trust. Hoping that maybe Joe just hadn't heard him correctly, Richard repeated, "Something... ah unexplainable is going on with the number of people that keep showing up around here. I've been—"

"I heard you the first time." Joe's eyes probed Richard. "Are you OK?"

"I feel fine." Angry at being cut off mid-sentence, Richard frowned at his friend. Shadows from the humming florescent lights in what was once a gift shop in the mall made him look older than his forty-four years.

"Okay, then I'm confused. So now, what were you saying?"

Richard's foot was tapping rhythmically, trying to give the building adrenaline an outlet. The growing paranoia on top of his persistent anxiety was exhausting. No longer able to handle Joe's intense stare, Richard looked at the bulletin board. It was a collage of flyers for past events in the town of New Bremen. "This isn't easy to say."

"Hey man, slow down. Take a deep breath."

"I'm sorry. It's been a long day." He thought of the last woman who left their weekly support group for chronic anxiety and depression and how she stared at him with penetrating eyes before disappearing to who knows where. Her eyes burned through him, seeing something inside he didn't know was there. "Two meetings ago, old man Brighton asked me to print out more pamphlets." His fingers traced the shiny paper that was on the folding table to his right.

"And... ?"

"I had just printed some out last week, so I was a little confused about how we could use so many up."

"Well, isn't it obvious that people maybe took more than one? Or that they were discarded."

"Sure, I thought of that, but last week, as everyone entered, out of curiosity, I counted how many people came in."

"Why would you do that?!" Anger flashed over Joe's face, and then his eyes scanned the room as if he were searching for an emergency exit. He clenched both of his fists and then let out a deep breath. "Sorry, I didn't mean for that to come out that way. What I meant was that's really a waste of your time and a good way to feed the obsessive thought."

Even knowing Joe had to be right, Richard had difficulty processing the response of his mentor. Over the past meetings, he had never seen Joe act the least bit angry. His demeanor was usually so calm, Richard often wondered what drugs he was taking. Richard sipped stale coffee from a Styrofoam cup, the acidic liquid stinging his tongue. Grimacing, he continued, hoping he could make his friend's scowl disappear. "Yes, well maybe, but I discovered that forty-four people entered when I did."

"And... ?"

Richard watched a vein appear from nowhere. Defensively, he stepped back, knocking over a metal folding chair. The clang as it fell to the floor set his nerves on edge and made him jump. He smiled painfully, attempting to cover up his jitters—feeling that, if he didn't, the volunteer who had been helping him learn to cope with his mental health could turn on him. "Well, I don't know why—" His eyes went to the floor. Richard never could stare at someone when he wasn't being truthful. "But for some reason, I counted the number of people that left. Joe, there were only twenty-two."

"You obviously miscounted," Joe replied dismissively as he went back to folding the legs on the worn laminate and metal table.

Staring at Joe's expansive back as he hefted the table on its side, Richard fought the urge to call out and insist he pay attention. "Yeah, that's what I thought at first. So tonight, I counted again." He paused, willing Joe to look his way. He got his wish. Joe's harsh stare was back. The shadows from the dim lighting made his pupils appear to dance. "I came up with the same number." His voice cracked on the last words. His anxiety was always a struggle, but he never remembered it being this constantly intense. It was like he was made up of nothing but raw fear.

Joe turned away again and kept working, pushing the table over after it was folded. It struck the floor with a resounding boom. "Richard, please, look around you. Does this place look big enough for that many people?"

As he had been doing for the last hour, Richard looked over the walls. He had come here every Tuesday night for nearly two years, yet today, the walls that desperately needed fresh paint looked new to him. "No, I know it's not." He fought against the instinct to keep quiet, afraid he was taking the thought beyond a sane point, but needing to get it out. Breathing deeply, he added, "But everyone was sitting during the meeting."

"So?!"

"There were no empty chairs, Joe." He pointed to the pile of chairs on the rolling cart at the end of the room. "There are forty-four, if you count the ones we haven't put away yet."

Joe's eyes flashed to the pile, and then he spoke so quickly it was as if the sentence was one long word. "There were some already on the cart then."

Richard began to say "No," but the look in Joe's eyes held it back. The normal warmth and compassion had been replaced with disappointment. Concerned he had lost the goodwill of someone he felt anchored him to sanity, he lied again. "Yeah, I guess maybe you're right." He rubbed his sweaty palms over his thighs.

Despite himself, Richard added, "But besides that, everyone had a doll in their hand." He inclined his head toward the cardboard box that housed the artist's dolls. Nude wooden limbs were jutting out over the top. The doctor who ran the sessions passed them out and had the members of the group hold them as they spoke about their anxiety. It was his way of making them look at their pain from a distance so they could separate and isolate all the negative emotions, making the dolls the recipients. At the end of each session, when the doctor collected the toys, he told the group to pretend the fear was gone forever. "There's forty-four in there, and after I passed them out, the box was empty."

Joe took a step toward him. "Hey, take it easy, man." He raised his hands palms out, in a gesture to halt. "You must be drinking too much of that cheap-ass coffee Doctor Brighton insists we brew. You look like you're about to jump outta your skin." He forced a laugh. It betrayed the concern in his eyes. "You're making me hyper with ya, pal. What'd you think is going on here? People are disappearing into the walls... " He made a mock scared expression as he waved his fingers like an apparition from beyond the grave. "Or are you getting a little paranoid and miscounted?"

Richard knew he was right about how many people were there, but he also knew there was a menace in Joe's stare that he wasn't prepared to learn more about. "Yeah, I guess that's it... caffeine overload." A dull, constant vibrating noise seemed to come from all around him. "You hear that?"

"Don't tell me you're hearing things now too?"

"No. Must have been the heat clicking on." He knew better. The mall's massive furnace had an unmistakable noise if the heat clicked on. This was much quieter. It was like something heavy being dragged along a smooth surface.

"Since we got that settled, what'd you say we double time getting this stuff out of here?"

"Sure." Ignoring the mental anguish, he grabbed the nearest chair and folded it. As he lifted it onto the cart, against his will, he silently counted twenty-four. He knew there were still twenty left to be put away. Cursing under his breath, he wished he had taken a picture to prove what he knew. Dr. Brighton didn't allow the use of phones during his sessions, and Richard, despite his confusion, would never disobey the rules. His heart picked up as sweat rolled down his sides.

"You sure your head's settled up on this?"

"Yeah, I don't, ah... don't know what I was thinking."

Joe lifted the heavy table effortlessly with one hand as he said, "Bit of advice, friend. I'm always here for you, but before you say things like that, I encourage you to think them through before speaking them out loud. Paranoid talk like that around Brighton can make you a quick candidate for the Forever House."

The left side of Richard's stomach felt like a sharp object was being inserted at the mention of the psychiatric institute. The real name was Furver House, named after the founder, yet the patients came up with the menacing nickname. Bending forward, trying to relieve the numbing pain, Richard said, "I appreciate your guidance." Fumbling, he grabbed the next chair, feeling exposed. Richard always felt this way when he shared any of his odd thoughts. It stung more than usual this time because this felt so real. He knew how many people were in the room, and despite there being no logical explanation, he was sure of himself. *If you're so sure that many people were here, where did the others go?*

He continued to stack up the chairs, doing his best not to look at or touch the walls, which he couldn't stop thinking were expanding.

Richard finished a cheeseburger. It already felt like a gut bomb, even as it had just settled in his already upset stomach. He was looking out the window of Gatlet's Diner, staring at the mall's north entrance. At this hour, only a few cars were in the parking lot. Squinting, he thought he saw a man in a large Stetson hat disappear into the shadows of the entrance. Remembering all the stories he had heard of odd occurrences in the mall, he could picture the walls shifting, enveloping all the other stores surrounding the room the town was allowed to use for a tax credit. He was absorbed in this deeply plausible vision of the mall eating up the rooms when Marci pulled him from his rumination.

"Earth to Richard." She had an onion ring wrapped around her finger and was eating only the breading.

"Sorry, I was a bit distracted."

"Distracted?" Having removed all the breading, she grabbed a new onion ring. "I don't think you've said more than ten words."

He always loved watching her eat. She was never shy like most were. Staring at the increasing grease stains on her T-shirt, he said, "Well, I was eating."

"So am I, but I keep talking."

He raised his eyebrows and pointed with his head to the crumbs on her chest. Smiling, she flicked them away. "I don't mind a little grease if it allows me to keep talking. It's a good trade-off for this very stimulating conversation." She smirked as she pulled her leg onto the bench seat, leaning onto her knee. "So, really? Why so glum, chum?"

"I had an odd conversation with Joe." Guilt consumed the little energy he had left, zapping him of any ability to enjoy being there. Sharing his feelings was never easy or without consequence. Sighing, he continued. "I probably said some things I shouldn't have."

"Is that new? Don't you talk to him about everything that goes on in that overheated noggin of yours?"

"Yeah." He raised his hands, rubbing the palms into his eyes. The anxiety was trying to take over again, making his forehead heat up. "He was just... different this time. When he looked at me, it was like he was... I don't know, he was disappointed or something."

"You sure you're not being a little paranoid?" She scrunched up her face before adding, "Sorry, not trying to be rude."

"No, you're fine. Yeah, maybe you're right." He wished it could be that simple. Deep in the back of his brain, he knew it wasn't. A lifetime of studying others' expressions had honed a keen ability to sense emotions. His mother's violent mood swings before she disappeared had been the preliminary masterclass, and he'd continued his training with diligence in the time since. It was also his mother who gave him the first insights into how to both physically and mentally heal himself after being the recipient of the outbursts.

"What did you say to him?"

"I was, ah... " He stopped, staring at a trucker in the next booth, rocking back and forth, nearly asleep as he ate a hamburger. There was a tingling deep inside Richard. *Don't alienate her as well, dummy. Then who will you have left?* "It's not important."

"Obviously, it is. You've been moping since you showed up."

"I'm not supposed to engage the content of the cause of my anxiety." *Even if it means you discovered a room that eats up people.*

"Okay."

Seeing the hurt look, Richard added, "It's not that I don't want to share it. The program encourages us not to."

"I get it. I go to the Thursday meetings, remember? The cool night, not like all you Tuesday dorks." She wiped the grease from her hand on her pant leg, then leaned across the table and placed her hand over Richard's. "I really do get it."

Her hands were ice cold, making him flinch. She pulled her hand back, seeing his reaction. They had been hanging out together more and more for the last few weeks, and still, whenever she made any contact, he wanted to run. "Look, I'm sorry. I don't mean to be so... standoffish." *Smooth, Richard, that will really attract her to you.*

"I know."

She flipped her hair back, jerking her neck, and it went perfectly in place. He was always amazed at how easily she could do that.

"I really like you." She opened her lips to respond. Quickly, he continued, "I just have to work out a few things still before I can, you know... show it." She blushed. Seeing the bashful smile, Richard reached across, placing his hand on hers. He couldn't quite make eye contact. Fighting not to shut his eyes, he looked back at the trucker. He was now sound asleep, sucking on his hamburger pacifier.

"You're worth the wait, Richard."

For the first time that evening, he forgot about Joe. Her look and knowing that she had once been as anxiety-ridden as him brought some relief. It was like lying in a warm bath, knowing you had to get out soon and feel the cold once again.

"I know you said you don't want to talk about the anxiety with me, but would it help you to talk to Joe some more?"

With the calm mood disrupted, he said, "Yeah, probably." *She's like all the others, Richard. She doesn't care about you at all.*

"Then why don't you?"

See? Pushy, too. "Tried. He isn't answering my texts."

"Why don't you stop by his place? You know you're not going to sleep, not if you're thinking about him."

She sure is eager to get rid of you, ain't she? "That's probably not a bad idea."

"Probably?! It's genius."

Although self-conscious over his sweaty palms, he squeezed her hand. "You up for a short walk?"

"With you? Of course. But I can't. I'm already late to my grandma's."

Told you. "Oh, yeah, I forgot. Why do you have to go there again?"

"My sister's out of town. My gram refuses to sleep in her house alone."

Richard couldn't remember her speaking about her grandmother before. *That's because she's making it up to get away from you.* "You can't blow her off once?"

"She won't sleep if no one's there with her."

You going to buy that, dummy? "She's never been alone a single night?"

"That's what she says. Since Grandpa died, it's been a struggle to keep the streak going. We're always taking turns."

Sure—you... Stay out of my head!! Squeezing his eyes tightly, he said, "Well, it's good of you to do that."

"She deserves it." She glanced at her phone. "Hate to say it, but it's time we get going."

"Yeah, I guess so." Richard wished he had the courage to lean over and kiss her. Instead, he got up, buttoned up his jacket and looked at the light snow through the glass. Thinking of the walls of the recreation room expanding again, he shivered as he led the way out.

———

After Richard knocked the second time, Joe's door opened on its own. Richard thought he had heard a muffled voice say, "Come in," followed by a high-pitched whistle. Looking into the darkness of the apartment, he covered his ears and called out, "Joe?"

Hearing nothing for several seconds, Richard walked further into the darkness. He was flooded by a gushing warmth. Richard called out louder, "Joe!" He held his breath as he tried to hear anything other than the persistent rattling heat from the radiator. "You here?" He took a tentative step onto a carpet that looked like it hadn't been vacuumed in a decade.

The only light in the dingy room was from a small bulb connected to a worn electric cord that ran the length of the ceiling. On a piece of plywood overhanging a round table was a scale model of the recreation room. Inside were wooden figures posed in the room, sitting and standing amongst the miniature table and chairs. The walls were painted to match, and there was even a bulletin board with flyers.

They were like the artist dolls Dr. Brighton used in his sessions. Looking at the faces Joe had painted onto the wooden figures, Richard felt that if he came into contact with one of them, he would scream. Examining all the intricate pieces, it was obvious Joe had spent countless hours making his odd pretend world. Keeping a safe distance from the model, Richard called out, "Joe!"

His eyes never left the tiny dolls dressed in their tiny clothes. *Did one of them just answer you?* Shuddering, he jerked back, bumping into the counter. The more he stared, the more he realized each figure was made up to resemble the regular members of his group. The replica of Joe was standing in the doorway that led to the mall. Clutching the counter, he fought the growing dizziness that felt like a cloud floating inside his brain.

Leave now. Richard put both palms on his temples, willing the voice away. There was a whistling noise coming from the door on his left. Swallowing hard, he walked to the bedroom. The single bed was covered in trash, mostly discarded fast-food wrappers strewn about the wrinkled sheets. Everything smelled like onions and the cheap aftershave Joe had always worn. Navigating the piles of dirty clothes, he tried to come up with a reason for the model to be there. Could Brighton have asked him to build it?

Wondering where Joe slept, Richard walked carefully to the bathroom, each step feeling like a circular crank of a wind-up jack-in-the-box. Every inch built the anticipation that something was going to attack him.

Behind the plain white shower curtain, he saw the silhouette of his friend. Despite himself, he smirked, knowing this had to be some crazy joke. He grabbed the plastic and pulled, saying, "You motherfuc—"

Richard nearly bit his tongue off as he stared at a life-sized wooden doll with a painted-on face. Bushy eyebrows were arched over wide blue eyes, matching Joe's. There was a cheap wig on the wooden figure parted to the side unevenly, the same as his friend's. The face looked nothing like Joe, but somehow exactly like him.

It felt like a switch was flipped deep inside Richard, freezing him. His thought came out in light, uneven whispers, "Please don't move." *Ohhh, but it will.* Sweat beaded on his forehead, cooling the intense heat that was making his skin feel as if it was burning. As he let the curtain go, the metallic rings rattled against the hanging rod. Walking backward, his heart rate ticked higher and higher. The reflection of the Joe doll in the mirror in the corner of his eye gave the impression that more than one doll was in the room, closing in on him.

Richard backed out, slamming the bathroom door behind him with the phantom feel of a wooden hand clutching at him. As he tried to catch his breath, the vibrating noise he had heard back at the mall returned.

He made his way back to the main room, focusing on the cause of the noise to keep his thoughts away from the thing in the bathroom coming after him. When he flipped the switch, the overhead lights on the ceiling fan did not come on. Flicking the switch again, he grunted, "Come on!"

Needing proof of what was happening, Richard found the courage to walk to the model once again, examining it more closely. Each doll had a small piece of tape on it displaying a number. The highest was forty-four. *Get out of here before you become forty-five.* The thought felt like a blow to his throat. "There has to be a reason for this."

There were notes in Joe's handwriting scribbled on the exposed edges of the plywood, each equally illegible. Squinting, he thought he made out "the others going to the higher place."

As he tried to make sense of the insane ramblings, Richard's phone dinged. It made him jump, bumping into the plywood and causing the dolls to shake. He pulled the phone from his pants. As he did so, the dolls appeared to dance as they settled back to their positions, and he fought the urge to urinate. It was a message from Marci informing him that she had made it to her grandmother's. He thought to take a picture and send it to her but couldn't. *What? Are you afraid you'll scare her off? She's as nuts as you, she might like it.*

Holding the phone over the diorama, he snapped a picture. He was sickened at how each part matched the tiniest details, including the worn vinyl squares on the floor. Unable to be there alone any longer, he took a picture of the notes. The flash from the camera glistened off the wooden figures. In the last picture he took, he noticed the two male figures standing in the doorway of the replicated room. He knew they were duplicates of him and Joe. With effort, he restrained himself from running and made his way to the front door, never looking back, wondering what type of madness his closest friend had slipped into.

Calling in a favor, he was able to get an appointment with the psychologist who organized the meetings. Richard sat in the waiting room, noticing the strong resemblance of Dr. Brighton's secretary to one of the dolls he had seen in Joe's apartment. He wanted to get the picture out, to make the direct comparison, but thought better of it. He promised himself not to look again until he saw the doctor and could settle himself down. The phone felt like it was burning against his skin as the echo played in his mind. *But where do they go?*

He was compulsively brushing his pant leg when a woman and her child entered the waiting area from the back room. She was wearing a short tan dress and had long blonde hair flowing over her shoulders. He recognized her from the diorama as the doll that was sitting on the edge of the desk with the dress pulled up well past her mid-thigh. Staring at her nyloned legs, Richard was sickened by the tingling in his groin. He looked away, making eye contact with Dr. Brighton's secretary, who was staring, giving him a sly smile.

The clock above her head ticked, the noise bouncing off the walls jarring his already taut nerves. This wasn't the strongest panic attack he'd ever had, but they'd never lasted this long. Exhausted, he leaned back against the leather straps of the ultra-modern chair. Tick... tick... tick... reverberated through his brain. Richard clenched his teeth, grinding them to the same fixed rhythm. When the secretary spoke, telling him the doctor was available, he nearly jumped out of the chair, running to the door that led to Brighton's office. It took effort, but he forced a smile as he passed her. He inadvertently looked down her slightly opened shirt and grimaced when he thought he saw a woodgrain pattern on her chest.

He whispered under his breath, "That's not what you saw," and entered the doctor's office. Brighton was sitting on his leather chair, like he always did, with a small notepad resting on his arm, smiling.

Richard entered and sat down in the middle of the couch to the left of the doctor. Embarrassment overcame him as he settled in. This often happened when there was slight relief from the anxiety. Being in this room typically calmed him. Knowing he was being judged, he fought the urge to brush his pants.

"Hello, Richard."

With a quick nod, he said, "Doctor." His eyes traced the doctor's face and neck, looking for anything that hinted he was wooden. Richard knew the obsession was growing out of control, but couldn't stop indulging it. Everything appeared normal, yet his temple throbbed. Richard tried to blink the tension away.

"So, what brings you here so... urgently."

Richard took a breath so deep he coughed. "I, I ah, am struggling some today."

"Is this because of Joe?"

"What?" He pushed back, digging into the cushion, trying to gain distance from the man. The cold leather squeaked as he did.

The doctor leaned forward and, with a trained sympathetic look, said, "Hey, take it easy. Everything's going to be all right."

"What do you know about Joe?!" Richard wished he could pull the words back as he heard the panic in them. The doctor tilted his head sideways, scrunching his eyebrows together. *He's gonna send you to the Forever House.* The doctor scribbled into his notes. *That's the committal slip.*

"I assumed he contacted you. Yesterday, after you guys separated, he called me. I can't get into the exact details, but he was very... distressed."

"Where is he now?" The shower and the smiling dummy danced inside his mind. He bit down so hard his fillings hurt.

"He went to Furver House."

"You admitted him into Forever House!"

"I really wish you wouldn't call it that." He took off his glasses and placed them on the arm of the chair, examining them carefully as if it was the first time he had ever seen them. "It's not appropriate. Nearly all of the patients who are voluntarily committed leave within a week. And yes, before you ask, I don't mind sharing: he went there willingly."

"Then why didn't he tell anyone? When I called her on my way over here, not even his mother knew."

"I have no idea. I was with him just before they took his phone, and he said he was calling you. Didn't he?"

Richard couldn't remember a missed call. He pulled out his phone, hoping there was a voicemail. It wouldn't explain the macabre display, but at least he would know for certain where his friend was and hopefully get rid of the paranoid thoughts. There were no messages. Richard looked up at the doctor. "No." He raised the phone. "I just checked again."

"Well, maybe something happened to the message." The doctor glanced at his notes. "I could understand why he wouldn't call his mother that late. He was most likely counting on you to handle that in the morning."

Richard wanted out of the room. Anxiety was making his skin crawl. He looked at the door and thought of just making a run for it. The steady voice that he had heard for an hour weekly since he was eighteen stopped him.

"Okay, so was that the reason you came in today? Just over concern for Joe?"

For the first time in his life, he stared at the man who was like a surrogate father to him, and he didn't trust him. Remembering all he had done to help him through his life, Richard ignored his instinct and continued to open up. "Have you been to his apartment?"

"No. We met at a coffee shop last night, then went to the hospital later."

"I know you can't talk about the specifics, but I'm telling you he's in trouble."

"You're right. I can't discuss that with you. I can, however, listen to why you think he is."

"He's lost touch with reality."

"In what way, specifically?" The doctor put his glasses back on. "Did you see his project?"

"The model?!" Richard's heart raced, bringing familiar dizziness. "You, you, know about it?" Richard massaged his hands over his thighs.

"Yes. He's been working on it for some weeks now."

"And that's normal to do that?" *Sure, for a lunatic.*

"Not a word I use. We cannot easily define normal, so it is useless here."

"It was a perfect replica. Like perfect." Every detail came to him, the tiny eyes of the dolls coming alive. "It's very different to put that kind of time into a model like that, wouldn't you agree?"

"Aren't all hobbies, as you say, different? Obsessions to some, harmless pastimes to others?"

"Why would he do it?"

"He finds it calming."

Feeling he wasn't getting anywhere, Richard asked, "When can I see Joe?"

"Probably not for a few days."

"But why not?"

"He needs his rest."

Get out of here before he sends you there formally and permanently. "Have you seen the model?" *And the big doll?* Joe's hands went forward to rub his legs.

"No. He has told me about it, though. Look, I can see you are upset. Going there to meet him and not being able to reach him is understandably upsetting for you. But you mustn't judge him for having a unique hobby."

Coming here was a mistake. He needed to leave and sort out what he saw at Joe's apartment in silence. "I'm sorry to come in here like this. I just didn't know what else to do."

"You never have to apologize. This is what I do." His voice became deeper. "You do know Joe will be all right. This is a momentary lapse. I will ask one thing of you, Richard."

"What's that?"

"You do your best to forget what you think you... saw."

"What do you mean?"

"Thinking there were more people at our meeting than there actually were."

"Wait. He told you?"

"Yes, he told me. Richard, ideas like this can be infectious. He will be back in a few days, and things can return to normal. That is, if you don't remind him of your obsession."

Something was off in the doctor's stare. "Of course. I know you have another patient waiting, so I really must be going now."

"As long as you feel that you are okay."

"Yes, I'll be fine."

"Richard, I can see the stress on your face, it worries me. It's important that you realize that you might not be seeing reality as clearly as you should right now. The talk of people disappearing and being overconcerned about Joe's hobby has an obvious cause. You do realize that your fear of abandonment is possibly contributing to that? Joe didn't leave you like your mother did. He just went away temporarily. You understand that, correct?"

His face felt as if it was on fire. Whenever the doctor brought up his past, deep shame quickly flashed into anger. "Yes, I'm sure that's it."

"Good, get some rest. I'll see you at the next session."

"Yes." Richard left the room, the whole time having expected the doctor to stand and move like a wooden figure.

Just as he was about to close the door, the doctor called out, "Richard, promise me you'll keep your theory to yourself. I think it would be potentially harmful for you to share it with anyone else. Especially Marci."

Richard nodded yes as he closed the door. He bypassed the elevator and took the steps two at a time, with the familiar panic he thought he had conquered coursing through him.

When he returned to his apartment, the light in the kitchen was on. He stopped, knowing someone had been there. It wasn't possible for him to leave it on. He always carried out his rituals when leaving. He took off his sweatshirt and hung it next to the door. Feeling an overwhelming presence, he called out, "Is anybody there?"

The words were swallowed by the shadows. It took effort to walk forward. Ambling along, he saw the plywood edge hanging over his kitchen table. Turning the corner with his head leaning back, he stepped into the room, and his heart stopped.

A ceiling-less replica of the fast-food restaurant in which he had eaten with Marci was sitting on the raw wood. Richard clutched the back of his neck, gripping tight as he let out a whisper of a laugh that ended in a whine.

"No... no, no." Shaking his head, he saw the doll version of the trucker holding a hamburger near its puckered doll lips. A replica of Marci was in the next booth, and a doll sat across from her. Richard was too afraid to look at its face, but he whispered, "I know it's me." *Of course it is, dummy.* He pinched the back of his neck hard enough that the flesh opened, letting out a slow trickle of blood. Clutching his chest, he asked into the room, "What is this?"

There was a shuffling noise behind him. Dashing across the kitchen, Richard pressed himself tightly in the tiny space between the fridge and the wall. His shoes squeaked as he fought to push as hard as he could against the outdated wallpaper, hoping to make it through the plaster and away from what was creeping through the darkness. *Smart, pin yourself in, doll bait.*

He desperately clutched at the wall, wishing he could get away from whatever was stalking him. His heart pounded relentlessly in his ears, as if it had crawled into his overheated brain.

Just as he thought this was it, it was his time to leave this world, he heard a familiar voice. "Richard, it's going to be okay."

It was Marci, yet he still fought to shrink himself deeper into his dark corner. When her face peeked around the edge of the appliance, his jaw went slack. Her skin was waxed, and her eyes looked like shiny beads. "Who are you?!" *You know, lover boy.*

"It's me, silly." She lifted her clubbed hand and then, glaring at it, quickly hid it behind her dress.

His stomach ached. "Please make this stop." Pushing as hard as he could, he pressed his head against the wall as if the extra inch away from the moving abomination would protect him.

"Oh, Richard, why must you be so inquisitive?" She shook her head. "Now, you will learn sooner than you're ready for."

"Learn what?!"

"The real truth of the room." She stepped away, revealing an unobstructed view of the model. "There's no reason to be afraid... really. Where we're going isn't that bad."

She stepped towards him, hooked his arm with her clublike fist, and pulled him from his temporary cocoon. He wanted to get away but couldn't. It was like he was outside of himself, an observer of whatever madness was taking place around him. The wooden hand pressed against his flesh. Grimacing, he allowed himself to be guided closer to the table and the model. "What're you doing?" *Run!* He tried to dig in, but his feet wouldn't cooperate.

"I've always found it better to show than tell Richard." Closer to the light, her face suddenly looked more human—still unlike the real Marci, but less like an oversized wooden artist's doll. She hooked his arm tighter and reached inside the display, opening the tiny door that led to the kitchen.

She whistled in a tone that made Richard's head hurt, feeling as if someone had jammed a knife into his earlobe, poking deep inside his brain. The tune was familiar yet distant, like a chorus from a song he never wanted to hear again. The tiny door in the back of the miniature room creaked open, and a female artist's doll saun-tered through the shadow on wobbly legs. Once she was halfway through the model, she looked up at Richard. It was Dr. Brighton's secretary. She gave the same sly look he had grown accustomed to. Pulling away from Marci, he whined, "This can't be happening."

"I know it's difficult to understand."

Every second that went by, she looked more and more like the girl he was beginning to love.

She explained, "You're in the labyrinth now, Richard. This is where our fear lives after we're cured."

Richard thought of the room and the people who disappeared. The memories of all of their faces reminded him that they could all be relatives of the recurring group. The same, yet somehow different. Amazed that he never realized that during the meetings, he said, "What'd you mean?"

"Dr. Brighton's method of talking to the dolls separates us from the fear that has plagued us... creating them." She looked down bashfully at her shoes. "But then our other version of ourselves needs somewhere to go. Afterward."

Get far away from her! "What're you talking about? How're you doing... this!" Richard's thoughts were a jumble. It was hard to concentrate, it was hard to breathe. The dolls looked up at him in unison. *Get out of here now!*

"When we split away from our other fearful self, there's residual energy. That constant worry is so strong it lives on. It lives in there." She pointed at the box on the table. "Doctor Brighton keeps the dolls in that wheeled suitcase he's always dragging around with him. When all our emotions are out in therapy, they reside inside the dolls."

Richard looked up for the first time, realizing the room had no ceiling. "Then why do you look like that?" He considered running, but quickly realized that where he might end up could be much worse. He tried to will the now wooden texture of his skin to life. *She's crazier than you!*

"Richard, I'm not doing anything. I'm just showing you how Dr. Brighton's method changes things. If you enter the labyrinth with me, you will finally know what it is to be without the fear that has been weighing you down your entire life. Once you enter, you will finally be free."

Her eyes glanced at the diorama as she pointed with frozen wooden fingers. "Living here, it's not that bad. I promise. It's like a dream where you watch yourself from a distance."

Richard looked at the doll of the secretary. She had moved to the booth, sitting next to Marci. "I won't do it."

A high, shrill whistle filled the room, emanating from the diorama. Richard covered his ears, wincing. He watched as she leaned forward and placed her hand inside the miniature room. As her hand went through the door, she shrunk. As she did, a wooden version of her came out. With its fixed smile, it stared at him, tilting its head sideways. The wooden woman advanced slowly toward him. Richard moved back into the tight cavity between the wall and the fridge as she drew closer. Her face was slowly transforming, becoming more human. She looked not like Marci, but like a close relative. Without warning, her hand clamped around his forearm. Whistling, she pulled him toward his miniature counterpart, who stood looking up at him from inside the tiny labyrinth.

Richard felt cold silk surrounding him as he was slowly enveloped in darkness. A calm he had never experienced washed over him until he tried to breathe, and it felt like a wet cloth was covering his mouth, sucking deeper down his throat. He coughed, but no sound came out as he struggled to fight against his unseen captor.

He knew his eyes were wide open, yet there was nothing, not even a light the size of a pin's head. Panic had no place in wherever he had slipped into, but there was still fear and pain. After what felt like an hour, the cloak of darkness lifted, and when he took a step to run, he toppled over. He felt stiff, as if his entire being had fallen asleep. Looking at his hands, he saw they were fixed in the shape of the letter C, the fingers conjoined like those of the action figures he used to play with as a child. When he tried to talk, it felt as if his lips were fused together.

Slapping at his face, he noticed the walls. He was in the recreation room in New Bremen. Marci was at his side, smiling. Her lips finally parted as she said, "Relax, you'll be yourself in no time, Richard."

He looked up and saw no ceiling to the room; it was familiar, yet not. The sights, sounds, and smells were all shockingly similar, but not quite the same. Searching the room, he suddenly felt very alone. Trying to navigate his new wooden legs, he made his way to a miniature chair.

Marci came and sat across from him.

"Why did you bring me here like this?" He tried to cry, but nothing came out. Looking at the miniature walls, he caressed his face with fingers that were just starting to become flesh again.

"Because you were going to end it for all of us, Richard. You almost bridged the gap between them and us. Now that you are here, the only way back is through that door. It will take you anywhere in our world. There's only one catch: you must never speak of this again, and you must show up every Tuesday."

"Why?"

"Because if you don't, the anxiety people... "

Footsteps sounded from the direction of the hallway that led to the room. The beginning of a shadow was filling the doorway.

"You must choose now."

The shadow was growing, wobbling closer. Richard stepped backward, his eyes glued to the moving shadow. Marci grabbed his hand and pulled him back through the same door they had entered. Blackness came over Richard. When he awoke, he was back in his apartment, staring at the diorama. His normal constant fear was gone, replaced with a deep emptiness. It took a moment to realize what was truly missing. It was his anxiety. For the first time he could remember, his dark, hidden friend was not there whispering in his ear, filling him with unwanted emotions. He looked down at his club hands and felt nothing but emptiness. It was like devouring food and tasting nothing. The anticipation of panic that didn't come made him unsteady. He hugged himself, only feeling warm flesh. "What the fuc—" He covered his mouth, and his eyes traced the room, seeing the model on the table.

He took tentative steps to the diorama. His doll was gone. There was only the trucker left in the tiny space. "Who are you?" A feeling like someone was about to grab him from behind caused him to spin. "Marci?" In the darkness, no one was there.

It was shocking not to feel fear, but depressing in a way. It was like a long-lost friend was found and lost again, rekindling old, buried feelings and experiences. Turning back, he used the tip of his finger to open the door through which they had entered. Peering through the opening, he saw Dr. Brighton's waiting room. His secretary looked up and gave him a knowing nod. Richard closed the door. He looked up; there was no ceiling to his apartment. When he turned to look out the front door, Joe's huge eye was looking in at him.

He instantly knew he was still caught in the labyrinth. Taking a deep breath, he opened the door of the model and stepped inside.

This time, the transformation felt like it only took seconds. Immediately, he looked up. There was no ceiling. Blinking, he stared at the room, realizing it was Joe's apartment. Joe came out of the bedroom, reeking of cologne. "You alright?"

"What's going on?!" The look of defeat on his friend's face brought the fear back in a solid wave.

"It's easier if you don't ask so many questions and just accept it."

"Accept what!"

He stepped forward, the dim bulb illuminating his wooden face. "You aren't who you think you are."

"Really? Then who am I?!"

"You know why you counted so many people?" He was stiffening as he spoke. "Because you counted the dolls as people."

"No!"

"Yes, friend. That's what you did."

"Why would I do that?!"

"Because to you, the dolls are people now. I'm sorry, but all you are is Richards's fear trapped inside the doll." Joe raised his club hand. "You came to life in the last session. The last days of your old memories mixed with your new form are creating mental distortions, making you see yourself and others as a human. It's your way of processing what's going on. You've created a fantasy world where you still remember things as they were instead of what's real. Many react this way."

"No, no. No!" His face ached from the scream. He rushed to the front door and burst through. Instantly, he was back in the mall, in Gatlet's Diner. Looking up, there was no ceiling. Frantically, he tried to run on wooden legs that were so stiff he wobbled.

Joe came into the room. "Don't fight it. Your life, as you know it, is gone. Be here now."

Richard burst through the back door and found himself in the doctor's office. The lobby was empty. He made his way to the worn chair, struggling to navigate his new wooden body. There was the now familiar noise off in the distance. It sounded like a ball rolling along a tiled floor, making lapping noises as it struck obstacles. Richard looked up, remembering what Marci said about the dolls being transported in the doctor's rolling suitcase. There was no ceiling; it was replaced with a large zipper. He could feel the wooden dolls around him vibrating as they rolled through the mall's corridor. His scream was held inside his new wooden mouth. The last thing he heard before he went off to permanent darkness was organ music blaring through the speaker system.

PRESENCE FROM THE MALL

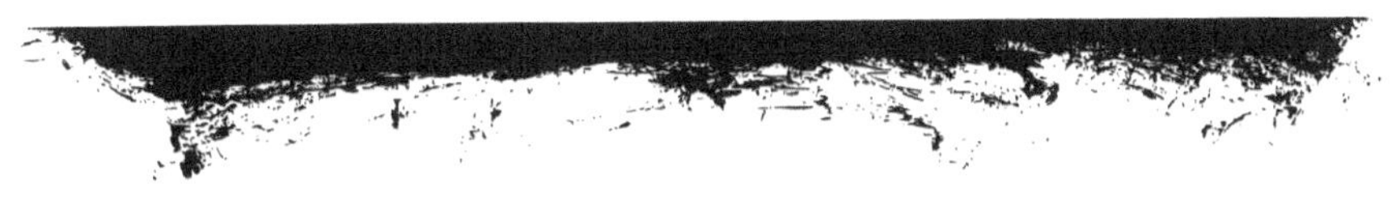

The sun beat down on the four-bedroom house surrounded by grass well overdue for the sprinklers. Inside, every shade was drawn, and the air was like a mid-December chill. This enhanced the ambiance of the artificial tree, lights, and assorted decorations surrounding the animated Mr. and Mrs. Claus flanking the fireplace. Barely audible choir music played on a single speaker on the fireplace mantle between two artistically hand-sewn stockings.

In the corner, Vincent sat with his laptop balancing on a wobbly TV tray. Its aluminum surface had a winter scene displaying reindeer flying over an old-fashioned town. The relic had belonged to his grandmother and never failed to bring back fond memories of over-cooked ham, the smell of tape, and the crinkling noise made from discarded wrapping paper.

Trying to determine if the song in the background playing on the record player was the Mormon Tabernacle Choir or some unknown group, he heard his girlfriend through his earbuds. "Seriously, are you even listening?"

"Huh? Yeah, of course." He was dreaming of a cake he once ate at his great-grandmother's house with a frosting that tasted of maple syrup and fruit adorning the top.

"So, you plan on spending the next two weeks locked inside pretending it's December?"

"Maybe not two weeks, but pretty much, yes, I'll be here until I finish the story."

"You're a nut."

"You knew that long before we started dating."

Her laugh had a high-pitched cooing quality. He imagined the woman who was nearly half his age wrinkling up her nose and flashing her bright smile.

"Yes, yes, I did." There was a slight pause, and the choir filled the silence with a rising pitch. Kellie's tone took on a slightly more serious note.

"Joking aside, is it really necessary to hang out in the dark like that? You know how you can get around the holidays. I know this isn't really Christmas, but I don't know if it's wise for you to be there all alone."

"It will be fine. I need to get myself in the right mood to pull this off." Hoping to get her off the topic of the seasonal depression he had been doing his best to ignore, he added, "Besides, this is only temporary, and I can stop whenever I want."

"How much do you get paid for this?"

"Practically nothing."

"Then why aren't you out here with me by the pool in the beautiful sun? Instead of sitting in the dark, you could watch me in my bikini."

The coo was there again, making him miss her more than he thought possible. "I owe the story to Marvin; my name got him the go-ahead for the short story collection."

"Yes, well, with a name like *Xmas Extremities*, I could see why he is guilting you into the story."

"I won't argue with you there. It is far from his best, but he has to take work where he can get it these days." He looked at his bookshelf, seeing the first collection he had ever been published in. "The truth is, I am living out my little world here where reality only exists as far as my imagination will take it."

"You are a weirdo, you know that?"

Yes, a weirdo whose weirdness is paying for your third vacation this year, while I work. Thinking better of it, he let it drop. "Well, let's hope I can harness some of that. It's been quite some time since I've written a straight horror story."

"I know it will be great, just like everything else you do. Hey, if you are not planning on going outside, what are you eating?"

"I have TV dinners and frozen pizzas to carry me through, and I have a stack of old VHS Christmas movies for entertainment. I picked them up for eight bucks at the donation center next to BMart."

"Great! Darkness, blurry movies, and unlimited junk food. Sounds awesome." After a sigh, she added, "Anyway, here's hoping you finish early and can get back to modern times quickly."

"You never know. Sometimes it goes that way."

"I hate to do it, but I got to go. Steph is waiting, and we're stepping out to dinner."

"Enjoy. I will call you tomorrow around the same time."

"Love you."

With that, the line went silent. Vincent leaned back in his recliner and stared at the animated decorations until he could imagine the eyes staring back. The game had been a favorite of his since he was very young. To him, imagining the miniature Mr. and Mrs. Claus coming alive was like a jack-in-the-box with a stronger bite. Feeling tired, he leaned back, smiling at the decorations as the eyes glistened, giving the plastic more depth. He slowly pulled the afghan over his head, deciding the writing could wait until after a short nap.

A few hours later, the first pages came in a flourish. After correcting the spelling, he headed into the kitchen for a TV dinner. Thinking turkey with mashed potatoes would be appropriate for the first night in his private holiday land, he realized how cold it was. He went to the thermostat: fifty-four degrees. Confused, he switched the system off. As he was closing the house earlier that morning, the outdoor temperature was already nearly seventy. He figured the house would warm up within the hour with the air off.

Walking back through the front room toward the kitchen, he noticed a present wrapped in silver paper under the tree, with the corners covered in red ribbon. It sat amongst the pile of decorative boxes that had been a fixture under his tree since he was a child. Staring at the reflective surface, he was confused, knowing it wasn't there before his nap. Slowly, he scanned the room, looking at the garland, candles, and other holiday heirlooms. Everything else was exactly as he remembered arranging it. He kneeled before the tree and poked the box as if it was alive. It slid a quarter of an inch on the silk tree skirt. Pulling it toward him by the ribbon, he saw his distorted reflection flash across the smooth surface. Vincent was cold. Drawing his arms nearer his body, he lifted the gift, shaking it. The silent weight inside shifted. There was a small tag on the edge of the ribbon. In almost illegible handwriting, it read:

"To: My Liebchen

From: Mom."

As his brain tried to process the emotion, he carefully peeled back the corner of the wrapping paper to reveal a plain box with the insignia of Gatlet's Department Store stamped in the center. He couldn't remember the last time he had seen anything from the store. Vincent lifted the top slowly with his thumb and forefinger, careful to make as little contact as possible. The thick, painted cardboard top came free with a swooshing sound, revealing a blue-collared dress shirt. It was an exact duplicate of the uniform he wore as a child.

Feeling even colder, he shivered and looked around the room. The only movement was the cloth statues of Mr. and Mrs. Claus twirling their heads and making their mechanical clicking noises. Still unable to think, he touched the shirt.

In a flash, he was sitting in Mrs. Vaglar's history class. He was at his assigned window seat, four back from the front, occupying the desk chair in which he spent so many hours wishing he were somewhere else. Directly in front of him was Kristen Delgrassi with her ridiculously thick, curly hair. Looking at her brought back the countless hours he spent staring at her bra strap through her thin uniform and wondering what it would be like to touch it.

Not a thing had changed from his memories of the room. He heard the voice that was always there, somewhere where logic was stored. *That's because this is a dream.* He ignored the voice and took in the room, seeing faces he thought he would never see again except in faded photos. Desperate to run up and down the aisle and recapture the long-lost feeling of complete freedom with the last group of people he would honestly call friends, something close to fear anchored him.

The clock above Mrs. Vaglar's desk showed that it was less than a minute before the bell. Vincent looked down at himself for the first time. He was wearing a heavy jacket and a scarf. It was the one his grandmother had made for him, which she called a "muffler." Looking out the window at the snow, Vincent saw his mother smoking a cigarette in her galoshes and oversized jacket. He wanted the bell to ring more than he ever had. Even if it wasn't real, if he could have even a few seconds feeling her arms around him, he would accept it disappearing when he woke up. The bell rang. Sprinting, he dodged the many friends he had longed to speak to just moments ago. Running down the painted brick hallway that always smelled of wax, he made it to the stairway. Taking the stairs two at a time, he made it to the exit. He pushed with all his might, but he did not have the strength to open the large glass door against the blowing wind. Frantic to get to his mother, he looked back.

In a wave behind him, the other children were catching up. They pushed against the doors as a group, letting in the frigid air and freeing Vincent.

The vision ended abruptly, leaving him kneeling by the tree, freezing, his hands extended. Disoriented, he leaned back and sat on his heels. Loudly he said to the empty room, "What the crap was that?!" He shook his head. Walking toward the kitchen, he passed the fireplace. A small, nearly extinguished flame was rolling along the final edge of silver wrapping paper. Exhausted, he kept walking, wanting to ignore the remnant of his dream. Hoping some food would straighten out his distorted thinking, he entered the kitchen.

His ringtone pulled him from his typing. It was Kellie. He answered with a sigh.

"How're things in Christmas Land?"

"Good, really good." His voice was monotone. He spoke into his chest as he slumped down on the recliner.

"Well, you are really selling the point with that emphatic delivery. What's going on with you? You didn't respond to any of my texts today."

"Nothing really, just distracted with waves of nostalgia."

"I told you it's not a good idea to be there alone, hidden away from the world like that. Vincent, I can catch a flight back in the morning if you want."

He equally wanted to say yes and no. Deep down, he knew how close the depression was to derailing him, but thinking of the dream, he wouldn't risk changing anything. "I appreciate it, but I'll be fine. At the pace I'm going, I could be done very soon. No point in spoiling your trip."

"I'm going to have to trust you on that, but please promise me that if you need me, you will call."

"That I can do." After twenty minutes of listening to her tales of her adventures in the Bahamas, Vincent ended the call. The room was still freezing despite the air having been off since yesterday. Wondering how they built this place, he pulled the afghan over his head and attempted to doze off, listening to Burl Ives belting out a ballad.

After several restless minutes, with ruminating thoughts of the house, his mother, and the work he needed to complete, he sat up. Vincent instinctively felt like there was something wrong. Slowly, he leaned forward and looked under the tree. In the same spot was another box wrapped in paper with Santa's face in a repeated pattern covering the surface. He walked to the tree with anticipation he had not felt in years. Faintly in the background, he heard organ music. Picking up the package, he shook it once, holding it to his ear. Whatever the contents were, they felt light and made a lot of noise. Tearing open the paper revealed a puzzle of a space station.

The second he took hold of it, he was in the basement of his childhood home they used to call the rec room. The walls were surrounded by cheaply painted bookshelves covered in puzzles, board games, and miscellaneous toys, all found in garage sales and donation centers. Sitting cross-legged, he spread the puzzle across the cheap vinyl floor. As he realized it was missing pieces, he thought he smelled cookies. He sprinted up the stairs to an empty kitchen. Standing on his toes, he looked out the window over the sink. It was a sea of white. The window itself had a decal of Rudolph's face with a shiny nose surrounded by spray-on snowflakes. Vincent and his mother applied the foam using aerosol cans they would buy at Drexel's drugstore. From behind him, he heard high heels clicking on the linoleum floor. He spun to see his mother still in her work clothes. She smiled as she bent to hug him. Smelling her perfume before she reached him, Vincent teared up. "Oh, how I have missed you." His voice was that of a child.

She pulled him tight into her chest and whispered, "Come now, I was only gone for a few hours, my dear."

Confused, he tried to pull himself free, becoming aware of how much stronger she was than his childhood self. Muffled in her blouse, he said, "But Mom, what's happening?"

She pulled him away. In her slight German accent, she asked, "Did you open your gift?"

"Yes."

"That's good. When I am not here, play with your gifts, and it will pass the time until you can see me again."

"Mom, what's happening?" The words died into the empty room of his home, getting lost in accompaniment to a violin version of "Santa, Please Come Home." Vincent looked at the fireplace. Again, the flame was finishing off the gift he had just opened. Frustrated, he walked to the picture window, pulled the drape to the side, and began removing the aluminum foil panels he used to keep out the light. There was no sun, only gray skies, and snow everywhere he looked. The drifts stood at least two feet high.

Holding in panicked laughter, he quickly went to his computer. It was four in the afternoon in mid-June. In the corner of the screen was a bright sun, and the temperature showed ninety-eight degrees. Inside the room he created as an artificial winter holiday, everything was as it had been, except for a pile of ashes in the fireplace. Disoriented, he leaned back in his recliner, trying to understand. Everything felt so real that he was afraid to challenge what he hoped was sleep. Suspecting that he may be awake and close to a place he didn't belong, he did as he had when he was a child. Pulling the afghan over his head, he closed his eyes tightly, trying to wish away whatever was happening. Laying there alone with small patches of light coming through the needlework of the fabric, Vincent stared at the decorations and felt more alone than he ever had.

By the time his phone rang the next day, Vincent had been staring at the snow accumulating outside, wondering how long a dream could last. He was afraid to answer the call, unsure what was real anymore. Knowing he should let it go to voicemail, he answered instead.

"Well, thank you for finally picking up!"

"What's that?" His voice was an octave higher. Vincent did not understand the change any better than he understood why when he used the bathroom, his pubic hair was gone, along with his beard stubble.

"Dude, I called you like ten times. I was just about to have someone stop in and check on you."

Feeling out of place, he absent-mindedly asked, "What song was playing the first time we danced?"

"Are you drinking?"

"No, just humor me, please."

"Peter Gabriel, 'In Your Eyes.'"

He remembered the retro eighties party as if it was yesterday. In a near whisper, he said, "That's right." He felt no validation. If this was his dream, that was knowledge he would be able to fill in. He was staring under the tree at the new present. The tag was slightly open. He could see it was from his mother.

"What's going on with you, Vincent?"

"Nothing at all." *Other than transporting back in time using old gifts as the catalyst.* "I was sleeping. That's why I didn't answer." Filling in the lie to give it substance, he continued, "I was dreaming about the first time we met. That is why I was talking about the song."

"You *need* to go outside."

Would love to, but I don't know who I will be if I do. "Yeah, I plan to, in a little while."

"How's the story going?"

"It's almost done." It wasn't a lie. He had the story mapped in his head after the first night. All he had to do now was type it out.

"Well, that's great news!" He heard her shout, pulling the phone from her mouth, "Not now, I will catch up with you later."

"Sorry to scream in your ear like that. Were you serious? Do you plan on going out later?"

"Yeah." *Right after I open this gift and try to figure out whatever I slipped into over here.* "So, what have you been up to?"

The concern went out of her voice as she talked about her day on the beach.

When the call was finished, an Italian crooner struggled through "Holy Night." Leaving the chair he had spent most of the last day sitting in, Vincent went to the package. This time it was all white paper with a snowman dancing, kicking up his heels. With trepidation, he tore into the decorative paper. Inside the box was a thin fabric blanket. Sewn into the quilts was a Martian landscape with retro spaceships and men floating away, tethered only by long tubes connected to their helmets.

As soon as he touched the fabric, he found himself lying in his old bed. The mattress was still uncomfortable, bringing back hundreds of memories of restless nights. There was a very uneven hump that always pushed against his back. Immediately, he stood up and saw his poster collection hanging across the walls. He was in awe, staring at the collage of classic science fiction and horror movie cards. Having no choice but to forgo the nostalgia he so desperately wanted to relish, Vincent ran from the room into the hallway.

It was hard to navigate the much smaller body. Every step seemed unsure. Awkwardly, he made it to his parents' bedroom. He could hear his father's deep snore. Even in his agitated state, Vincent wondered how his mother could sleep through it. Making it to her side of the bed nearest the window, he shook her bare shoulder, "Mom, wake up. I need you."

She opened her eyes, and they seemed to shine in the dim moonlight the drapes allowed into the room. "What are you doing here, honey?"

Her breath smelled of menthol, as it always did. Vincent froze, thinking of the cigarettes that had taken her from him. Finally, he regained his sense of urgency. "I can't figure out what is going on."

The words came out in a whine. Quickly, he added, "What should I do?"

She calmly said, "All you have to do is follow your heart, and all will be good. Where do you want to be, here or there?"

"Where is here... " The second the words left his mouth, he was back in Christmas Land. Staring at the glittering aluminum-colored tree, he wanted to scream away all the pent-up frustration. Shaking, he made a fist and hit the pile of fake boxes. They scattered across the hardwood floor. Vincent stood and walked to the front door.

Flinging it open, he stepped out onto the snowy walkway. Two steps in, he tripped over his pants leg and fell into the deep snow. His legs were those of an eight-year-old. It was as if the transformation had happened as he crossed the threshold. Continuing down the path to the street, his shirt hung almost to the ground. The house next door had been replaced with the home of the Buxleys, his former childhood neighbors. Vincent slapped himself across the face. It stung hard, but nothing around him changed. Looking back at his house through the open door, the interior looked like his childhood home. The exterior looked nearly the same as when he bought it with the royalties of *When the Laughter Stops*.

Running full speed, his socks came free from his feet. The front door was slowly closing as he got nearer. He fought through the snow and ice, slipping as he jumped over the single step of the front porch. At the last second, he reached his tiny hand out, preventing it from shutting completely. With all the strength in his tiny body, he pried the door open and jumped inside.

The interior was back to its original form as he left it. Between exhausted breaths, he could hear "Silent Night" playing. He was almost back to his actual height, but not quite. The sleeves of his shirt hung down past his fingers. With his pants off, he looked at his groin, and the hair was still missing. Panicked, hands shaking, he returned to his recliner and covered his frozen, almost hairless body with the afghan. His breath came out in short, interrupted wheezes as he tried to make sense of what was happening. Looking around the room, he saw a tiny flame in the fireplace. For several seconds that felt frozen in time, he watched the flame dance across the snowman, making the paper wrapping disappear entirely. Quietly, he said in a childlike voice, "I know how you feel."

Over the next few hours, he lay in his cocoon on his recliner and struggled between fitful bouts of what he believed to be sleep. Feeling too exhausted to continue running from or to the realm he had been thrust into, he was going numb from an overworked mind. Even in his anxiety-ridden state, he believed he had no choice but to wait for the next gift.

The room was still bitterly cold, and the heat would not kick on. Vincent had put on an overcoat and several pairs of socks. They all dwarfed his half-man, half-child body. His girlfriend called. He sent the message to voicemail and simply replied in a text explaining he was deep in a scene and would call her later. She replied with a smiley face and a picture of her tanned face showing cleavage.

As it had every other day, the gift came at the same time. Reflecting the dim light of the room, the present had a glittering silver paper like the first gift, but this time it had candy canes displayed in sporadic patterns. Knowing he may have been going completely mad, he knelt before the present. In his current childlike state, his memories were so vivid it was as if his past was measured in hours, not decades. No matter how much he tried to convince himself that being young and with his mother was perfect, he struggled with the thought of letting go. He had spent a lifetime trying to leave the loneliness and angst behind. Finally, he thought of his books and knew that his work, much like himself, was a byproduct of all he had been through in his formative years. Feeling like it was a betrayal of everything he was and had been through, he knew what needed to be done. Thinking of the person who always made him feel safe, he fought to say words that felt determined to stay hidden in him. "Mother, I love you. Please forgive me." He grabbed the ice-cold box and put it into the fireplace on top of the kindling. Working a match out of the box, his hands shook. He didn't know if it was from cold or fear. As it ignited with a familiar smell, he placed the match across the edge of the paper, and in seconds, it burst into flames.

Vincent sat on his heels, knowing he had made the right decision. As much as he thought he wanted it, he knew the present was where he belonged. Thinking of his mother's touch, he watched the flames turn to smoke and escape up the chimney. Nothing was distinct about the stream of gray smoke, but like the animatronic toys surrounding him, the longer he stared, the more he saw the form of his mother's face dancing through the mist, free to go on wherever her journey would take her now.

The lid of the box slowly disappeared as the flame ate away the cardboard, revealing the contents.

Inside, he saw the sports jacket he had worn the day of her funeral. There was no doubting the cheap fabric he buried in his closet the day after she went into the ground. Feeling the weight of her death and all the months caring for her leading up to it, Vincent sobbed uncontrollably, his clothes tightening as he returned to his true self. Watching the jacket go up in flames, he said in his normal deeper voice, "I will always miss you."

He slowly stood, wanting to distance himself from the barrage of memories that the sports jacket, the room, and the decorations had thrown at him. Walking toward the front door, he hoped to find the sun shining again and everything back to normal. Behind him, the fire popped loudly, and there was the sound of the fireplace screen rattling. Quickly, he spun.

Standing a foot behind him was the shape of his mother. With her features looking like an abstract painting, the mist expanded. It added enough distinction to make an impression but was still not defined enough to conjure any tangible connection except for her piercing eyes that, even as smoke, matched her living self. With almost transparent arms, she reached for him, and through parted lips, tiny flames escaped, creating whispered words, "I am so sorry, my Liebchen."

The dense smoke quickly enveloped him. As he inhaled the thick fog, he could feel all her desperation since she left this Earth as if it were his own. Her memories overwhelmed him. As he transformed into smoke, he stared into her almost human face as she became alive. Her expression changed from shame to elation as she gripped her new flesh.

Vincent thrust his arms forward, trying to grab her and take back his old self. The effort was useless. His smoke form dissipated with the movement and then slowly reassembled. Full of rage, he tried to yell, causing smoke to stream from the area his mouth used to occupy.

His mother slowly stepped back from the vapor wide-eyed, staring at her son. Her look of relief devastated him. Still fighting against the smoke, he could no longer feel contact with the floor as he floated aimlessly into the air. The smoke rose to the ceiling, making him feel one with the room. For the first time, he felt fear as he wondered what his mother had been through to make her betray him. He took one last look at the only person he felt had ever truly loved him, then eternal darkness overcame him.

THE FILM

Detective Bradley sat patiently in the passenger seat of the police cruiser next to an officer who looked like he was still a senior in high school. After reading the case history, she flipped through her phone to find an article about the movie playing in the theater they were racing toward. The first headline at the top of the search was from *The San Francisco Examiner*. The article was dated October 1980, and headed *"A Look Back on a Curious Film Premiere."*

The officer next to her spoke loudly over the wailing siren. She looked at him. The reflection of headlights in the rear-view mirror highlighted the upper half of his face, making him look like just a floating set of eyes in the dark.

Bradley, trying to hide her annoyance at being pulled from her research, politely said, "Sorry, I didn't catch that."

"I said, what's it like to work homicide?"

"Officer." She paused, trying to remember his name. Usually, names stuck in her mind longer than they should. After working for nearly twelve hours and then being lent out to help the suburban team, she felt like a shadow of herself. "Daniels. That's not something I can easily answer."

"Oh." He sounded hurt.

She engaged him, feeling somewhat guilty even though she didn't need the distraction. "I would assume you don't get too many out here?"

"Shit, no. Been on the force for nearly two years. Only deaths are in the old folk's home over on Forest Street. I guess that's why they had me pick you up. We don't have much experience out here in the burbs. Then again, who does with this type of thing?"

They were about ten minutes out. The officer picked her up from her townhome in Beverly. It was as far south in Chicago as she could live and still be considered a resident, meeting the city's requirements. Leading a somewhat suburban life outside of the city was usually worth it, but being called into their cases was a price she had to pay to raise her daughter in a house with a yard instead of a concrete jungle. Looking at the unfamiliar streets, she let out a sigh. "To answer your question, working in homicide is not something I would recommend. Of the dozens of weekly cases that come across my desk, most are just a pile of paperwork that goes over to the gang unit. The others are baffling, and even when you track down the perpetrator, it doesn't give you much of a sense that you did anything to help anyone." As politely as she could, she continued, "I have to catch up on this." She raised her phone. "So, if you don't mind, can you turn the siren off the rest of the way?" Hoping he got the hint that she wanted silence, she began reading the article.

With a quick flick of his wrist, he hit a switch, and the persistent wail disappeared. "Yeah, I know how it is. I can't read with lots of noises either." Less than ten seconds later, he added, "Hey, you've heard all the rumors about the mall, haven't you?" He glanced in her direction with a boyish grin. "We get some of the craziest calls down there. People saying they saw insane stuff. Dolls in hallways, a weird guy who juggles, and a skeleton boy in a weird suit. I guess it's fitting that there was a mass murder. Par for the course for the weirdos that hang out there." The smile suddenly faded from his face as if someone had drawn a curtain over his joy. Quietly he added, "I... I didn't mean it the way it sounded."

He was growing on her, even if he was keeping her from her work. She grunted with a laugh, "I know what you meant." She covered the yawn she had been fighting off with the back of her hand. The officer put both hands on the wheel as he slowed through a red light. Detective Bradley let the silence hang and read the article from 1980.

The night of horror that made national headlines on October 8, 1978 still bewilders. At the impromptu premiere of Spontaneous Revulsion, *a B horror movie in its director's home, all the viewers were apparently tortured, then abducted. As if it wasn't sensational enough, the investigators could only find blood puddled in the seats. There wasn't a single clue that could lead to the unknown assailants.*

In an interview, the lead investigator stated, "It was as if everyone involved vanished into thin air. We had teams searching day and night, and whoever did this did not leave a single shred of usable evidence behind."

As days became weeks, all parties involved came to the abhorrent realization that this was not a hoax. There were rumors the blood was from a hospital and the attendees were hiding out to promote a film that would not otherwise receive any publicity. When weeks became a month, the terror of the night became real.

The events quickly triggered a media frenzy, keeping the story going for almost the entire summer. The coverage pushed the boundaries of good taste when they published leaked crime scene photos.

There was a black-and-white picture of a large room with rows of chairs descending to a pull-down vinyl screen. The screen was half covered in blood, looking like a grotesque, giant Rorschach image. Bradley enlarged the photo, moving her phone inches from her face. All she saw was a pixelated space covered in dark liquid with small pieces of what resembled cloth mixed in. Pulling the phone back to the proper perspective, it looked like something from a horror movie. She was amazed she had never heard of this happening until now.

Out of respect to the presumed dead, Spontaneous Revulsion opened a year after the murders took place. Most critics found its release in bad taste and refused to write about it. The movie wasn't quite a B film, but closer to a drive-in special, made to play for a limited time for mostly teenage audiences. After the extensive media ramp-up, it had a huge opening, then the independent film faded away, quickly becoming a quick byline to all but its very few most ardent fans. For the few that still clung to the belief that the events of that evening were an ill-advised publicity stunt by a group starved for fame, there are still showings trying to draw out anyone who can shed light on the tragic event. More than two years later, the case is listed as unsolved. As of this report, not a single member of the crew has resurfaced, making us all wonder what really happened.

Bradley was pulled from her reading when they approached the theater entrance at the back of the aging mall. Detective Cliffe walked up to the car, flicking a cigarette into the brick wall as he did so. Bradley zipped up her jacket. "Thanks for the lift, officer."

"My pleasure." He gave a slight nod.

Detective Cliffe offered a meaty hand as she stepped out of the cruiser. It was sticky, and it felt like he was trying to crush her fingers as they shook.

"Thanks for coming out so quick."

Like I had a choice. "Of course."

"Have you been briefed?"

"The desk sergeant told me you got a theater full of bloody seats, no bodies, and what could be small bits of flesh. There are no witnesses other than an older gentleman who says he saw the whole thing."

"Yeah."

"Blood been tested?"

"You thinking it's fake, right?" With an enormous fist, he pulled his collar up as he added, "Thought the same thing. It ain't.

The swab showed it's human, or at least most of it." He ran his hand over his face, pulling out the wrinkles. "There's a lot like a swimming pool a lot. The lab folks couldn't make out the foreign substance mixed in with the blood. The swabs were taken in ten different areas. We sent multiple samples back to the lab for more analysis after we got here. Results ain't back yet. Had to send it several towns over. We ain't got the proper facilities here."

"Yeah, figured as much. Even if it's real, this all sounds like a BS publicity stunt gone way too far. What else could it be?" She stamped her feet, trying to generate some warmth. "You know about the first showing of the movie, right?"

"Yeah, I read about it when I got over here. To be honest, I thought the same thing. But now I really don't know." He looked at the ambulance driver and the few police officers congregated outside. His paunch made him wheeze as he leaned forward and whispered in her ear, "You see, the lab folks say the film ain't made of normal film stuff."

She looked at him inquisitively. In a near whisper, she said, "What does that mean? Exactly."

"The film ain't celluloid." The word came out with a few extra syllables, his south side accent making it sound foreign. "They couldn't say for sure, but it looked a whole lot like human flesh."

"Cliffe, I'm not in the mood if you are trying to pull a joke here."

He stepped back and shrugged his shoulders. "Believe me, I wish I were joking."

She wanted to believe he was teasing her, maybe because she was coming to take over his case. But looking at him, she knew he was very skilled if he was lying. "Well, I guess we'll have to see what they actually find out then." She thought of what kind of mind it took to splice flesh, making her grimace. "Wait, so this theater isn't digital? They play actual films?"

"Yeah, probably why it's in this dilapidated mall. They didn't keep up with the times. Guy who owns it's kinda a weirdo. We found a cot in the back office; from what I saw it looks like he lives in there. Strange thing about it, he's well off. Used to own an architecture company here in town."

She looked up at the marquee. It looked original. Half the show lights surrounding the "Towne Point Theater" sign were out, making it look like *Tow P i t Th a r* in the darkness. "Was he in the building tonight?"

"Making assumptions, yeah. But we only got one person to interview. Everyone else seemingly has vanished into thin air."

"Did you interview the man who witnessed the murders?"

"Got some basics out of him, then heard you were coming. He was pretty shook up, so we got him some coffee and figured it wouldn't hurt to wait the ten extra minutes for you to get here."

She didn't know if she should compliment him for the clear-headedness or judge him for being lazy. Doing neither, she pointed with her head to the glass doors that led into the mall behind him. "I guess we better get in there, then."

With Bradley following the overweight man through the glass doors, they entered the mall through the glass-enclosed vestibule. On the brick wall, there were vacant bays for payphones and dozens of caricatures and phrases etched in the marker of the remaining plexiglass. The modern hieroglyphics brought back memories of hanging out with the kind of people her parents tried to shield her from. There was a closed-down storefront to her left. The dark brick had the outline of the word "Starcade" stenciled in it with a worn picture of a spaceship blasting an asteroid. Across from the vacant store was the theater.

It had a large marquee with hundreds of bright lights, across which were draped layers of cobwebs. There were faded movie posters displaying long forgotten films in bright colors and bold images. One was a slasher movie that had women's body parts lying beneath a chainsaw next to the byline *"Yeah, it's what you think it is!"* Raising her eyebrow, she shook her head slightly. The walls of the lobby were covered in red velvet drapes that looked as if they hadn't been cleaned in a few decades. To the right, there was a concession stand ahead with a huge popcorn bin encased in glass sitting on a long counter with assorted candies beneath it on shelves, filling the lobby with the smell of butter and grease. Above the concession stand were two signs pointing in opposite directions, indicating Theater 1 and Theater 2.

They took a right and, after a short walk down a narrow-draped hallway, entered the rows of seats with puck lights built into a red carpeted walkway. As she slipped on cloth booties, the dim overhead lights were on, making the liquid that was drenching the seats glitter in the dull reflection. A few rows down was a female officer standing in front of an elderly man with a full head of white hair.

Bradley caught up to the officer with a long stride. Tugging at his sleeve to stop him, she said, "You didn't remove him from the crime scene?"

"Look, don't start, okay?" He arched his eyebrows and looked down at her hand on his shirt. After she removed it, he smoothed the wrinkled material fastidiously before speaking again, as if he could not focus on anything else until the task was complete. "Of course, I tried that right away. The man refused to go." Cliffe waved both of his hands in the air, selling his point. "He started hollering like someone was killing him! When we gently tried to... you know, physically remove him after he refused to go, he got even louder." Talking from the side of his mouth, his accent got stronger, sounding as if the letter t was not part of his phonetic repertoire as he added, "I know it ain't procedure and all, but he is the only witness and hasn't said a word about a lawyer. So, I took a gamble and figured you could make the call. Now that the scene is yours, you know." His face showed his resentment as he pushed his tongue in his cheek, biting his lower lip.

"Got it." Knowing she might need him, she added, "You did good, I would have done the same." Looking at the blood staining the fabric chairs, she thought again that it had to be bovine intermixed with human or some other source that was easily accessible, giving the lab techs a false reading. Even though it was elaborate, she felt little doubt that this was some hoax. As they got to where the man was seated, she walked sideways down the aisle, carefully avoiding stains on the floor. Standing next to the female officer, she looked at the man. She wanted to be angry at him for pulling her away from her daughter to aid in a case that the suburban squad could have handled without her if they had any sense. But when she saw his face, she couldn't help but feel pity. Beyond the terror, there were telltale signs of terminal illness. His face was ashen, and his eyes set way too deep. Leaning on the chair back, she said, "I am Detective Bradley, Mr. Cromwell. Is it okay if I ask you a few questions?"

His mouth worked furiously, as if it was chewing something. Looking up, he said in a shaky, wheezing voice, "Is the projector unplugged?"

Between his bites, she could see he was working over his dental plate. She gave him a polite smile. "What's that?"

His eyes came alive, and he lunged forward, reaching for her with shaking hands. "Upstairs! Did your men unplug the projector?"

Bradley pulled back. "I honestly don't know." He was so distressed she considered calling in the paramedics.

Before she could ask how he was feeling, he leaned back. "I asked your man here." He hooked his long thumb toward Detective Cliffe. "He gave me the runaround. I'm not going to answer any of your questions until you assure me it's unplugged."

Groaning, the detective responded, "Sir, as I told you earlier, it's unplugged. As a matter of fact, it wasn't plugged in when we entered the projectionist room."

Bradley thought of the article and the earlier comment about the film being made from flesh. The old man shook his head up and down, whispering under his breath. "Good, good." His eyes stared past Bradley at the large white screen behind her.

Bradley asked, "Would you mind telling me why that's so important to you?"

His eyes opened wide, and he gave an appalled look. "Because the film ate up everyone."

As a reflex she gasped, "Huh." Narrowing her eyes to slits, she quickly regained her composure. "How does that work... exactly?"

"Please don't look at me like that." His words came out in a whine, like a child begging for something they knew they couldn't have.

"Like what?"

"Like I am senile." Before she had a chance to respond, he quickly added, "There is no way you are ever going to understand or believe me, so we might as well stop right here." He hunched forward and let out a long, sad sigh.

"That's your right." Her eyes traced him. She knew better than to have a personal reaction to someone she was interviewing, but something made her want to get him out of there immediately—perhaps his age, or her fatigue. "The other option is, if you're up to it, we keep talking so we can figure out what happened. Right now, you're either part of a... charade, or you witnessed something so horrific that you maybe need some medical attention." Bradley could see the fear growing. "Would you like for us to get you some help?"

"Oh, you are just like the rest." The old man slumped in his chair with a deep sigh.

"Look, if someone tricked you into staying here and telling us a story, it's going to come out eventually. We always get to the truth. Are you up to continuing the conversation? If not, we can get you to the hospital." He stared silently. She felt enough time had already been wasted waiting for her arrival. "Sir. Where is everybody?"

"I told you, the film took them!"

"Where did it take them?" She was fighting not to sound sarcastic.

"I don't know. Once it started, I covered my eyes after I saw it take them." His eyes glanced at the ceiling.

"Okay, so help me understand. After you covered your eyes, what happened?"

"I heard... I heard horrible things."

"How long did that last?"

He bit at his dentures again. "It was a long while."

"And that whole time, you didn't feel anyone touch you? You just heard the others screaming?"

He nodded almost imperceptibly.

"No other voices, names, someone saying, 'Look out!'?"

"No, just... screaming."

He ran his shaking hand across the top of his head. Bradley wondered if she was staring at a killer. Her gut told her no, but long and hard experience had taught her to base her opinions on only what she could prove. "When your eyes were closed, could you see any light from the film? Or anything else."

He let out an exasperated chuckle. "No. It wasn't like that at all."

"In your opinion, then, why didn't the film... How did you put it? Eat you up like the others?"

"Because whatever was in the film thought it already got me. You see, I was borrowing someone else's time when it all happened."

Bradley closed her eyes for a second and then leaned forward, fighting the growing frustration at Cliffe for keeping a senile man in the middle of a horrific crime scene. With her hands on her thighs, she opened her eyes. "Sir, do you have family we can call? Someone who can possibly come by?" She studied his eyes and knew deep down he understood everything she was saying. "Would you be okay with that?"

The old man rubbed his face. It pulled out his wrinkles for a second, making him look nearly a decade younger. "I told you that you wouldn't believe me. But if you let me talk, I will tell you all that I know."

Bradley took a deep breath. Figuring she would give him another few minutes she said, "Please continue with your story, sir."

The old man looked up at Detective Cliffe. Staring at him distrustfully, he wiped his nose with the back of his dirty shirt sleeve. "I am going to end up in the looney bin, which means I will be dead in a few days, so I guess it's time to let you in on the secret I have been carrying around since I was a young boy. I have never told a soul my trick to keep myself alive long past my given time." He paused, leaning back in his chair. His eyes became narrow, making him look as if he was nearly asleep. Finally, he continued. His voice was barely louder than the hum of the heating unit above them.

Looking up bashfully, he said, "Having a weak heart growing up, I was excluded by necessity from the normal activities of a child. Running, swimming, and playing ball were never available to me. To make up for these deficiencies, I visited the movie theater every afternoon for entertainment. Our next-door neighbor was a manager there and used to let me sneak in the back for the feature films. There, I entered a world where a young boy with a heart condition could experience great adventures like everyone else had the opportunity to do. The strange part of it was that as I sat there, I somehow got healthier. My parents, doctors, and clergy all had different theories, but over time I was able to piece together the truth."

Bradley looked at Detective Cliffe. She couldn't say for sure, but thought she saw him smirking. Knowing she had no choice but to listen, she leaned slightly back, hoping the lab techs got a report back soon so she could finally get something tangible to work with. Crossing her arms with the heat blowing on her, she thought of her warm bed and her wife.

"Every time, about halfway through the movie, I could see the beam of light from the movie in the theater... kind of... glow. It wasn't like the normal light you see from the projectionist's room.

The light was like a flashlight with a gold filter covered by a heavy cloth—dull but with obvious power. Except the heavy cloth was transparent. It had a kind of dull illumination all over." He looked at the three officers in front of him, the sincerity showing in his eyes. "Over time, I learned that while everyone was so caught up in what was on the screen, they were less guarded. All that pure emotion did something. I learned that somehow, the other moviegoers' subconscious minds while the film was running made it something else. They became so engrossed that for a few minutes they lived inside the film. It was as if their focus on the story had transported them away from their own life and experiences. In those brief moments, I was able to absorb the spirit of the film for a few minutes at a time."

He paused, chewing on his dentures, and shifted in his chair. The slight motion made his face look like he was sitting on a needle as he finally settled in. "As crazy as it sounds, I learned then that all I need to stay ahead of the reaper is a full movie theater of excited moviegoers. At these times, I could borrow just a little bit of their time. I wasn't really hurting them. Just borrowing a few minutes of theirs to keep me living.'"

As she listened, Bradley pulled up the notes for the funny little man on her phone. Cliffe had reported that he lived alone in Orland, about forty minutes away. Retired machinist, no family, or priors. The gentlemen apparently had led a very quiet life.

Bradley looked at him, and her eye twitched as she examined the self-satisfied look on his face.

"May I continue, Missus Officer?"

There was a large clanging noise in the projectionist room above. They all jerked their heads in that direction, but when nothing further transpired, Bradley said, "Please continue."

The old man continued, his voice sounding like it was running out of steam. "This became life support to me. Those stolen moments keep me going. It occurred to me that perhaps I was just outliving the expectations of my doctors, and my fanciful thoughts about what I had come to call 'borrowing' was just a device to help me forget that I was born with an unfair expiration date. A lifetime of feeling all those films has changed my view. I now view this gift as a counterbalance to my heart—a gift, in a way, from above."

Detective Bradley interrupted. "Sir. What happened here tonight? I don't need to know anything else. I'm sorry that you have to deal with your medical condition and am glad you have overcome the odds, but now I'm going to ask you to please focus on the last few hours." It was becoming painful to keep indulging him. Thinking about her grandmother, she fought to keep calm. "Now, from when you came in until the other theatergoers disappeared. Let's please focus on only that. Okay?"

"I ain't dumb, ma'am. I wouldn't presume to waste your time on information that you wouldn't believe if it wasn't relevant to what you need to know. So, you want me to continue or not?"

Bradly nodded. "Please, just get to the point as quickly as possible." She racked her brain, trying to figure out why this man was stalling. The press was here. If this was a ploy for publicity, what possible purpose was there to have this old man carry on now?

"I have been coming to your theater here for several weeks now. From the first day, I found that the patrons are some of the most passionate I have ever seen. That is why I, at first... I wasn't concerned by the presence I was feeling. I just assumed it was a result of the zealous nature of the people that come here. That was until I started to feel... him."

"Who?"

"The skeletal boy."

Bradley's mind raced back to the car ride over. She was about to ask Cliffe if he was orchestrating some kind of ridiculous joke. Just as she was about to give the order, Cliffe's ringtone—""La Bamba"—echoed loudly in the sound chamber of the theater.

"Cliffe here." The officer shook his head, wiggling the fat beneath his double chin. "You're sure?" He exhaled between pursed lips with a low whistle. "You better be. Type it up and let the sergeant know. Yeah, I know he's at a wedding, but I don't care. Get him on it! Now!" He clicked the end button, staring at the screen as if it was a poisonous snake.

"What is it, Cliffe?"

"Bradley, could you please follow me?"

Bradley made her way down the long aisle, using the chair tops to keep her balance as she stepped over the thick liquid that was all over the floor. The backs of the fabric chairs felt like sticky, worn carpeting. With every touch, she fought the feeling that something bigger was happening. Her unwelcome intuition, up until now, had been held at bay. After listening to the old man, she was feeling small waves of something she couldn't quite understand. Cliffe's odd reaction wasn't helping.

When they were in the carpeted aisleway, Cliffe stopped. For the first time since she had met him, he didn't look in control. "All the blood is real. Gets better: the foreign substance is aged celluloid."

Bradley scanned the room, looking over every chair and portions of the floor. Her mind filled with images of a Stephen King movie she had seen when she was a child, in which there was an elevator filled with blood. "How can that be? Where did they get that much from?" Years of practice did little to stop her rising anxiety. "Wait, did you say celluloid, like film?"

"Yeah. I can't believe it. Whatever's happening, that old man's got to be in on it. It's demented!" The comment seemed to change him. His normally arrogant face was replaced with a look of fear.

"How many people exactly were in here?"

"By the ticket stubs and the security cameras, somewhere around twenty-eight, maybe more." His hand went to the handle of his gun in his holster. "This had to be some cult stuff. Like that James Jones deal all those years ago. Remember the guy with the spiked Kool-Aid?" He rubbed his hand against the stubble of his face, his eyes looking like they were going to shoot out from their sockets. "Here, a cult! Can you believe it?"

The Blue Oyster Cult song "Don't Fear the Reaper" played in her head. It had been playing when she got the call. Like an earworm, it burrowed deeper into her subconscious mind. "If it was a mass suicide, where are the bodies?" She chewed her curled index finger. The habit becoming an unconscious ritual first appeared when she quit smoking over a year ago. "The report said there was no usable security footage outside, right?"

"There was footage, but nothing unusual. Just a few folks coming and going. Nobody with a wheelbarrow full of bodies or anything like that." He cringed, drawing in his shoulders. "Shit, didn't mean it like that."

Speaking out louder than she intended, she said, "Let's keep our wits about us here. This could still be a hoax. They might have just gone too far with the blood." Her mind raced, frantically trying to figure out where someone could access that much blood.

"Where did they go then?"

"Maybe slowly, one by one, they left using other exits."

"The cameras from Gatlet's Diner were on the entrance the whole time. They say nobody left."

"We sure they entered in the first place? They didn't just mill about in the lobby?"

"Yeah, had the same thought already. The security footage shows them going in slowly, starting a half hour before the film was due to start."

Looking toward the projectionist's window above, she asked, "The lab guys are still up there with the film?"

"Yeah. Unless they snuck out without reporting it."

The glass obscuring half the opening was coated in dust. Behind, there were moving shadows. "Radio up there and tell them to sit tight. After we finish with Mr. Cromwell's statement, we will head up there."

"Got it." He pulled the radio from his belt.

Listening to his instructions, Bradley walked on tiptoes, avoiding the blood. Fighting the hypnotic guitar rhythm that was taking over her head, she came upon the old man. No longer finding his wild tale completely unreal, she cleared her throat, feeling her heart pound against her ribcage. "Mr. Cromwell, before you say anything else, I must inform you that you are going to be held as a material witness. This entitles you t—"

"Spare me your mumbo jumbo. I don't care. Don't you see what is at stake!"

"Sir, whatever is going on here could end up putting you in harm's way if you are not truthful. Do you understand?"

"I'm being truthful. That's why I was telling you what happened after I made this discovery when I was a young boy."

"Tonight! Mr. Cromwell, what happened tonight? Were the others drinking or doing drugs? You said you saw a skeletal boy. Did the other theater-goers dress in costumes as well?"

"No! The boy wasn't there at first. At least not like you and I are here right now. I could just feel him when I saw an oddly shaped man who was wearing a bad hairpiece sit down. The second I saw him, something inside me was different."

"So, what does the man have to do with the boy?" The man looked frantic, his sunken chest rising and falling as he spoke. Bradley was seconds away from getting him to an ambulance, but she felt stuck like something was holding her to this spot. Feeling like a rookie, she hung on his words as she chewed on the insides of her lips, using the pain to keep focus.

"When the movie started glowing, it was like nothing I had ever seen before. Usually, it glows, then the screen glows, and I feel elated. This time, when I got close to him, it was like I could see through him and live out his experiences." A single tear ran down his face. With the back of a liver-spotted hand, he wiped it away. "I saw things no one should ever see. Terrible, horrible things." As his bottom lip quivered, he leaned forward, hanging his head down.

She knew the answer but asked anyway. "Did this man have anything to do with the killing in the theater tonight?"

"No! He wasn't really here, he was, was like a... ghost. Everything I saw was memories. I could see his past, and I could see him being drawn here by the skeleton." He leaned forward, placing his elbows on his thin legs. "I've had some time to think about—or more accurately, feel it. Spirits like him are drawn to stronger spirits. They can't help themselves. It's like a moth to a flame. That skeletal boy, for some reason, drew him here, and he lived out the last few decades in these walls." His eyes traced the room as his dental plate fished between his lips once more. His nervous habit seemed to steady him.

"I know how that sounds, but I could feel him, the same as I can feel the clothes on my back." His hand flashed up to his shoulder and lifted the fabric of his wrinkled shirt. "He sat right there in the seat you are leaning against. I'm telling you, I could feel and see everything!"

Instinctively, Bradley stood up, pulling her hands from the seat. She wiped her palms across her pants, trying to get the imagined dirt off her. Staring at the fear in the man's gaze, it felt tangible hanging in the stale air. She knew she would have to coax him. "And what did you feel, exactly?"

"All that he had done was as if I was doing it myself." His dental plate made an odd slurping noise as he sucked on it. After a few bites, he used his thumb to put it securely back in place. "As I was borrowing from the film, the man turned and stared at me with knowing eyes. It was the first time I had ever been with someone where I thought they knew what I was doing. He didn't say anything or make a fuss, he just turned around and smiled, then licked his fingertips and touched my hand." He stared at the veiny skin.

"Did you leave?"

"Wanted to, couldn't. It was like eating tainted fruit. You know it has flavor and nutrition, but you paid for it with its spoiled taste." His voice squeaked as he continued with tears streaming down his worn face. "He knew he had me, and he just sat there with his awful stare and chuckled as I saw the images of him tormenting others." His voice cracked. "That is until the film changed."

Bradley could feel the man's fear, as if it was infectious. She wanted to leave, make up any excuse, feeling no good would come from her staying. She asked, "How did it change?"

"It was no longer the scene in the church. It became a scene of the interior of this theater! Next thing I knew, everyone started screaming and there was blood everywhere."

"Was it a group of men harming the other patrons?"

"Listen to me!" He scooted to the edge of his seat and stared with pleading eyes. "It was the film!"

Spittle flew onto her sleeve and hand. As she used her arm to wipe it away, the old man leaned forward and grabbed her fingers. He was cold as ice. His touch was like electricity coursing through her. In a flash, she saw what he saw. In painful waves between pitch blackness, she saw glimpses of the pear-shaped man alternating with a vapor flying through the theater. As the mist ran through everyone, they disappeared as if they had never existed, leaving only blood and parts of their flesh behind. Bradley, stunned, tried to pull her hand away, but the old man's grip was like a vice. When she gripped the chair behind her to gain leverage, touching the damp fabric, she saw the pear-shaped man and the things he had done. Each disgusting act was like watching a video with bad reception, pausing, and playing, showing images that were worse than anything she could imagine. With her free hand, she clutched the side of her head to alleviate the pain radiating down her spine, making her stomach feel like it was filled with acid. Mercifully, the man let go of her, causing her to almost tumble over the seat behind her as she pulled herself away from him.

She massaged the fingers that he held, trying to work in circulation. An image of a tall, skinny man with a cowboy hat leaning against the fabric walls still in her head. It shook her deeply. The old man stared through her, biting away at his false teeth in a rhythmic cadence.

In a monotone, he whispered, "You can see too now, can't ya? First the tingling, then the visions." He smiled, showing his exposed gums. "That intuition, that feeling you always thought was just intelligence followed by scrupulous attention to detail." He leaned forward, tightening his lips so that his words sounded like a grunt. "That's... what my glow is like."

To her left, Cliffe nearly shouted, "What was that? You alright, Bradley? You don't look so hot."

Defensively, she turned her head, staring at Cliffe, nearly snarling. Not wanting to share this piece of herself with the man she considered an imbecile, she said, "Nothing."

"Like hell!" He folded his beefy arms and raised his chin. "What did you see?" His eyes moved between Bradley and the elderly man. After nearly a half minute of silence, he grunted. "Well, what're we going to do? Should we haul him in? The man's obviously not all there."

She looked into the eyes of Mr. Cromwell and saw a depth she couldn't comprehend. "No, not now." She placed both hands on the seats behind her, trying to keep her balance as waves of light-headedness drained her of strength. Touching the fabric brought vivid images of the spirit running through the theater. It was a glowing mist drifting from the projector's beam, devastating everything in its path. As if it was red hot, she pulled her hands away, shaking her fingers, hoping to make the images disappear. This wasn't the first time she'd had a spell like this, where she was overwhelmed by a perceived thought, but she had never felt anything this strong or vivid.

"Seriously, Bradley, you got the flu or something? You look terrible."

"I'm... fine." She motioned with her head quickly toward the main aisle, directing him to leave. Cromwell reached once again for her hand, and Bradley jerked away like she would from a swarm of bees. Cliffe turned and walked up the narrow passage between the folded seats. She followed, feeling like a zombie. It took conscious effort to keep placing one foot before the other. As she walked, she was careful not to touch anything, fearful of triggering a repeat of the terror that had overwhelmed her. Her chest felt like it was wrapped in a tight band, each breath becoming a chore. When they were in the main aisle she asked, "When you arrived on scene, was the movie still playing?" The fear in her voice made her cringe.

"Don't you start too!"

"Please, just answer the question."

"No, I obviously wasn't the first on scene, but the officers that were walked into an empty, dark theater with the exception of the old man. At least, that is what they reported."

Bradley recalled the notes. They stated that, after Mr. Cromwell called, he said he never left his seat. She reached into her back pocket, pulling her phone out. It had no reception. She looked up at the metal beams of the tall ceiling of the theater, wondering how he made the call at all. She couldn't understand why he wouldn't bolt out of there in the first place. If the images were anything like she had seen, she couldn't comprehend why he would stay. The fear inside her grew. She felt if she remained in the theater, she was allowing an unseen force to take something from her. Something she couldn't easily get back.

"What're you thinking?"

Ignoring his question, she responded in a tired voice, "Let's get up to the projectionist room."

Upon entering, she was immediately overtaken by the smell of heated celluloid and caked dust from the soundproof fabric walls. The room was close to pitch black, with only a single low-wattage bulb above. Some additional ambient light made its way through the two windows that opened into the theater, where the projector beamed the images onto the screen, but it was not enough to add so much as a shadow. She was about to ask why they didn't turn on the battery powered light, but then she looked at the film hanging out of the projector and thought better of it. Forensic experts, in her experience, could be extremely sensitive.

On the wall furthest from her, she saw piles of film canisters holding the many imaginary worlds that the movies created. Her gaze was drawn toward the theater and the vastness of the screen on the back wall.

The two forensics workers were so focused on their work that they didn't even nod when Bradley and Cliffe entered. Cliffe said to the shorter of the two, "Hey, Parker, this's Bradley with Chicago homicide. She's here to assist in the investigation."

The older woman, who had the face of a teenager, looked over the rim of her thick glasses. "Ya got a doozy here, detective." She stood from her bent position at the projectionist table and side-stepped the seventies-style projector. "Been at this job for some time now. Never seen anything remotely like this here." She pointed to what looked like a long glass straw at the spool of film. "Whatever the nutcase who perpetrated this deal here did, he certainly will end up in the looney bin hall of fame." With the glass wand, she carefully pulled at the film. The tail end was hanging out of the projector, flittering in the air like a snake's tail. "Come here, Detective." She looked at Bradley's face and smiled. "Come now, don't be shy. I don't bite."

Bradley stepped next to the oddly shaped woman.

"I don't know how this was done, but someone spliced this film here or overlayed it with images from the interior of the theater. I am not going to lie to you, I don't know the first thing about how this works, but I have taken a crash course on Google over the last half-hour. The original movie sold a few months ago, and I think we have it." She lifted the film to the light. "You see, the first few frames are from the original film. At least they appear to be from what I saw online. But then, after the pretty girl enters the church with her monstrous bujumbas hanging out, something happens." With her free hand, she pushed her glasses in place, slowly scanning Bradley's form. The thick lenses made her eyes look twice the size they should be as they openly gawked. "You see this next part? Just as the bimbo walks through the door, the next frame is of the inside of this theater."

Bradley interrupted. "And you know this film was altered, or more precisely cut?"

"Film is an interesting word choice. The sprockets on the film are slightly different in diameter from standard film. I fed it into the machine, and it appears to still work. But when I was comparing it, I noticed something else. This film here is twice the thickness of any other film in this room." She looked at the shelving full of piles of canisters. "Gets better. I did something I shouldn't." She looked at Detective Cliffe. "Sorry, Cliffy. I touched the film with my bare hand to get an idea of the texture. I know it's unprofessional, but after unspooling the film and realizing how thick it was, it immediately reminded me of a case I worked a long time ago where I came across human skin that had been pressed to make a flag." She raised a hand that looked too small in relation to the body waving it. "Don't ask, it's a long story. Anyway, this film here also had an odd texture that reminded me of overdried winter skin just after lotion was applied. You know, equally rough and sticky. And then there is the smell." She lifted it toward Bradley's face.

The detective jumped back. "Don't!"

"Well, suit yourself, but I am tellin' ya, it smells exactly like barbecue." She dexterously continued to unspool the film, the large wheel turning as the thin material was pulled away. "Anyway, the film for a spell is the interior shot of theater. It's real dark, so hard to make out the people in the seats... that is until you get to here." With the wand, she pointed to a tiny rectangle that had a clip on it. "You see here, things get, well, weird. It would be better to run this through the projector, and you can see for yourself, but I don't know what it would do to the film, and Cliffe gave very specific instructions to not plug the projector back in. But here, if you hold it up to this light, you can see what I'm talking about." The technician removed a pair of gloves from her coat and handed them to Bradley.

Reluctant to come in contact with anyone after what she had experienced downstairs, she grabbed the very tips of the latex and tugged them away. After she pulled them onto her hands, she carefully took the film with thumb and forefinger, mimicking what she saw the technician do. Holding it up to the light, the first rectangle she looked at was of a pear-shaped man wearing a ridiculous toupee. With a look of fury, he took up most of the space on the spool of film. The face, now frozen, was identical to that of the man she had seen when Mr. Cromwell touched her. She fought to control herself, knowing all eyes were on her. She then looked down to the next rectangle, seeing a pair of dolls that were dressed in sailor's suits. They were holding hands with jagged smiles painted in red.

"What am I looking at exactly?"

"Exactly? Beats me, but if you keep going a few more frames, you will see a mousy-looking guy who looks like he is constipated. I'll betcha dollars to donuts that he's the owner. I saw a picture of him on a poster from a news article from when he bought this place." She tapped the side of her bob hairdo. "It's getting more selective as I get older, but I got a somewhat photographic memory."

"So, you think he made this doctored version of the film?"

"Honey, I don't know what I think. Frankly, after looking over the next couple of frames, it was kinda hard to concentrate to be honest."

Bradley saw the spirit from the film absorbing all that was in its path. The images were like a memory, a memory of an experience she had never had. Carefully, she lowered her arms. As she was about to hand the film back to the technician, she saw a skeletal boy in the frame next to the children. Without thinking, she let go of the film, not wanting to be in contact with it for a second more.

"Woah, slow down there, cowpoke!" Parker, using her wand, quickly swooped up the film before it made contact with the floor. "Evidence, ya know? Can't have you contaminating everything."

Sharply Bradley barked, "Why did you say cowpoke?"

"I don't know." She shrugged her square shoulders and gave a bewildered smile. "Never used that term before in my life."

Bradley thought of the smiling cowboy. She walked out of the room, back toward the small stairway.

Cliffe from behind her called out, "Hey, where're you going, boss?"

As she reemerged into the theater, she ignored the panic and strode down the main aisle back to the old man. Bradley said to the female officer who was stationed there to watch him, "Please excuse us."

"I'm supposed to not let him out of my sight, Detective."

"Now!" her voice echoed in the cavernous space.

Taking the hint, the officer raised her eyebrows and walked away, murmuring something under her breath.

Sitting next to Mr. Cromwell, she made sure to keep enough distance, so they were not touching. She quietly said, "The spirit took everyone and brought them back into the film, didn't it?"

"Yes, that's what I was trying to tell you."

She knew it couldn't be true, but she also knew that it was. No longer interested in trying to struggle with logic in a realm where it had no place, she said, "Who were the others that're trapped in the film?"

He rubbed his nose with the back of his hand. Pulling away, he looked at the snot as if it was something of great interest. His response came out in a wheeze. "Some kinda ghosts, I figure. I know they have been here a long time, trapped in this mall. I could feel it. From what I saw that boy called them here originally. I can't figure any more than that out, though. It's like an old memory of mine, I can only see pieces of it."

"Do you think the film has them now? For good?" She wanted to laugh at what she just said, realizing she was looking for advice about spirits from a man who, a few minutes ago, she thought was crazy. Watching him process the question, she looked around the room. Every chair was covered in blood. The walls were surrounded by fabric drapes. Thinking of all the pleasant evenings that had been spent here, she took a deep breath, stopping the tears that had been threatening.

"I only felt the spirit that lived in that film for a second. But yes, I think so."

Bradley saw Cliffe approaching out of the corner of her eye. She turned, holding up her index finger to tell him to give her a minute. Before she could turn around, the old man grabbed her shoulder. Like electricity, his touch ignited her mind, making her feel the spirit and its torment as it had been trapped within the film since the premiere. In tiny windows in her mind, she saw the original crew being devoured as it viciously flew through the room. As the flying mist went drifting back into the projector's lens, the old man released his grip.

"I am sorry, but I had to. So that you understand that you have to make sure that film is never played again."

"I know." She got up, pulling free without looking back. Thinking of how she was going to make the film disappear forever, she did her best to look straight forward and not allow the room to take any more of her sanity. There was suddenly a ticking noise echoing through the room. Even before she saw the beam of light, she knew it was the film. The overhead lights clicked off as the grainy test pattern attacked the white screen. In the distance, there was organ music accompanied by a wave of shrill cries.

Cromwell screamed, "You idiots! Stop the film!"

She watched him cover his eyes like a child hiding from the boogeyman.

Spinning, she yelled, "Cliffe! Shut that off!"

His chubby face poked out through the oblong rectangle to the right of the film's glaring beam. "We didn't turn it on!" He turned, his image gobbled up by the booth's shadow. "Is there a remote or something?"

From the room she heard the lab tech call out, "It ain't even plugged in!"

Flickering, the movie played out with a panning shot of the theater she was standing in. Every few seconds the film would stutter, revealing a screaming face pounding against an unseen barrier surrounded in darkness. In the corner of her eye, she saw the shadow of a cowboy sauntering down the aisle. His elongated shadow stretched across the red carpet walkway, making him appear a giant.

Cromwell gripped her wrist, pulling her into the seat next to him. "Shut your eyes!"

Obeying, she saw what he saw. It was an image of a skeletal boy being forced into a flesh suit. Cringing, her feet ground into the sticky floor as she braced herself. From above, over the organ music, she heard a cry like she never had before. At the ending gurgle, she thought she recognized Cliffe's voice.

Quickly, an image of the boy sitting in a beautifully decorated room ran in her mind's eye. His eyes became hers. They looked at the television screen, seeing a clown juggler. The room was papered with images of a tall cowboy. She could feel the deadness inside the skull come alive as he tried to smile. She knew then that the child's surroundings were pulled from the boy's imagination, following him to his pit in the belly of the mall.

Seconds became years as she saw through the grate of the bottom of the escalator. His spirit bringing every neighboring soul to his new home. Bradley wanted to open her eyes, but couldn't. A cold hand gripped her wrist, she knew it wasn't Cromwell's. Recognizing it had to be the boy's cowboy lackey, she fought to pull away but made no ground.

"Hey, ma'am. Come along nice and easy. We got room for one more."

Bradley remembered the last empty square of the film.

Cromwell, in a shaky voice, said, "Take me."

"All the same to me... cowpoke."

The noise of the film going through the projector exploded in her ears. She tried to scream 'No!' but her voice wouldn't come out. It was as if fear gobbled it up, protecting its host. She felt the death grip release from her arm, instantly refilling her head with the child's fragmented memories. She could feel his pull to the pit that his father created. The isolation he experienced over decades came over her in a rush. Needing to be free of it all, she opened her eyes, screaming, "Noooo!"

It was too late. A black mist was enveloping the cowboy and Mr. Cromwell. The regret on his face was the last thing she saw before he became one with the dark entity the film released. For a brief moment, she could feel the angst of all those trapped in the human celluloid. As the light above extinguished and the noise died away, Bradley knew she had to get upstairs and get the film in the can and out of the theater. It took all the strength she had to stand and shuffle up the walkway. From off in the distance there was the faint sound of organ music winding down, sounding like a radio with the batteries going dead. She knew deep in her bones that this would be the end of the theater and the mall it had sat in for so long. She made her way up the curtain-lined stairs, she tried to think of where to seal the evil she could never understand. Looking up, she thought she saw a shadow of the cowboy. Hearing the lapping of the film on its spool come to an end, it slowly evaporated into the darkness of the room.

FAN'S FICTION

Steven sat listening to how his book changed the life of the very pretty girl in front of him. All he could think of was hand sanitizer. The thought burrowed through his head like a worm as he smiled and listened to his fan's triumph over depression. He had shaken more hands in the last hour than in his entire life before that, and if he concentrated hard enough, he felt like he could remember the texture of each one along with the imagined germs. He categorized the germs by the grooming of each individual, those with beards and tattoos rating the highest on his list to be avoided. As the girl was finishing her story, the part of his brain that registered subtle things like anxiety labeled her as moderately clean. "Well, thank you for your kind words. It's readers like you that keep me writing."

Over his shoulder, Linda, his publicist with her expensive haircut and way too revealing pantsuit, whispered, "We already are fifteen minutes late for the photo ops. We have to wrap this up pronto."

Steven looked back to the girl, handing her the signed first edition of his debut novel, now a valuable collectible as a result of his subsequent success and celebrity. He was careful not to contact her. His hand was already feeling harder to lift, weighed down by the collection of heavy germs. "Thanks again. I hope you enjoy the convention." Grabbing his insulated cup, filled with the only brand of coffee he would drink, he started to stand when a very thin man pushed his way past the volunteer security guard, who appeared as if he couldn't be more than sixteen and thrust a copy of *The Stranger's Heart* onto the table. Staring at the cover art displaying a dark, veiny hand reaching toward an enormous heart brought back fond memories of when Steven still felt like a writer and not part of a media machine.

The security guard grabbed the man by the arm. "Sir, you need to get back in line until after the intermission." With his pimply smile, he looked at the author. "My apologies Mr. Hall."

Steven made eye contact with the volunteer and then the wiry man. "It's okay. I have a minute for one more signing." Purposely, he looked back at Linda and gave a wide, antagonizing smile.

"So, how would you like me to sign it?" Steven quickly glanced at the man's hand. It was covered in what looked like Cheeto dust and grime. Steven, grabbing a pen with both hands, made a production out of removing the cap, hoping the gesture evoked an unspoken agreement that there would be no handshake.

"Could you sign it 'To my close friend, Jack'?" The man clutched at his worn messenger bag as if it contained precious jewels. His deep-set eyes scanned the crowd. The back of his hand looked almost skeletal, matching the artist's rendition of the book cover. "Oh wait! Very."

"I don't follow?"

The man shook his head violently. "I am not going to lie to you. I am really nervous. I've wanted to meet you for some time now."

"I'm glad we can finally meet then. So, you said very... "

"Yes, please sign the book to my *very* close friend... Jack."

"Ah, yes, of course. I would be happy to."

"You know, nobody writes horror like you. I always feel like I am living in the world of your characters. Like they are born somewhere, that can't be, but I sure would like to find."

Quickly scribbling the note—he always felt bad when folks asked for personal inscriptions, his handwriting was nearly illegible—he closed the book and slid it toward Jack. Steven saw him reaching under the flap of the messenger bag with his non-Cheeto hand. Caught between the demands of etiquette and the imperatives of fear, he stared at the back of the young security guard. In a flash, he saw the cover of a book make its way across the canvas bag. Taking a deep breath, relief came over him. "I'm sorry, but I'm only signing one book per conventioneer."

"Oh, I didn't want you to sign this. It is a gift for you. You see, I am a writer myself. Not a big shot like you, of course, but if I do say so myself, an important one—at least to a few." He placed the book on the table cover—side down and slid it forward, littering the glossy book jacket with Cheeto dust.

"Well, thank you." Something inside Steven wanted this man gone. It wasn't the fact that he was unclean. The feeling was similar to the reluctant responsibility you felt around a stray dog that you knew would bite you the first chance it had.

Linda stepped forward. "Okay then, thank you for coming, sir. Mr. Hall needs to move on to his next commitment now."

As if she hadn't spoken at all, the thin man looked to Steven. "I am sure you get a lot of people trying to get you to read things, but I promise you, if you read the first paragraph, you will find the book... most enlightening." He looked down at his hand and, as if for the first time, noticed the remnants of his lunch. He quickly rubbed his bony fingers on his shirt, embedding reddish streaks into the wrinkled fabric. "It certainly was nice to meet you after all this time."

"Well, thanks again for the gift. It's always nice to meet another writer." Steven watched the man walk away, his limp leading him to wonder if he was ill. His tight jeans clung to him, fully accentuating his nearly skeletal frame. As Steven stood and walked away from the table, there was a collective sigh from the line of folks who would now be forced to wait out the two-hour intermission or forfeit their place in line. Even though he had nothing to do with the scheduling, Steven cringed. Now eight books into his career, it had been some time since he was on the other side of the table, but he was familiar with the feeling of waiting for someone you idolized. Pulling the hand sanitizing wipes from his pocket, he wiped away both the germs and some of the anxiety as he followed Linda to his next commitment.

Two hours and what felt like a hundred pictures later, Steven sat behind the curtain of signing area A, eating a slice of very greasy pizza. Thankfully, he was alone. It was the first time since very early this morning when he left his home. He stared at the tiny folding table he was using as a makeshift display covered by piles of his book. Just in front of the stack was the dirty surface of Jack's book. Pulling it toward him with his knuckle, he noticed that the cover bore an image of a very large house at night. The photograph, below a very blurry title, was colorless and slightly out of focus. Looking at the arched gables in disbelief, he thought he was staring at his vacation home. Through the window he could see his bed and two hard to make out characters lying under the covers. Forgetting about whatever germs could be on the cover, he picked up the book, bringing it inches from his face. Squinting at the photo, he thought he could see the shadowbox that his wife had made of the first book he ever published. Steven swallowed hard and quickly pulled the drapes back an inch, scanning the line of fans, hoping to see someone holding a camera and everyone pointing and laughing, saying, "Gotcha!" Instead, all he saw were hundreds of eager faces of a group most would label misfits, but whom he considered his people, with their dark clothing and love of dark entertainment. The small area felt like it was spinning. Quickly flipping the book open, he remembered what the man had said about the first paragraph.

Steven sat at the convention table holding a very valuable book that was given to him by a very important man. The book held secrets to his future, a future that could only come true by reading further.

Removing his glasses, Steven cleaned them on his shirt and frantically looked back down. Except for the first word, *What*, the remainder of the next sentence was blurry. It was like reading small type through a magnifying glass. Only once the word was passed over it remained clear. Wondering if maybe someone put something in his drink, he continued reading.

What Steven was about to learn was that he was entering a very special time, one in which he would be able to see the remainder of his life chapter for chapter if he chose to follow the warning. As he read further, he couldn't decide if what he was receiving was a gift or not. In his very sharp intellect, a very obvious question did not take long to form. If he could know what was going to happen, would he want to know, and if he did know could he change the outcome? With thousands of possibilities and probabilities running through his mind, the author was amused as much as he was afraid of the clever trick that the man named Jack had left behind for him. Steven, although wanting to read ahead, was unable to, as the blurriness would not subside. Eventually, knowing the trick could not be easily figured out, he went back to his signing feeling apprehensive, unaware that in less than a half-hour he would be dead at the hand of the girl with a tattoo of a snake, who decided to stab him as he signed a copy of his book. The action was one of love. She was quoted as saying: "I wanted to have an effect on his life that was as profound as his on mine."

Steven felt as if he was in the twilight of a deep sleep, when you stir, and all of your experiences could be real or just fragments of your dreams. Swallowing hard, he flipped forward. All the pages were blurry, except for the chapter headings, which were dates displayed not as numbers but as words written perfectly clearly. The ink appeared to be normal. He racked his brain trying to figure out what was creating a reaction with the paper to cause the blurriness.

All he could think of was his children's coloring books, the ones where rubbing a marker over them made images appear. Smearing his hand over the pages, leaving smudges of grease from the pizza, tension built in his shoulders, leaving him foolishly staring at the unchanging text.

Absentmindedly, he wiped his hand with a sanitizing cloth. As he stared, the word "unaware" had changed to "aware." His thoughts sped up, making his overactive imagination conjure up all that could be wrong with him. From his left, a loud metallic noise suddenly sounded. Jumping, he realized it was only the loud clicking of the separating curtain flying open.

Linda entered the makeshift tent. "So, you ready to get back at it?"

Steven looked at her as if she were an alien. It was a habit of his to ignore everything around him when he was deep in thought. Through the dizziness, he said, "What?" The word was less than a whisper, barely audible over the roar of the immense crowd surrounding them.

In a mockingly loud voice, she said, "Are you ready to go back out there?"

The thought of leaving the tiny cocoon of the draped area made his stomach turn over. Looking once more at the pages of blurry words, he answered out of reflex, trying to make sense of all that was happening. "Yeah, I guess so." He fought to keep the fear out of his voice. "Hey, does this look blurry to you?" Lifting the book open, he held it out. The cover was inches from his face, forcing the realization that, if nothing else, the lunatic knew where he lived and had been close enough to photograph it.

Adjusting her glasses, she said, "Yes. Whoever printed that should be let go pronto!"

Quickly pulling the book back to the table, he went back to the first chapter. The words he'd already read were still legible to him. "What about this?" He leaned to the side, letting her peek. As she came nearer, her perfume, which oddly smelled of peaches, made him cough.

"Same." She twirled the badge around her neck that had "exhibitor" printed beneath the plastic coating, straightening it. "How could a printer let that out like that? Where did it come from?"

"One of the conventioneers gave it to me."

"Well, he should demand his money back." Linda pulled the drape all the way open, walking toward the crowd. "We really have to get back to it."

"Yeah, I guess." Steven closed the book, his fingers lingering on the cover. Tracing the outline of his second home, he thought he could hear the ocean lapping on the beach. Then, with a deep sigh, he followed her through the curtain.

The room was alive with kinetic energy. Everywhere he looked was a sea of costumes, movement, and noise. Looking through his line, he squinted, specifically trying to find a woman with a tattoo. The pragmatic part of him was trying to calculate how far back someone would be in line to wait a half-hour. Not coming up with an easy solution, he sat, doing his best to smile as a mother and her young son approached his table. Listening with half an ear to her rave, he nodded, feigning interest, still calculating. If each signing took around four minutes, that would put his surprise guest to him in about eight people.

Trying to decide if four minutes was a legitimate time frame, he looked beyond the young mother and saw the eighth person. He was a Black man wearing a psychedelic T-shirt, towering over everyone surrounding him. Slightly relieved, it was easier to concentrate as he scribbled the note "to my biggest fan." Looking down at the reflection of his silver coffee mug, he saw the tiny tattoo of a snake on the inside of her wrist.

Something propelled him backward. Pushing himself back from the table, the chair leg caught the thick carpet, toppling the seat over. Just before he made contact with the floor, the knife blade penetrated the exact spot where his chest had just been. Lying on the floor, his back ached. Turning, he stared into the shocked eyes of his assailant, who glared wide-eyed from across the table. Seconds later, the junior security guard tackled her. Steven stood up, watching him pin her to the ground. Although everything was operating as if it were on fire, it felt like the entire room was in slow motion. The hundreds of voices surrounding him seemed to be drowned out, leaving only the commotion around his table. Unable to speak, Steven backed slowly through the curtain. Grabbing the book, he opened it.

Panicked, he flipped through the sea of blurry pages, seeing the chapter headings. Each written number now had titles beneath. The first title he encountered was, "Another child," immediately preceded by the next labeled, "A death."

Hearing what he thought was the security guard barking out instructions, the words sounded as blurred as the text below the titles was. Flipping to the next chapter felt like moving closer to danger as he read the next heading, "A Time of Peril." He let go of the book, placing it on the tabletop. It opened toward the middle, showing blurry pictures of his house and family while they slept. The most disturbing was of his youngest son in his mobile bassinet. The picture was taken from inside the house, in the laundry room. When the four-month-old wouldn't sleep, he and his wife referred to the room as the calming place since the sound of the dryer rarely failed to lull him to sleep. Thinking of a lunatic penetrating such an intimate place with his child present, Steven flipped to the masthead page. It was difficult to focus, but scanning the fine print, he found the copyright was registered to A. Friend, and the book had been published a year ago to the day.

Linda entered the makeshift room with her eyes wide open. "Are you okay?"

Pulled from the images, he glanced up, trying to find words. Her face ramped up his own anxious feelings, her fear making what just happened more real. The task of making up words, which was usually so easy for him, felt like lifting a heavy weight. Finally, he spit out, "I, I... am okay."

"How did that happen?"

"I don't know."

She poked her head back through the curtain, then looked back at Steven. "The security guard said the police will be here to speak with you in a few minutes. Are you going to be up to it?"

"I need a minute to compose myself."

"I understand. I'll be right out front when you're ready."

Feeling like the ground wasn't stable, he grabbed his phone. Stationed almost dead center in the belly of the convention center, there was no reception. Trying anyway, he hit the number and watched as the call screen was frozen in place. Silently, he willed it to go through, holding it up and waving the instrument back and forth. After seconds that felt like an hour, he gave up, pressing the end button. He thought of waiting for a police officer or someone else who could help, but for now, reason was taken over by the obsessive need to hear his wife's voice. Unsure of himself, he left unseen through the back curtain.

Jogging frantically around the overwhelmingly large crowd, panic made it hard to think. Even in the expansive space, he felt more claustrophobic with every new person he rubbed against. Fighting his way through to the restaurant he remembered seeing in the east corridor, he cut through the line, ignoring the protests of those around him. Heading to a revolving glass door and clear reception, a man in an enormous homemade Halo costume turned sideways and caught his backpack in the door, jamming it. Wanting to scream, Steven dodged past the revolving glass to the door just to the right.

Outside, a crowd jabbered about the convention while sucking on cigarettes, adding a dense cloud to the already heavy air. Finally, seeing the three bars of his phone, he dialed. The call went right to voicemail. In a pleading voice, he left a message. "Honey, please call me as soon as you get this!"

The phone vibrated in his hand. Flinching, he glanced down. The screen was a picture of his wife. Tears stung his eyes as he remembered taking the picture at the beach. It felt like a lifetime ago. Before he had a chance to speak, he heard her familiar voice. "Shouldn't you be signing books right now?"

"Jodi! Are you okay?"

"Yeah, why? You sound weird."

"Are the kids with you?"

"Yes, they're watching some obnoxious show with the worst singing I have ever heard. What's going on?"

"I'm not sure." He chewed at his bottom lip, trying to think how to say what he needed to say without causing panic. Knowing there was no time, he finally blurted out, "Can you please take the kids to your sister's and stay until I get there?"

"Are you joking? You won't be back until after nine! What's going on?"

Steven lifted the phone away from his mouth, not wanting her to hear him gasping for air. "Humor me and go. I'm leaving in a few minutes."

"What about the convention?"

"Don't worry about that. I promise you I'm alright. Please pack up and go *right* now. I will stay on the line."

"What's going on?"

"I can't get into it right now. Please trust me. I need you to go now." There was a pause. He could picture her standing at the kitchen island where they ate most of their meals, trying to process why he acted this way. His heart hurt thinking of her pain.

"Should I be worried, and if so, how much?"

"Probably not at all. I might be overacting."

"Okay." There was a long sigh. "Alright." She sighed again, deeply. "I'll get going right away."

"Thank you." In the background, he heard her tell the boys to get their shoes on. Steven continued to scan everyone around him, expecting to see the skeletal man in every face he examined.

The thick cigarette smoke made him woozy and brought back a strong craving for a habit he quit over a decade ago. Listening to the shrieking that always came when television time was interrupted, Steven moved away from the smoking section and found the edge of a large stone planter to sit on. It was damp from the recent rain, and his brain sent alarms that it was covered with disease. He stood up, fighting the urge to pull his pants off and stop any contact from the wetness with his skin. The adrenaline was making him exhausted, so much so that his eyelids felt heavy. Needing something to occupy himself, he went through the book again, opening it to the pictures. Staring in disbelief at a tiny casket, he instantly shut the book, pretending he had not seen the heading above the disturbing image; however, it was too late. Placing the book cover down next to him, he lifted the phone to his ear, hearing muffled laughter. He called into the phone. "Are you in the car yet?!"

"Hey, Dad!"

"Hi, Ray." Hearing his son's voice made him feel weak, quickly uncorking all that he was trying to keep inside.

"We aren't in the car yet. Henry can't find his shoes."

"Well, put your mother on the phone, please." He clenched his teeth together, trying to hold in the terror that was growing inside him.

"Why do we got to go to Auntie Karen's, Dad?"

Steven, struggling, screamed. "Please! Just put your mother on!" A man in a stormtrooper costume stopped momentarily, staring him down. Steven turned away, hunching over, and pressing the phone closer to his face.

"Alright, alright, hold your horses over there!" There was insane giggling after his new favorite phrase, which he'd acquired from *The Spaceman Cowboy Spectacular*. Muffled in the background, he heard, "Mom, hey, Mom! Here, take this."

After hearing the fumbling of the phone, he yelled, "Jodi! Please forget shoes. Just grab your purse and keys and go."

"Okay... you're freakin' me out now."

In the background, Ray shouted, "Henry, better find your shoes quick! Mom's freakin' out!"

"Honey, what's going on?"

Steven put his hand to his forehead and slowly rubbed, trying to find what was best to share. "I met a very strange man." He fought to keep the panic out of his voice, yet the words came out uneven, betraying his attempt at a calm facade.

"At the convention?"

"Yeah."

"Recently?"

"About two hours ago."

"He couldn't make it out here that quick."

"I know, but I'll feel a lot better once you're with someone else." He bit off "and a place he doesn't know about."

"Did he." Her voice dropped. "Um, you know." Her voice went down an octave. "Threaten you?"

The image of their blurry house flashed through his mind. "No, nothing like that." *At least I don't think so.* Somewhere deep in his subconscious, it occurred to him the man had saved him. His skin felt instantly cold as he contemplated the how and why of what had happened over the last few minutes. "Please, please. Go, now."

"Alright. The boys are here. We're going to go get buckled in and get out of here. What did the man do, then?"

Steven glanced at the book and came close to telling her everything. Concerned with her driving the kids while hysterical, he said, "He was just *intense*. Please, honey, go now. I'm just doing this for my peace of mind. Everything is going to be fine."

"Okay, hang tight, I have the troops corralled, just need to get them in the garage."

Steven could picture the passageway to the garage with its glossy white wainscoting and old wood floors. He then saw the mudroom and the closet door. Imagining the thin man waiting there for his family, Steven sat back down and, forgetting about germs for a second, grabbed the stone planter with his free hand, squeezing it to relieve the tension. His breathing was labored as he imagined his family being attacked by the deranged man. Feeling the gritty texture of the concrete, he thought of the germs living on the mildewy surface, then quickly let go and jumped up. The crowd was watching him now. He could feel all their eyes burning into him.

He knew Jodi was right. There was no way someone could make it that far in this traffic that fast, yet logic brought no solace to his overtaxed mind. When he heard the familiar rattle of the garage door, he felt like he could almost breathe again until he heard Ray. Listening to the sounds of the kids getting settled in, his imagination kicked in. He could see the thin man lying under the car, leaving a trail of Cheeto handprints to his hiding spot. The car's ignition pushed the thought away. A few seconds later, he could hear the kids arguing.

"Are you guys out of the house?"

"Yes."

Steven felt a wave of relief wash over him. "I'm going to let you go now. I will call you as soon as I can."

"But what happened?"

"Not with the kids in earshot. Everything's fine. I love you, but I really do have to go right now." Steven hung up, the guilt of the abrupt disconnection settling on him like a weight. He surveyed the group that was assembled around him when he quickly made his way back into the convention center, his head on a swivel, looking for threats, real or perceived, in the constant circular logic that was his subconscious mind. He navigated through the crowd, feeling electricity from the excited throngs of convention-goers. The noise of the room was nearly deafening to his ringing ears.

Exhausted, he made it back to the signing booth. The crowd was held back by a mixture of security and police. Watching the gawkers try to see what was going on reminded him of a Ray Bradbury story, where the same crowd would assemble to view accidents. The thought of the supernatural entities added to the growing dread. From behind the curtain, Linda spotted him and made her way to the officer nearest him. Before he had a chance to poke his head through the group of onlookers, Linda stepped up, telling the officer to let him through. Once he was free, he strode quickly to the booth. From behind, coming within inches of his face, Linda gripped his arm. "What happened? Where did you go? Are you okay?"

He jerked away, not needing anyone touching him when he was this amped up. "Physically, I'm fine." Steven took the stairs and ducked behind the curtain. Looking back, he watched as a police officer whose radio was screaming out what sounded like a foreign language held back the crowd. Another officer, out of uniform, was taking notes as she spoke to the security guard. She looked through the drape and made her way to Steven.

Without offering her hand, in a Southern drawl, she said, "Heard you had a pretty close call today, Mr. Hall. Do you need medical attention?"

"No, I'm fine. I need you to send someone out to watch over my family right now."

"Why's that?"

"I think that woman might have been working in tandem with someone else."

He spent the next two hours giving his story to waves of law enforcement who continually asked the same questions. Steven made no progress, trying to convince them that the thin man had orchestrated the attack. The book, to them, was just a blurred leaflet, not a clue as to what was really happening.

At a hotel that night, Steven passed through the connecting door to his room after getting the kids settled. There was enough distraction with the kids to avoid any meaningful conversation with

Jodi about the day's events. He knew the brief reprieve was going to end. Before he made it into bed, his wife sat up like a bolt.

"Why would someone do that?"

On the drive back from the convention center, he had decided how to handle the conversation. Until he understood what was going on with the book, he chose not to say anything. "I don't know." He sat on the bed, pulling the sheet back. It felt cold and damp. He knew it was dry—expensive places like this had to be well maintained—yet he yanked his hands to his lap, trying to protect them.

She leaned in and hugged him as he sat next to her. "That had to be awful. I'm so sorry you had to go through that."

"It's over now." He closed his eyes, hoping he could believe that, but knowing it wasn't possible. Her warmth brought the anxiety down almost enough that the ringing in his ears subsided.

She pulled back, staring into his eyes. "Do you want to talk about it?"

"Honestly, no. It's over, and I would like to forget it." She began chewing on her hair, darkening the blonde ends to brown. He knew something big was coming: the nervous tic always gave him notice.

"I don't want you doing any more signings."

"We have plenty of time to think about that."

"When I think we could have lost you today... " Her voice trailed off as she wept into his T-shirt.

Caressing her back he said, "You didn't, that's all that matters." Gently, he kissed the top of her head. He thought of the book, knowing he wouldn't be here without the warning. The reprieve from the anxiety lifted, making him feel like he wanted to run. "Why don't you get some sleep?" He hugged her closer, hoping to feel something other than the dull confusion and growing anxiety.

After a few seconds, she whispered, "Okay."

He lay there in the dark, listening as her dull sobbing turned to her shallow breathing. Once he was confident she was asleep, he carefully headed into the bathroom with the book and put two towels over the edge of the tub. Terrified equally of reading further and of not reading further, Steven sat on the edge and opened the book. The practical part of his brain tried to keep his imagination under control, reminding him that there was no way any of this could be happening, but the words in front of him did not allow him to consider anything else. Steven picked up where he left off in the first chapter.

After the author had left the convention and was safely at the hotel, he snuck into the bathroom to read the book that he received earlier in the day.

Steven rubbed his forehead, fighting off the tears. Even if the skeletal man staged the attempt on his life, there was no way he could have known for certain that Steven was now in a hotel. The certainty that the unexplainable was happening was like a crushing weight. Looking back at the blurry letters, his stomach ached from the constant contraction of his muscles.

He knew he was at a threshold that he could not easily get back from and had to decide if it was time to destroy the book or embrace it, knowing if he continued, it would own him.

Steven, taking off his glasses, leaned back. He placed the book on the toilet, carefully avoiding contact with the lid, feeling like he couldn't stand to hold the book for even a second longer. It felt alive, as if it possessed the ability to harm him physically. Staring at the picture on the cover, he felt suddenly as if he did not belong in the life he was leading—like everything he had ever been told was a lie, and the new truth was behind the blurry photo on this cover.

It was what he had often wished for, a roadmap to a certain future that would allow him to ignore all anxious thoughts about sickness and ritualistic cleanliness. Yet now that it was in front of him, it didn't bring relief. All he felt was the weight of responsibility and the devastating fear surrounding it. For the hundredth time, he wrestled with the idea of what would have happened if he hadn't read the book while he ate his lunch. It brought the realization that the words were blurry because his future had many possibilities and realities. Wondering what the price would be for cheating death, he picked up the book, knowing each word indebted him more deeply to a force he wanted nothing to do with.

Accepting his place in the macabre arrangement, Steven searched the author and the publisher and discovered neither existed. He looked up the address given for the publisher. The location was an old vacant mall in New Bremen on the south side. At this time of night, it would take him less than a half-hour to get there. Something deep inside Steven gave him the knowledge that's where he would find answers.

Steven followed the book's instructions, coming to the same conclusion as his fictional version. He then went to the table of contents and looked over the chapter list. The last chapter was dated eight months from now, with the heading "The great author's exit."

He tried to process why the words were visible. If he was able to make choices that could change the future, then why was there now an end date when all the other chapters were blurry?

He got dressed and left the hotel room. Once he walked out of the lobby, he looked at the book's table of contents. The date of the final chapter had changed. It was now over a year away. Steven got into his car, knowing he was not ready to face whatever he was about to encounter.

***

A half-hour later, he found himself in a littered alley in front of a massive building that appeared as if it hadn't been maintained for several years. It was a collection of graffiti, grime, and boarded windows. Standing beneath what appeared like the former marquee of a movie theater, he used his phone's flashlight to look for an opening. Finally deciding his best bet was a small window that had a sizable gap in the plywood covering it, he pulled his sleeves over his hand and lifted a discarded pallet. Leaning it at an angle against the wall, he fashioned a makeshift stepladder and pulled himself up. As he stared into the darkness, he felt a second of perfect calm before his thoughts ran wild, sending his heart racing. He traced the edges of the battered piece of wood, examining it.

The gap was just large enough that if he turned sideways, he thought he could enter. With a deep sigh, he pulled his sleeves over both hands, wishing he had brought gloves. Gripping the edges of the plywood, the jagged edges tingled his flesh as he imagined a thousand splinters penetrating his skin, infecting him with who knew what. Struggling to get through, the space was barely large enough for his shoulders.

The light swept across the floor. Instantly, he heard the scurrying of dozens of tiny feet. Smelling what he assumed was urine, he fought the suffocating claustrophobia when he got stuck halfway through the opening. Imagining creatures of the night covering him, Steven pulled with all his strength. Wiggling ferociously, he finally freed himself from the jagged edge of the plywood, sending him toppling into a pile of cardboard boxes. He felt a sharp pain on the back of his hand. Looking down, he saw a solid stream of blood where the edge of the decaying wood had opened his flesh. He kicked at the mounds of junk lying around him, desperately wishing he had been more careful.

As it always did, his germaphobia kicked in, causing him to shake and beat at his clothing with his good hand, wiping off germs. A cloud of thick dust made him cough uncontrollably, spewing phlegm as the heavy, damp air settled deep inside his lungs. The loud booming of his cough echoed against the former mall's high-beamed ceiling and long hallway. Pounding on his chest, he finally got his breathing under control. He pulled his sanitizing wipes from his pocket and furiously scrubbed every exposed surface of his skin. Steven pulled the book from his back pocket, knowing he couldn't take much more.

The author, standing amongst a sea of rodents, looked desperately for some path that would lead him to the answers he desperately sought. Once inside, the realization of all he had been through weighed him down as he stared upwards towards the second floor. He met...

The words become blurry again. Putting the book inches from his face, it was no use. There was nothing else he could discern. Steven was no longer able to fool himself. Whatever this book was, he knew it was controlling his fate. Frustrated at the sea of blurriness, he looked down. In the small beam of light, he saw what he thought was a trail. Tracing it toward a dark corridor in his periphery, he saw the gleam of hungry, tiny eyes, followed by the sound of scratching nails as the creatures ran from the light. Steven slowly moved forward with shuffling tentative steps, feeling imagined nips and scratches with each step. Cringing, he forced himself to move forward, knowing he had to find answers.

The disturbed dust ended before it reached the escalator. He decided to walk further down the corridor, passing the stairway. The light from his phone flashed against the many windows, creating dancing shadows in the decrepit building. Every nerve in his body was preparing him for a jump scare. He kept lifting the light up and making an arc around himself, expecting to see a face inches from his own.

When he came to what he thought was a food court, he opened the book again. The words were still blurry. The surrounding shadows moved. He knew it wasn't the light, but rodents staying just outside the beam. Up ahead, he saw a triangular information board. Going down the legend, he saw a listing for a community center on the second floor. His brain told him that was where he needed to be. He went back towards the escalator.

As he passed an aged store with a decaying sign labeled *Fashionation*, he saw the trail could actually lead up a rusty escalator. He glanced at the book. The words were filling in again.

The great author's instinct was right. Now he needed to find out if he had the courage to go deeper into the darkness to meet a being that could control his fate.

Steven squeezed the book, shaking it. "Why can't you just give me a complete picture?" The words traveled along the darkness, coming back in a taunting reverb. He put the book under his arm and, using a new wipe, dabbed at the blood on his hand. The surrounding skin looked puffy. He tried to remember if that was good or bad. Something in his memory told him it meant it was healing, but he wasn't sure. The momentary distraction slowed the pace of his heart slightly. It was as if using his brain for something useful took up space that had been occupied by fear, pushing it away.

When he came to the platform that led to the once moving stairway, he wanted to leave but, in his mind, he saw the title, "The Great Author's Exit," bringing thoughts of Jodi and the kids. He put the book back in his pocket and tentatively stepped on the first metallic stair.

It creaked so loudly he recoiled backward, clutching his ears. He carefully took another step. He lightly jumped up and down with both feet on the surface, testing the sturdiness. Amazingly, there was little give. Almost confident that the aging, rusted machine was safe, he slowly made his way upward, listening to the creaking and groaning of the internal mechanisms with every slight movement. As he came to the second-floor landing, the dust trail went off into the vast darkness. Steven lifted the beam of light, expecting to see rodents the size of cats lining the walls. Instead, he saw worn out, shuttered storefronts running in every direction, layered in thick dust and cobwebs across the expansive rooms that used to hold happiness. Steven made his way, following the trail that ended behind a closed door that was labeled *"Custodial Staff Only,"* nestled between a store and a sunken seating area. The sign for the custodian was hanging sideways, held intact by a single rusty nail.

Just to the right was a cloth sign that read "New Bremen Community Center." Glancing back at the book, the chapters changed, and it was now twice as thick. The final chapter was now labeled.

Everlasting Life.

"What?" Gripping the book tightly, he took a step closer to the room, and the book swelled in his hand. Steven closed his eyes, trying to wish the anxiety away.

Steven used a sanitizing wipe to grab the handle and open the door that was just to the right of a rolling gate. The light revealed a rectangular room with rows of desks. There was a narrow corridor and off to the right, just beyond an enormous plastic plant. Following the path along the dirty tile floor, he came to a room opening. The light's thin beam revealed a pair of eyes behind a desk stacked with junk food wrappers. The thin man who went by the name Jack was chewing on a pretzel. His tight skin looked as if it had been flayed off with a potato slicer. The flesh hung in erratic ribbons, moving with each bite. In a gravelly voice he moaned. "Good to see you again."

Staring at the talking skeletal figure, Steven yanked the book from his pocket. Waving it in the air, he shouted, "What's happening?!"

The thin man swallowed hard, jerking his neck back as if it took great effort. His exposed throat appeared like it had been torn open by a claw. As Jack coughed, pieces of the pretzel violently spewed out of the side of his neck in a crumbly cloud. "I take it you read the book. Well... I guess that is not a very bright observation." Jack smiled, exposing jagged teeth that were nearly concealed by the peeling skin. His deep laughter echoed in the cocoon of the empty building. "If you didn't, not only would you not be alive, you also wouldn't know to be here."

"How're you doing this?" Fear closed his throat, making his tongue stick to the top of his mouth. The abomination he was staring at looked like an attraction at a cheap carnival ride. A ghoul that would greet you as you entered the dark world of a haunted house. Steven slowly lowered the beam of light, no longer wanting to look directly at the evil face, grinning a nearly lipless smile.

Jack's voice pierced the darkness. "The more relevant question would be, what happens next?" The thin man's shadow looked at his hand. It was coated with the remains of the mounds of junk food sitting before him. Staring at Steven, he put his index finger into his mouth and, with a smacking noise, licked it clean. As he pulled it loose, the wrinkled skin came free. The loose flesh hung from his mouth, looking like a snake's tongue dangling against his chin. When he spoke, the wrinkled mess dropped to the desktop. With a sharp chuckle, he grabbed the skin flap between thumb and forefinger and tossed it to the floor. It landed inches from a hole in the wall. There was a loud scratching sound, and then the strip of flesh quickly disappeared through the hole, gripped by a furry claw. "Please excuse my eating. I expect you consider me uncouth, but please understand that it is very rare that I get to taste what I eat. You see, it is difficult when you don't have a tongue most of the time." Jack looked down and noticed the skinless finger. In a quick motion, he covered it from view with his other hand as if he was embarrassed by the lack of flesh. "As to your question, I've given you a gift."

"A gift!"

"You don't think prolonged life is a gift?" He raised his eyebrow over his right eye. It accentuated the fact that he was missing the eyelid, making it look like he was staring through an enormous magnifying glass.

"This can't be happening."

"But yet it is."

"Where'd you get this book from?!"

"As I told you earlier today, I wrote it."

"How do you know what's going to happen?" Steven could hear scurrying behind him. He wanted to close the door. The thought of being stuck inside the small space with the skeletal form stopped him.

"A time ago, when I entered this room, I came across your first novel. The second I touched it, an urge to consume it overwhelmed me. As I read it, I became... inspired to write. It was as if your words were filling in a story inside my head. I could see moments from your past and then your future. But they were always blurry. I would get a sentence here and there. I wrote every one of them down. It took me quite some time to piece everything together. Even longer to realize that I was connecting to you through your subconscious." Leaning back, the chair squeaked as he stared at the book in Steven's hand. "You see, that's why everything was blurry, because the future can change."

"I can't believe any of this. Why would you have this power?"

"Somehow, I was chosen. By who or what, I do not know. All I know is that parts of me returned with each word I wrote." The skeletal figure paused, looking at the back of his hands. "The words came from somewhere outside of me. I felt as if I was just a vessel for them to make their way onto the page. Over the course of a month, I continued to read your books, and I became nearly whole. Every time I finished a paragraph, I stopped and added to my growing work. It was as if you wrote your books only for me. Today when I saw you, I wanted to ask if you actually did."

"But why me?"

"Because you are gifted, and that gift through your work extended to me so I can now live out my destiny."

"And what is that?"

"You will see... in time."

Steven glanced at the book. It was still as thick as it had been when he crossed the threshold. He wanted to open it and read what was to come next, but he froze. Dread felt like a blanket wrapping him tight. *Please, how do I stop this?* He opened his lips, but the words would not come out. Desperately, he looked back at Jack. "How are you doing this?"

"You see, recently I... passed. Well, to me it seemed recent. To those alive, it might not. The experience wasn't like one might expect. There were no white lights or anything like that. I've lived outside the edges of society for some time, even before I became like this." His eyes traced his flesh. "Alcohol had its claws deeply into my... human form. Having nowhere to live, I snuck into this place with some vodka I purchased with money I'd begged on the street. I was amazed at how much I found here besides shelter. I had clothing, partially filled vending machines, and pooled rainwater. All that I needed to live, except for my chosen drug. Feeling like I had won the jackpot, I holed up inside a clothing store." The skeletal face seemed to smile for a quick second.

"That night, feeling safe for the first time in years, I stuffed myself full of junk food and enjoyed my drink. That was when I saw the darkness and then realized I was not in a mall, but in an oversized coffin. The darkness overtook me then and there. Honestly, I wasn't that sad. I knew the end was near, something hadn't felt right inside for some time. Once I was gone, I slowly made my way here."

Steven watched the skeletal face speak as if they were discussing a baseball game, not surviving death. He slowly inched himself back until he felt a cold wall behind him. "So, you know my future then?"

"It's not as simple as that. I see multiple versions and wrote them all."

"So, you know when I'll die."

"In a way, yes. Ultimately, it's up to you. Within reason."

"And you call this a gift!"

"Don't you?"

"No, not like this."

"Well, I guess that depends on... perspective. You need not view this situation with such a narrow lens. Think of it this way. If you decide to keep the book, you will be given notice of what is about to happen. If you choose, you can alter the outcome as you did today."

"And if I don't?"

"Then you will get another visit from me, and nature will take its course as it was supposed to today." Jack eyed the cellophane wrapped brownies. He quickly grabbed one, pulled away the covering, and started to eat it. The creamy filling oozed out the sides of his mouth in the gaps that were growing slightly larger with each bite. "Of course, that meeting will not be as pleasant as this is."

"How can this be happening?"

"I stopped asking those questions after I realized I had survived death."

"What are you?!"

"A man like you. Or at least I was... until I wasn't, that is." He emitted a mirthless grunt of laughter. "I like to think of myself as the keeper of the books." His eyes darted to the desk.

"Books? Plural."

"Oh yes. I'm working on alternate volumes."

"Why did you choose to give the gift?" Steven slowly lifted the light, getting a better view of the creature.

"My reward is I get my flesh back. At least for a short time." The words sounded garbled. Slowly, his fingers fished inside his mouth. The sinewy flesh stretched as it fought to extract his tongue. The decayed material made a wet slurping noise as it went through what was left of his lips. He held it, staring at it for a moment as if trying to identify an unknown foreign object. With a sigh he said, "But alas, my reward is over for now." Staring longingly at his mountain of food in the dim light, he said, "But at least I got to taste all of my goodies for a short time." His lidless eye looked off into space.

Steven, disgusted, found the courage to toss the book on the desk, scattering the empty wrappers. "I don't want any of this! Take this away. Return it to wherever it came from."

"All the books come from this desk. When it is complete, the second drawer will contain the next book to be shared, depending on what decisions you make. Either way, this leaves me stuck in this building amongst my many furry minions. Possibly until another inspiration takes your place." He lovingly caressed the desktop. "If you want to leave it here, it certainly is no skin off my nose." He peeled off a strip from his nostril, letting out a contrasting joyous laugh. "But understand that your choice will no longer give you the opportunity to change anything. There is no going back once you leave this room without my gift to you."

He needed time to think, to reason, but knew he didn't have the luxury. "Can you see all that's written?"

"Not in a way that would benefit you. I see multiple end dates. The day that I am to pay you a visit, as I did today." In the shadows, the skeletal man no longer looked human. As if he sensed Steven's thoughts, Jack raised a dark hood over his head. The heavy material hung just above his eyes, accentuating his deadly stare.

"For how long will I be able to alter the ending?" The words came out slowly.

"For as long as you choose to heed the warnings."

"So, I'll have a chance to live longer?"

"Yes, until you don't."

"What happens when I reach the end?"

"You will take my place here amongst the rodents!" Jack stood quickly, raising his hand, and peeling a long strip of skin from his fingertip down beneath the sleeve of his robe. "The transformation began the minute you chose to extend your life. Look at your hand, you are now becoming like me." He pointed to Steven's hand with his long bony finger.

Steven looked at the puncture from the plywood when he entered the mall. The surrounding skin was gray and peeling upward, just like the atrocious being in front of him.

"No, this can't be happening!" Steven shook his head. The room suddenly felt like it was shrinking, pushing him closer to the laughing skeleton.

Jack cackled in the darkness, pulling back both his hood and the remainder of his skin mask. What was left of the flesh on his face hung like a scarf around his neck in a wrinkled heap.

Steven desperately wanted to leave the book but couldn't. Quickly swiping it from the desk, he ran from the room, following the dust trail and darting down the long hallway that was now filled with scrawny rats. They squeaked and scratched their claws against the tile floor, creating a nauseating squeal. The stairs of the escalator quickly filled with layers of rodents. Steven looked up and watched them fall from a hole in the ceiling. He did his best to avoid coming into contact with the throngs of furry beasts taking the stairs in quick leaps, narrowly avoiding snapping teeth.

When he reached the bottom, he went to the window. The boxes below were filled with rats crawling over one another in unison, snapping in the direction of their prey. Grabbing a discarded piece of wood, Steven swung. Instead of parting, they dug in with their noses high and mouths wide open. Turning around, Steven saw a sea of hairy creatures pouring out from the stairway running toward him.

He was no longer able to indulge his germaphobia, so he jumped up on the box, squishing the moving flesh beneath his shoes. Ignoring the queasiness in his stomach, he jammed the book into his pocket and pulled himself through the plywood opening. As he wiggled his way through, he felt rough fur make its way up his pant leg to near his groin. Shaking and screaming, he finally was able to free himself by wiggling sideways, causing him to fall onto the ground. Appalled, he pulled down his pants and swatted at a rodent nearly the length of a football. He sprinted to his car without looking back, leaving the rat spinning inside his pants. The door was unlocked, but nothing happened when he hit the start button.

Immediately, it came to him. His keys were in his pants, which were now covered in a blanket of rats climbing over one another. Screeching out tears, he punched the steering wheel. Without thinking, he pulled the book from his inside jacket pocket.

The great author, learning his fate, ran from the skeleton's army of rodents. When he got to his car, the realization came to him that he had to go recover his keys.

Hearing hundreds of tiny claws on his car, Steven looked up to see the hungry little faces quickly enveloping all the windows, extinguishing the moonlight. He took a deep breath and continued reading in the little light that was still coming through the window.

Hoping he could outrun them before they tore him to pieces, he summoned courage that he didn't know he had. After fighting through the herd, Steven made his way back to the car and saw his reflection. Most of his skin was gone, leaving him looking like the skeleton from which he had just escaped. When he was back inside the car, he knew he would survive the wounds, as he was on his way to becoming part of something larger than himself. He also knew that, in this hideous condition, he would not be able to spend the rest of his time on Earth with his children. The dark realization brought a deep sadness, knowing that the "gift" from the monster did nothing more than prolong a now meaningless everlasting existence.

Steven quickly went to the last chapter.

"Everlasting Life."

He removed his multitool from the armrest and clicked open the razor-sharp knife. With shaking hands, he brought the glistening metal to his wrist, feeling the cold metal on his skin. Outside, the rodents were scratching the car, sounding like nails across a chalkboard. Looking at the book that lay across his lap, he pressed the knife down with enough force to draw blood. Squinting, he could just see that the title had changed to the current day. Resigned to his fate and the realization that the last few hours of false hope had all possibly been for the amusement of the creature he had just encountered, Steven threw his head back and laughed sardonically.

Looking through the thick sea of rats fighting to climb the slick glass, he saw in the second-floor window of the dead mall the outline of the skeletal man. The dark silhouette of a robed figure holding a curved scythe loomed above. Steven, knowing the futility of trying to delay the inevitable, dropped the knife. Carefully, he clutched the book tightly over his chest, feeling it double in size as he did so. Thinking of his family, he wept as he slowly opened the door, crossing over to the other side.

ARE YOU REAL?

After finishing a very thorough orientation with Ms. Iblis, the sleep clinic's director, James sat alone, waiting for his escort to his home for the next two months. Looking at the glass eye of the camera in the corner, he cautiously put his notes away. As he shoved them into the briefcase, he saw the name of the man who committed the murder-suicide that he'd come here to investigate.

The walls of the empty room were pristine, white, so bright they were almost glowing. The only color besides his wet clothing—he'd arrived in a relentless downpour—was the insignia of The Forever Institute that stood above the door that was opening. With a mechanical whoosh, the doors opened, exposing walls that were covered by computer screens, dials, and switches. The lettering around the equipment was all in a language incomprehensible to him.

A very tall man entered the small room, obscuring the view of the technological contraptions. "Good evening, Mr. Aickman. I am Mr. Raybury." He stood with excellent posture and an amused look without extending his hand. "If you follow me, I will show you to your quarters." He gave a look that suggested the chore was interrupting something very important.

The word 'quarters' sent off a signal in his brain that James didn't like. He was fully knowledgeable of the inner workings of the facility, but here now, cold and wet, he felt an unexpected apprehension come over him in a wave. "Lead the way." Watching the tall man step closer to reach for his luggage, James turned, grabbing the bag himself. "Thanks, but I have it."

"Very well."

Once they were back in the main corridor, James noticed cameras spread out amongst the many former storefronts. "Where are we heading?"

"Second floor in the east corridor. Ms. Iblis has you in a former clothing store. It's a very nice space."

"Good view?"

"No, sir. None of the rooms have windows to the outside, and the interior windows are all clouded over for privacy."

"I was wondering why they all looked the same. How do they create that... smoky effect in the glass?"

"It's a gas that is infused between the panes. It is quite an efficient method to create a pleasant atmosphere as well as privacy and mood."

He wondered how much it cost to create such an elaborate effect. "Wouldn't it have been simpler to just build walls where the glass panels used to be?" His eyes moved across the aisles of glass surrounding them.

"Engineering is not part of my responsibilities here. Therefore, I wouldn't be able to answer that. However, I think you will find the smoke allows a more pleasing atmosphere for sleep. Or at least that's what most of our disciples say."

James, knowing the price of a prolonged stay at the exclusive sleep clinic, wasn't surprised by the answer. He had been fully briefed before being assigned to observe from within, as a guest of the clinic where there'd been two suicides in a span of less than one year. Staring down the cavernous hallway, it looked as if it had never ended. The walls were identical, with long corridors of glass and stainless-steel panels. The sleek decor reminded him of the cover art of a paperback of *The Martian Chronicles* that used to sit on his nightstand. James fought to stay a half step behind as the tall man strode along. Listening to the rhythmic thumping sound of the wheels of his luggage dragging along behind him, he said, "It must cost a fortune to keep this place lit."

Mr. Raybury whipped his head back. "What's that?"

"All the lights. The energy bill must be very significant."

"Oh, I wouldn't know of such things. The budget for utilities is not under my purview."

"Oh." As they approached the two-tiered main atrium, he looked up. "This place was a shopping mall, wasn't it?" He knew full well it was but was trying to keep him talking.

"Yes. Having a structure that has so many individual spaces is ideal for our needs."

"That's understandable." The large atrium was an intersection of the four connecting walkways and had a glass-paneled ceiling with an artificial tint. The rain pounded against the glass, creating a loud echo. As he was staring at the two-story intersection of the corridors, his host turned to their right and got on the escalator. Following behind, he asked, "I was expecting Mr. Craneshaw to be at the orientation. I thought he made it a habit to meet all his new... guests when they arrive."

As they rose, the man turned. "Yes, that's his typical custom. On his behalf, I would like to apologize for Mr. Craneshaw not being here to meet you." For a moment, he looked as if he was going to add something.

"That's quite all right. With... everything that's happened recently, I perfectly understand." His hinting at the murder didn't seem to register. The insurance company he worked for sent him there to investigate the practices of the secretive facility that was becoming a religion to those who stayed there to gain enlightenment. He knew what he was going to be up against. The woman who admitted him had a similar reaction when he made the same comment. The complete absence of emotion made him wonder if they had been coached on how to respond.

"His position as acting director keeps him very busy."

Catching up to him, James kept at it. "I'm here by recommendation of a close friend. He was tight-lipped about any specifics. I was hoping you could inform me of what to expect?"

"Sir, our secrecy is for the benefit of our disciples. If I reveal any part of the program, it will alter the experience and go against the creed." He absentmindedly put his hand on his bracelet.

"So, you are a disciple yourself?" Seeing the look of surprise, he quickly said, "Sorry, not prying. I just noticed your bracelet."

"Why yes, I am a disciple and wear this proudly." He lifted his arm, exposing the silver band with an iris in the center, reflecting the bright overhead light. "I have been here since a year after they opened. I started out taking treatment and then decided I didn't want to leave after that."

"So, they hired you on after?"

"Hired? No, I am a volunteer." The man turned to step off the escalator and walked briskly as they made their way down another corridor.

"And what do you do?"

"Maintenance, mostly."

"Do you enjoy your work?"

"Oh, yes, very much so. I would do anything to stay here."

James stepped off the moving stairway. "Do you have any family?"

"Not any longer." His face changed when he said those last words. The habitual hazy look showed a quick trace of anger.

"I'm sorry to hear that."

"No need to say that." He pointed quickly to his right. "This is your room. Please watch carefully as I press my hand against this interface. Immediately after I remove it, please press your hand against the screen, and you will be programmed for entry."

James followed the instruction, and the large glass panel opened inward, making a pneumatic hissing noise. The room was dark. The second they entered, lights above clicked on in succession until the expansive space was completely illuminated. There was low-set, very modern-looking furniture everywhere. The walls were plasma screens on which images like lava lamps moved. The floors were a collection of large white panels with rectangular stainless tracks separating them. White was the predominant color, making the room appear to glow. "You weren't joking when you said this was large." There was no response, just the same dull expression. "How do the lights work?"

"This controls all functions of the room." The enormous man waved his hand across a beam of light that was emanating from the floor. The solid stream was nearly two inches in diameter and rose all the way to the ceiling. Small specks of dust floated throughout its intense light. A pulsating beeping noise followed the motion. "Lights extinguish." In an instant, the room was dark except for the ambient light from the corridor. "Lights, full power, only in the sleeping chamber." The lights directly behind them lit up.

"Why not make everything voice-activated?" James placed his shoulder bag, which he used for his papers, onto the table next to his bed. Seeing the pillows, the tiredness he had been ignoring came over him in a wave. Adjusting his jacket, he looked back at the man.

"It was, until we discovered our disciples were activating the device unintentionally in their sleep." He quickly changed the subject. "In an hour, the door will close and lock for the night. After that, if you have a reason to leave, call using the light sensor so we can let you out."

"Wait. So, I will be locked in?"

"Well, no—I mean, yes, to the extent you will have to wait for one of our staff to come and activate the door. It is a precaution for the safety of our other guests."

"Sleepwalking?"

"It has happened."

James thought of his office and the last conversation before he reluctantly accepted the assignment. He was sure they didn't mention that the clinic had such unorthodox procedures. But he knew he would have come anyway: he was in no position to decline any work. He let the conversation drop. Scanning the room, he said, "Where can I get something to eat?" He hooked his thumb at the beam. "Is there a way to order food on that thing?"

"On the first floor, there is a cafeteria in the west wing. It will be open until ten when everyone is expected in their room."

"Okay then. I will head out as soon as we are finished." The hint didn't register.

The man gave a quick nod as if approving before he continued, "As I was saying, you will use our lighting activator to call us for any of your needs and to activate any normal controls in the room. Once the light is interrupted, speak to it as if it is any other voice-activated device. In the morning, the doors will open at precisely eight a.m. From there, feel free to roam around. We will expect you to go through our full orientation after you eat. The presentation will take place at ten a.m. sharp. I will meet you in the main atrium and take you to the presentation room. The only other request I would have for now is that you give me your phone."

"What?" Not sure if the dour man was joking, James raised his chin slightly, looking at the man as if he was crazy.

"Sir, I apologize, but it is a prerequisite for staying here. We cannot have outside interference. We published this information in the contract you signed." His face turned from anger to understanding. "Sorry, I didn't intend to sound confrontational. The request is for the comfort of all that stay here. It really is for the best."

"Is there someone I can speak to about this? Possibly Ms. Iblis?"

"Sorry, no."

James pulled his phone from his pocket. There was no signal. He knew he didn't have much of a choice, but looked at the entrance, thinking of leaving this place and the tension that had been growing. Remembering his debts, he reluctantly shut it off and handed it to the giant, thinking he would find Ms. Iblis in the morning and straighten everything out. With the wet clothes clinging to his back, his patience was growing very thin. "Well then, thank you for the tour, and I guess I will see you in the morning."

"Yes, sir. I hope you enjoy your journey to enlightenment." The man gave a slight nod and walked out into the main corridor.

James waved his hand through the light beam in the same way he would an open flame and with enough speed that it couldn't hurt him. Once the beep sounded, he said quietly, "Close the main door." With a swoosh, the door obeyed his command. "Please turn the temperature up eight degrees." Through vents that were cleverly concealed, he heard the air rush into the room, feeling like a warm breeze. Tired and hungry, he opened his bag, retrieving dry clothes.

***

The cafeteria was as sterile looking as everything else in the facility. Each food bay had a colored theme, and all the counters and walls seemed to lack a right angle, making them blend together like some large unfinished art project. After selecting the items on a touch screen, the food came out in glass compartments. In front of the serving area, there were half-moon booths spread throughout.

James was alone except for a man in wrinkled striped pajamas and a woman who looked like she could have easily still been in college. Not eager for any company, James sat across the room, facing in the opposite direction. As he sat down, he noticed that the man's left arm seemed to be pinned to the table. Trying not to stare, it appeared as if his Institute bracelet was holding him to the stainless tabletop.

Turning his head away from the other diner, he picked through the food on his tray, trying to ignore the distinct smell of overheated meat. As he took his first bite, he heard over his shoulder a high-pitched voice say, "What did you get?" After a brief pause, the female voice added, "Stay away from the beef here, buddy, believe me!" The young woman came around the table, holding her thin stomach and puffing out her cheeks as if she was trying to hold in gas.

She sat across from him in the curved booth and said, "Name's Shirley. How long have you been here?"

"Just—" The words came out muffled. He quickly covered his mouth with the back of his hand and chewed down beef that he wished he had never tasted. "I just arrived an hour ago."

She pulled her leg, which was covered in a tight, almost shiny material, up to her chin, hugging it. "Ohh, exciting. This is my second night. So far, no enlightenment, though." Shirley gave a wide, sarcastic smile.

"Well, I would think it could take a few days, at least." He grinned.

"So, how did you make your money?"

James smiled widely, squinting at the abruptness of the question. "What's that?"

"Your money. You obviously have a pile if you're here. Unless you know an insider and found a way past the ridiculously high entry fee."

Having already prepared a cover, he said, "No, no tricks. I'm a doctor. So, for me, the fee was slightly more reasonable." Although he had known her for less than a few seconds, James felt guilty for lying. He stared into her eyes and couldn't look away. She reminded him of someone he used to know, but he couldn't remember from when or where.

"Well, that explains it. Since you told me, I will tell you what you are probably too polite to ask. My father's got more dough than he knows what to do with. He owns like a thousand businesses. Not a single one of them is the least bit interesting or well-known, but together, they do quite well."

He was watching her rub her fingers together where a wedding ring would normally be. There was no partial tan line, but he would bet she recently removed a ring. Habits like that didn't change quickly. "So, you came at his insistence?"

"No. I wanted to come." She opened her eyes wide, leaning forward, trying to sell her point. "After he completed his stay, he was a very different guy. Although he wouldn't tell me what went down here, he practically begged me to come." She rubbed her nose. "If you knew him, you would know he doesn't beg anyone for anything. I guess, in the end, that is why I agreed. If it meant that much to him, I figured it must be pretty amazing."

She smelled like flowers after a downpour. As she spoke, he felt very close to her, so much so that it scared him. The intensity of her gaze forced him to look away. Looking back at the other diner, he saw him shoveling another plate of food into his mouth. His hand still did not move off the table. "From all I have heard, it must be beyond remarkable."

"So, you alone?"

"Here? Yes."

"What about when you aren't here?"

"Well, I have friends and family."

"Sorry I'm asking so much. I guess I'm kinda lonely and bored. I sleep most days."

With the tip of the fork, he pushed through what looked like pureed vegetables, letting steam escape.

"So far, it has worked well for me. But then again, what do I know? I am quite crazy most of the time."

James let out a quick chuckle. "What do you mean by that?"

"Nothing. Don't mind me; most don't." A darkness came over her face as if a light had been switched off. Shifting in her seat, she said, "Better finish up before your food gets colder."

James examined her changing face. The glow in her eyes extinguished, making her look much plainer. He dug into the vegetables. They tasted as if they had been blended with cardboard. Pushing the plate to the side, he whispered, "That's enough for tonight, I guess."

"Don't worry. The main meals are much better." Her thumb massaged her finger in a continuous rhythm. "It's nothing like the machine food you just had the pleasure of experiencing."

His stomach growled. Shifting in his seat, he said, "So, you said you slept most of the day. Is that typical for patients? Sorry, I mean guests."

"Not typical, but I would say typical for here. *This is* a sleep clinic, after all. They do everything they can here to help you sleep." She grabbed his napkin and began slowly twisting it, making it look like a rope.

"Maybe that's why the food tastes like that." James flicked the edge of the plate slightly, making it give off a solid metallic ding.

"Huh?"

"Drugs. You know... to make you sleep, for those that can't."

"Oh, no. I don't think they do that." Shirley shook her head quickly. "No, for sure... I don't see them doing that."

"Maybe not." With a slight shrug of the shoulders, he added, "So, what have you learned so far?"

"You know I can't tell you." She looked up at the camera over the food dispensary. "If I did, the robots would come and sequester us." Her eyes got wide, and she looked around slowly. "Ha! You should have seen your face, buddy!"

"Very amusing."

She laughed, exposing a pierced tongue that was missing a stud. "That was too easy." She fanned herself with shiny nails. "Honestly, though, so far, not much has happened. The orientation is a bit of a boring-ass history lesson, and they ask that you keep an open mind. So far, the only consistent thing I have experienced is that they are very much into keeping a somber, quiet atmosphere to keep everyone in a sleepy mood. You have only been here for a short time, but I am sure you will notice how much this place reminds you of floating in a cloud."

Loudly he said, "That's it!" James smacked his hands together. Shirley jumped, lowering her leg. The pajama man looked at them and then went back to his plate, shoveling the food down as he continued to stare. Reaching his hand across the table, James touched her very warm hand. "Sorry, you just helped me figure out what I have been trying to fill in for the last half-hour. This place reminds me of being on a plane and seeing the clouds. There is a weird hum, and everything is bright and airy."

Shirley let out a nice laugh. "That was funny. Yeah, I swear, a few times, I've felt like I was moving. When you are back in your room, ask your light waiter to play calming music. Then sit back, and I bet within a minute you will feel it as well."

"Light waiter?"

"You know that weird light you have to touch and talk to?"

"Oh."

"You saw it, didn't you?" Not waiting for an answer, she added, "Of course you did, duh, or you would have your luggage with you. When you were brought to your room, was it that Lurch-looking guy?"

"Tall, huge forehead?"

"That's him. Creepers man. Don't know his whole deal, but what a weirdo."

"Yes, he had an odd... demeanor."

Shirley rolled up her sleeve, checking her watch. It sat directly next to her bracelet. Noticing him staring, she said, "You will receive one of these lovely pieces of jewelry tomorrow. It's policy to wear it. If you don't, robots will come after you." With a wry smile, she added, "Sorry, I had to. Well, we better call it. Haven't much time before they want us to get to sleep."

"OK then. It was nice to meet you. Perhaps we can meet again tomorrow for lunch?"

"Are you asking me out on a date? Creepers, man." After a beat of uncomfortable silence, she smiled.

James felt himself blush and let out a gruff chuckle. "I... I didn't mean it like that."

"You are so easy, dude. Yes, I would be glad to eat with you tomorrow."

She quickly stood and headed down the corridor, adding color to the stark white surroundings. Feeling he should have, if nothing else, at least some interesting conversation until he could get out, James headed in the opposite direction for his first night of controlled sleep.

After a considerable walk, James was back in his room. At the built-in computer, he was filling out his daily questionnaire. The ceaseless humming had put him on edge. He hadn't noticed it until Shirley mentioned it, but since she did, he could think of little else. It was not loud but persistent enough to make concentrating very difficult. Doing his best to complete the questions, he found himself humming along to the odd noise.

After completing the section about his eating and exercise habits, he came to the sleep portion. There were a series of questions asking about the duration and quality. Then he came to the section that asked about the themes of his dreams. He typed in that he had no dreams. The screen would not let him advance. After re-entering the response several times, he went to the light beam and asked for help. After a beep and a brief pause, he heard an unfamiliar voice.

"Good evening, Doctor. How may I assist you?"

"I was filling out the questionnaire as you have requested, and the screen froze."

"Well, first, thank you for filling out the information. It is vital to your experience. Second, I would like to ask on what screen the computer, how do you say, 'froze'?"

"It asked me about what type of dreams I have. I responded that I didn't have any. After that, it will not go forward."

"That cannot be, Doctor."

"Feel free to come on by and take a look for yourself."

"I believe you that the screen stopped there, but why did you answer you do not dream?"

"Because I never do. I never have since I was a child." Suddenly, by the man's response, it occurred to him that the computer was being monitored.

"I don't understand how that can be possible. Everyone dreams, James. Especially here."

"Well then, maybe I am the exception."

"Well, I wouldn't know about that. The specifics of dreaming are not under my purview. Therefore, I would not be able to give you a conclusive answer. Would you please try to change your answer? Perhaps type that the dreams were nonspecific."

The humming seemed to increase to the point that it was affecting James's equilibrium, making him feel like the entire room was moving. He reached back and steadied himself on the edge of his bed. "I thought we were encouraged to answer truthfully."

"It is just to see if it... *unfreezes* your screen, sir. If you don't mind, could you please try now?"

"Sure." Shaking the cobwebs out of his head, James made his way to the computer. After he retyped the information, he hit enter, and the computer advanced. Raising his voice, he said, "That did it."

"Very well, then. Is there anything else I can do for you?"

"Yes, tell me how I go back and put in the right answer."

"There is no way to do that. I will let your leader know you had to fabricate the answer if you would like."

"I guess that would be the appropriate thing to do."

"Is there anything else you require?"

Like everyone else James encountered in the clinic, his speech was erratic, as if English was not his first language, but it was not as simple as that. The delays in word choice seemed somehow deliberate, like a computer processing data. "I don't... think so."

"Well, thank you again for calling. Please don't worry about contacting me. Have a wonderful sleep."

Before he could ask why he would worry about contacting them, the light flashed quickly, and there was the familiar beep. James spent the next ten minutes filling out more meaningless questions that he no longer felt compelled to answer honestly. When he was done, he listened to classical music and drifted off to sleep.

After hours of nothingness, suddenly, he felt like he was viewing a movie. Like an omnipresent force, he began seeing and feeling all that was around him, knowing it couldn't be real but feeling as if it was.

Bruce had just arrived in Chicago. As he stood just past the eased curb beyond the public transportation kiosk, he checked his phone. There was a text from the lawyer saying there would be a town car waiting for him near arrival gate B. The wind was chapping his face. His skin had not acclimated to the dry air after spending so much of his time on the beach. As he dodged the business travelers and their wheeled luggage, he sensed their anxiety as they navigated through the kinetic loading zones.

Next to a bench, where a mother was corralling her children, Bruce saw the bold letter B on the grimy sign. There were four mid-size Uber vehicles idling at the curb but no town car. As he waited, he stared at the haggard mother. He felt her desperation and fear of being alone and tasked with so much responsibility. Her frantic mind merged with his. The connection was so strong Bruce felt nauseous. He moved further away, trying to avoid her and her anxiety.

Looking down the covered corridor, he saw a town car make its way up the circular ramp, weaving past the checkered cabs, its headlights fighting the gray midday air and the flurries that were just forming, spiraling in erratic circles. The driver pulled up with a screech, inches away from Bruce. Minutes later, they were heading downtown; the flurries were rapidly turning into substantial snowflakes. Without speaking, Bruce knew the man driving the car was worried about the results of the pregnancy test his wife was going to take. The driver loved his daughter but knew they were in no position to have another, at least not right now. Bruce pressed the button, raising the tinted glass partition. He was too close to the man to stop the mental connection but did his best to ignore the driver's unwelcome fear. Instead, Bruce watched the other cars enter the great city and its cluttered skyline. Looking through the driving snow, he felt like he was in the center of a snow globe. It wasn't his first time in Chicago, but it had been so long since his last visit he had forgotten the breathtaking beauty of its skyscrapers.

An hour later, Bruce was in the lobby of the penthouse suite. He had just been asked to wait by a nurse with a thick accent. To his right were floor to ceiling windows. Through them was a spectacular view of the growing snowstorm swirling over Lake Michigan. He was contemplating how far out he would be able to see on a clear day when, in the glass's reflection, he saw a tall, overweight man enter the room.

Extending a hand, the man said with a deep voice, "Mr. Lloyd, glad you could make it."

Bruce could feel Walter's amazement at his appearance. To him, Bruce didn't appear to have aged a single day from their last meeting over a decade ago. There wasn't any recession to his hairline, or a wrinkle present anywhere on his face. Before Bruce took Walter's hand, he could feel the intensity of the lawyer's obsessiveness and drive. The emotion was so strong it made Bruce sweat. Fighting to remain focused, he shook the hand that dwarfed his own. "Nice to see you again." He didn't remember their previous meeting but saw it in the lawyers' memory, the same as he saw the reaction to his appearance.

"Can I offer you anything to drink or eat?"

"No, I am fine, thank you. If you don't mind, I would prefer to get down to business. I would like to fly out before the snow increases." He felt the man's amusement at Bruce's naivete about the possibility of travel in the snow.

With a polite smile, he said, "I understand. Mr. Dahlton is available. Please follow me."

Bruce did so. They passed several very large, brightly lit rooms, all decorated in classic muted tones. The floors were the only exception. They were heavily veined marble in varying wild shades of peach. Not a single item in any of the rooms looked practical, only chosen to impress guests with their considerable cost. As they approached the master bedroom, Bruce composed his thoughts and did his best to ignore the constant anxious energy coming from the lawyer. He respected the man's sincerity but needed to focus on the frail man lying under several blankets, surrounded by a sea of silk pillows.

Hal Dahlton was propped up, wearing a dress shirt without a tie. The shirt was intended to give the businessman an appearance of respectability. However, it did just the opposite. It made him look pathetic. Bruce walked up to the side of the bed and saw the full toll of the man's disease. His eyes were sunken, the sockets appearing as skeletal orbs. His heavily wrinkled face was dry and sagging and as white as the sheets he was lying on.

Bruce said, "Hello, Mr. Dahlton."

"Thank you for coming, Mr. Lloyd." Always the businessman, he shuffled in the bed, trying to make himself appear taller. With an arthritic hand, he pointed across the room. "Walter, if you don't mind, can you bring that chair over? I prefer eyes at level when I speak." Walter nodded and brought the chair a foot from the bed. Once Bruce was seated, Dahlton continued, "So, from what I hear, you have a... unique skill."

"Some would say that."

"So, what exactly are you capable of?"

Bruce was used to dealing with the wealthy and powerful. He was also used to the reaction he would receive when he responded to *that question. Through long and hard experiences, he had learned to be both concise and blunt. "I can guarantee to extend your life by six months."*

James woke to the sound of his front door. The loud banging noise brought his groggy attention to the glass doors at the front of the room. Wiping the sleep from his eyes, he fought the urge to yell out into the vast emptiness. There was a small amount of ambient light coming from the wall that was a barrier to the main hallway. Disoriented in unfamiliar surroundings, he carefully walked to the light beam that controlled the room. The humming, along with the faint memory of what he just witnessed in what he could only guess was a dream, was making his head pound, feeling like his heartbeat originated inside his eardrum. Fighting to keep his breathing under control, he quickly waved his hand over the light, his eyes never leaving the front door. "What time is it?!" Flinching at how loud his voice was, he glared at the light, trying to will it to respond immediately and make him feel less alone in the vast space.

The response finally came in a hypnotic, robotic voice. "It is two twenty-four in the a.m."

As he was about to ask for the main lights to come on, he heard a deafening thumping noise. James stood still as he watched an enormous shadow grow. Its silhouette was taking the shape of a man through the thick, obscured glass. Wondering if it had been there the whole time he slept, he waved his hand frantically over the light beam. "Open the door!"

There was silence.

Feeling foolish, he waved his hand repeatedly over the light, begging, "Please!" After the customary beep, he yelled, "Open the door!"

After a full second of feeling like he was going to pass out, the digital voice finally responded. "Unable to process that command, Doctor." There was a gap that felt like it lasted an hour but which, in reality, was mere seconds. "Please call your leader for that command, Doctor."

Angry, he clenched his fists before saying, "Call the leader."

"Hold, please." There was a digital beeping noise followed by a voice. "Dr. Aickman, are you all right?"

He recognized the voice as the man who had shown him his room earlier. "Someone is at my door."

"Interesting."

"Interesting? Interesting?! Is it normal to have someone peering into my room as I sleep?" Disoriented, he shouted, "What's going on here!"

"No one can see in, Sir."

"Be that as it may, I still don't like it!" Watching the shape, his temple throbbed, blurring his vision. Images from his dream ran through his mind, making James feel dizzy and exhausted. In his adult life, he couldn't recall having a single dream. Experiencing one here in this strange place made him feel hungover. Something deep inside told him the shadow had something to do with the dream. It was getting harder to breathe. Shaking his head, he nearly screamed, "Look! Just unlock my door."

"I am afraid I cannot do that."

"I demand it."

"Sir, the doors must be opened manually. I will come up at once and investigate."

"What about the cameras outside my room?"

"Yes. I am looking at them now." There was a nearly silent pause. "There has been no activity since you entered earlier. When did you say you heard or saw this... person?"

"It woke me up less than a minute ago!" James looked at the glass panel. The shape seemed like it was floating. "You're telling me that, right now, you don't see someone in front of my room?"

"No, sir."

Like smoke, the shadow slowly disappeared in glimmering waves. Staring at the obscured glass, he quietly said, "It's... gone now."

"Sir, would you like me to come up now? I can be there in less than five minutes."

James looked at the wall that was connected to the hallway. Through the fog, he stared at the glass, feeling exposed to something that he sensed, deep inside, could hurt him. He slowly pulled his arms into himself, instinctively trying to make himself smaller, hiding from a threat he knew couldn't be avoided.

"Sir, are you still there? If you don't keep speaking, the connection will be lost."

"Who was outside my door?"

"As I explained, I have seen nothing on the camera."

"Are you sure it is my front door you are looking at?"

"Hmph! Yes. Sir, very sure. There is no one there."

"Get someone up here, now!" James studied the wall of glass, looking for some way in or out before adding, "And it better be quicker than five minutes."

"Yes, sir. I will head up immediately."

James flashed his hand over the light beam. After the beep, he whispered, "Turn off the ambient lights."

"Sir, the remaining lights are there for your safety and convenience. They cannot be extinguished."

Angrily, he glared at the glass. The shadow was gone, yet he still felt a presence that was filling all his senses, reminding him of a firework that had gone off. His mind filled in the color, shape, and sound of the phantom even though it was gone.

When the light beam loudly beeped off, James felt like he was going to crawl out of his skin. Taking a deep breath, he screamed, "Who's there?" The words trailed off into an echo in the cold room. Wondering what he had got himself into, James waited over a half-hour for the tall man to enter the room.

The next morning, ten minutes before the appointed time for orientation, James was sitting on a bench in the main atrium. The memories of what he experienced last night drifted like a fog in his mind. Beyond the confusion of what he could only assume was his first remembered dream, he had woken up wearing a bracelet like the one Ms. Iblis had on.

Frantically, he rubbed the skin around it, making it turn a deeper red. He had spent twenty minutes trying to remove the bracelet, irritating the skin close to the point of bleeding. The eye that was the symbol of the organization stared directly back as if it was taunting James. Every time one of the other disciples staying in the facility went by, he pulled down his sleeve, hiding the symbol that would prove his devotion to something he did not believe in. There was a mixture of young and old moving throughout the expansive space. Everyone looked like they were moving in slow motion, as if the air was thicker, impeding their progress.

All the inhabitants looked docile, pleased to have a time where there was little to think about other than relaxing. From where he sat, he could count a dozen security cameras and four workers dressed all in white, like the man who showed him to his room, all of them silently watching those in their care. The slower pace, coupled with the disturbance last night, was making him frantic. With no connection to the outside world and nothing to do but wait for instructions that felt more mysterious with each passing minute, James now wished he had pushed harder last night for a meeting with Ms. Iblis. Now he was forced to see the tall man once again. He watched as he came up the corridor, standing more than half a foot taller than everyone else in the long hallway.

"Good morning, Sir."

Ignoring the salutation, he raised his arm up. "Who put this on me, and how did they do it?"

"Sir, that was given to you last night when you arrived at your meeting with Ms. Iblis."

"It was not!" The words were icy through clenched teeth. Holding his temper made his face feel warm as if he had a strong fever. In a way, he wished he did. It would at least allow him to explain away a few of the things he considered to be hallucinations. "Take this off. Right Now!"

"I will have to put in a request with maintenance for that. It requires a special tool. We found that necessary when a few of the bracelets were lost. The ore of which it is made is of great value."

"You told me you are maintenance. Take it off."

"That is not my exact department. Therefore, I would not be able to do that. Don't worry. It only takes a few hours for that type of request."

"I want to see Ms. Iblis." James took a step toward the man, immediately feeling foolish as he was dwarfed by him.

"I spoke to her this morning. She said she would meet you in the cafeteria after your orientation."

"I need to see her now." Not willing to show weakness to the giant standing before him, he struggled to arrange his face.

"Sir, that is not possible. The orientation is only a few minutes long. You might as well get it out of the way."

"When she comes, will she be able to show me the security footage from outside my room last night?"

"I couldn't say." The tall man took a half step closer, towering over James. "Shall we move on to the theater room for your orientation? If we don't, we will be late."

James felt physically threatened for the second time in the last twelve hours. Quickly, he said, "As soon as we finish, put the request in to have this removed." He raised his arm, holding the symbol inches from the man's face.

"As you wish. Please, the room is just this way."

Expecting a long walk—everywhere he had gone so far felt like at least a mile away—he was very surprised when they entered a door just beyond the escalator. There were lights in tubes running the length of the floor as they entered an enclosed draped area with theater seats. They were the old-fashioned fold-down kind that is bolted to the floor. "Please sit wherever you feel comfortable. I would, however, recommend the back seats. I will go start the film."

Sitting near the back, James settled in, staring at the large rectangular screen. The film began in total blackness after the running lights turned off. An attractive woman in an Institute suit sat behind a control desk like the one Ms. Iblis had sat at last night. The audio was not synchronized with the film, giving it a surreal quality. She opened with a brief history of the founder, explaining how their religion came from his extensive study in foreign lands. She then told of the great awakening that was about to come to anyone who was truly ready to receive enlightenment. After nearly twenty minutes of meaningless dialogue, James felt very disappointed, expecting some kind of rationalization for all that he had read and experienced up to this point. When the film was over, he sat alone in the barely lit room, waiting for the tall man to return. After a short time, he realized he would not. Feeling exhausted, he found his way back to the main hallway, wondering what type of trouble he had wandered into.

When he got to the cafeteria, hoping to find Ms. Iblis, Shirley was sitting in the same booth as they did last night. He sat down, and she loudly asked, "So, what did you think?"

It took him a second to process the simple question. "About?"

"Duh, the orientation." She gave a mock shocked expression.

"It was fine. Honestly, I was underwhelmed." Shifting in his seat, he felt like getting up and walking to release the anxiety that was building up inside him.

"I felt exactly the same way. After the buildup of coming here, I think it is natural to expect some kind of great display. Instead, it is a cheap film about how they expect complacency during your stay."

"Yeah." Although he wanted to shout and ask her if she knew what was going on, the word came out nearly in a whisper. He held everything inside, some part of him reluctant to confirm that something was very wrong.

"Have you met anyone else?"

"No. I slept pretty late, then went right to the orientation." He stared at her pretty eyes, looking for anything that would give him a clue if she could be trusted. All he saw was warmth, but instinct stopped him from saying anything else.

"Well. How did you sleep?"

"It wasn't much different from other nights." After his lie, he thought he saw a brief flicker of recognition.

"That will change." Her eyes narrowed, causing slight wrinkles in the corners of her eyes. The pain conflicted with the wide smile.

"How?"

"You will see for yourself." Her head darted to the right. "Hey, you see that guy over there with the long beard?" She pointed with a nod, making her hair flip.

James couldn't tell if he found the way she jumped from one topic to the next annoying or endearing. He glanced over his shoulder. "Yes."

"That's Captain Trepps. Do yourself a favor and stay as far away from him as possible. He is odd, and not in a good way odd. And an incredible bore."

"How did he get the designation of captain?" The humming seemed to increase, making it hard to concentrate. James rubbed his temples, trying to relieve the building tension.

"No clue, man. He talked to me for like an hour, and it never came up."

"Oh." Trying to sound casual, he changed the subject, attempting to get answers to the vastly building questions running through his mind. "So, what do you do all day?"

"Eat and sleep like everyone else."

"There are no other activities?"

"Not that I am aware of. Meals are big around here. It's the only time everyone comes out of their overpriced cocoons. That is why I got here so early, to get us a premium seat. I like it here because you can see down the long hallway." Her gaze drifted to her right.

"Don't you get bored?"

"Oddly... no. If I were home doing nothing like this, I would go crazy. But here, it feels calm and normal."

James had been hoping the feelings he'd had towards her in their first meeting would have gone away. The last thing he needed was the complication of a woman. Tired of holding it all in, he blurted out, "Are your dreams different here?" Hoping the words didn't show the anxiety increasing his heartbeat, he studied her. Her head twitched slightly after the question, and James thought he could see recognition in her eyes. Before she could answer, Ms. Iblis came to the booth, appearing as if from nowhere.

"I was told you needed to see me."

James nearly leaped out of his seat, grabbing the woman he saw as his salvation from whatever insanity he had inadvertently entered. "I need to speak to you in private."

She pulled out an ultra-thin tablet and slid her finger across the surface. "If this is about your... disturbance last night, it would be better if we met later this afternoon. By then, I will have had a chance to fully review the entire matter with my staff."

"I don't think you understand. It is vital that I speak to you now."

"As I said, it will be better to wait. I will be by in the afternoon, and we can discuss anything you would like." Turning, she looked at Shirley. "I would like to remind you that we encourage you to dine with different people at each meal."

"Yes, I remember you mentioning that." Shirley quickly looked away from the woman's piercing glare.

"Please keep that in mind. We have our rules for very specific reasons. Well, Dr. Aickman, I will leave you to enjoy your lunch.

Now that you have finished your orientation, the rest of the day is yours to do with as you wish." Abruptly, she turned and walked away.

James hopped out of the booth and nearly knocked over the thin woman. Leaning into her, he said, "What happened last night?"

Staring at him as if he was a venomous snake, she spoke sternly. "Doctor, please. As I mentioned, I do not have time for this."

She continued walking away, not waiting for any further comments. James, with his frustration bubbling over, tagged along. "You will make time, or I will be making a call to the authorities." He could no longer control his fear. The words came out much too loud, drawing the attention of the few who were slowly gathering in the cafeteria. Trying to appear as if he had some control, he quickly smiled and took a half step back.

She turned. "And say what? That you woke in the middle of the night because a dream startled you?"

James saw a door open next to the cafeteria bay. In the darkened opening, he could barely make out the outline of a man wearing a glass shield obscuring his face. The glass had the same foggy reflection that all the glass in the facility had, giving the guard an inhuman aspect. He took a half step back, becoming enveloped in a shadow from the beam above. Just as he was about to disappear completely, James noticed he was holding a long, truncheon-like object that resembled a cattle prod. He took a deep breath, saying, "You know that isn't true."

"I appreciate that you earnestly believe that you thought you heard something, but I assure you that nothing took place outside your room last night."

"Then show me the tape."

"To accomplish what? Do you really think if we were in a conspiracy to hide something from you, we wouldn't delete the footage? Please, Doctor, I really must go now." Slowly, she began walking toward the door that was now only open a few inches.

"As I said, later, we can meet and discuss the matter in greater depth. If you insist on speaking to the authorities, as you said, I can make those arrangements. But understand that after you do, I will require you to leave immediately. I can't have these disruptions interfering with my other guests' experiences."

"I am not the one causing disruptions." James raised his arm, waving the bracelet around. "Do all your guests have these placed on them against their will while they sleep? Is that a common policy for you to sneak into your guests' rooms?"

"Doctor. You put that on yesterday in my office. I don't know what you are trying to accomplish with these antics, but you really must stop." The tiny woman's face softened. With her free hand, she reached out and touched James's arm. "I am sorry that you had a rough night, but please, I ask that you keep your temper and be careful when making such claims. I really must go now."

"What did you put in my food?"

"Pardon?" Her voice rose.

"What do you put in the food to induce... hallucinations?"

"Doctor Aickman! I do not know what you are referring to."

"Last night, for the first time in my life, I had a dream." He leaned in close, lowering his voice. "It was so real that I thought I was actually living someone else's life."

"Doctor, as you know, an accusation like that is a very serious thing. I can assure you nothing is added to the food. Are you sure you are feeling all right? You don't look at all well."

"Besides being filled with anxiety by whatever it is you do here, I am just great." He waved his hands in the air.

Slowly scanning the room, he saw a small crowd gathering, including two very fit men wearing Institute shirts. Knowing that if he continued to push, the job would be over, and he couldn't afford to leave until it was, he added, "I apologize for any trouble I caused. I didn't sleep well and am a little out of sorts."

"Are you sure?"

James lowered his wrist and slowly pulled his sleeve over the bracelet. Fighting to sound sincere, he quietly said, "Yes. Let me catch up on my sleep, and I am sure I will be more myself."

James watched Ms. Iblis head to the door marked private. Her heels echoed on the polished floor. He walked the few steps back to the booth, trying to avoid the stares of the others in the room.

"What was that all about?" Shirley leaned in. The table, which had no visible means of support, made a creaking noise.

"Nothing." He leaned back as far as the booth would allow.

"Are you sure?"

"Really, it's nothing. I just had an issue with one of her people. It's taken care of now." James looked at the camera that was pointed directly at their table. The glass surface reflected only bright white as if the room had nothing to reflect.

"I don't care for her. In fact, I believe that woman has it in for me."

Feeling hopeful that his paranoia was not baseless, he responded, "Why is that?"

"Nothing I can quite explain. It's just a feeling. Kinda like you get when you first go out on a date. You know what I mean? It's like you like or dislike someone for no good reason."

"Yeah. I know what you mean." He wanted to open up and tell her everything he was thinking, but he couldn't. For a few quiet seconds, he watched her nibble the ends of her blonde hair, the dampness turning it a brownish color. "What was that about not eating with the same people?"

"They have some odd rules around here. I guess they think it is best if we don't compare notes, but I don't know for sure. She has a habit of appearing at every meal I am at. It makes me wonder if she was just coming by right now or if she intentionally was seeking me out." She glanced at the closed door. "I don't like the way the staff disappears behind those doors. It's very off-putting. Maybe I am just being paranoid, though."

James wanted to tell her he was the one being watched but thought better of it. In the distance, the rolling shutters opened, showing menus of various foods. James looked at her, asking, "I guess it's time to eat?"

With a smile, she got up and headed toward the Asian food section. Over the next hour, as they ate and talked, he learned very little from Shirley, except that he was growing fond of someone he couldn't be with.

Later that afternoon, alone in his room, James was near sleep. The room was dark and eerily empty, but James felt like the entire room was moving. The sensation was so strong that he slowly put his foot on the floor, thinking this would help him regain his equilibrium. Feeling cold metal and a very gentle vibration, he stopped fighting and let sleep overtake him. Within seconds, he was once again in someone else's memory, having the ability to both see and hear secret inner thoughts. The voices were at first foggy and distant, but then, the images became vividly clear as if he was in the room.

Hal did little to disguise his amusement. With a smirk, he said, "To be clear, you said guarantee to extend my life, right?"

"Yes, sir."

"And how do you go about doing that?"

Bruce looked at Walter. "Mr. Crenshaw, please don't take offense, but I have to ask you to leave the room before I continue."

Hal interrupted, "Anything you say to me can be said in Walter's presence."

"This will get very personal."

"I understand, and it is not an issue."

"I am warning both of you it would be in everyone's best interest for this conversation to be held between only you and me, sir." He knew Hal wasn't going to budge. A man in his position rarely did. "If you want him here, I am going to have to insist that Walter

allow me to retain his services as my temporary legal counsel to ensure confidentiality."

Reading Walter's thoughts, Bruce continued, "In our previous encounter, you were aware of the result, not my method. I am afraid I must insist." Bruce pulled out his wallet and removed a hundred-dollar bill—the smallest he had—and handed it to him. "Please accept this as a consultation fee." Quickly he added, "That is, of course, if Mr. Dahlton is still okay with the arrangement?"

"Take his damn money if it makes him feel better."

Walter did so with a sigh. "I accept."

"Thank you for indulging me. I know you might find it unnecessary, but to me, secrecy is of paramount importance."

In an irritated voice, Hal asked, "With that out of the way, please explain yourself."

Bruce crossed his legs and, with his thumb and forefinger, went over the crease in his dress pants with deliberation. "I am able to trade a year of my life for six months of yours. During that time, you and I will share a consciousness, and you will be in perfect health. Let me be clear about that, perfect health for a man of your age—"

Hal interrupted, "Walter, what kind of bullshit is this?"

"It isn't bullshit, Hal."

"How could it not be?"

Walter looked at Bruce. He continued, "There is no explanation I can give that you will accept, so let me say this first. Before I entered this room, you were dreaming of riding a horse through clouds. You weren't frightened at the thought of plummeting to the ground as you flew. You were frightened because the horse had no saddle. It reminded you of your childhood friend who was thrown from a horse riding bareback. You were there to witness the pain he suffered from that event, and it changed the way you saw the world. That was the first moment you realized the complete randomness of life and how little actual control you had. You have thought of your friend Charles's pain nearly every day since then and realized that it could have just as easily been you that day who fell and changed your entire future." Bruce could sense Hal's overwhelming sense of calm.

The shipping tycoon let his guard down and spoke with the slight Alabama accent he had fought so hard to hide from his many business acquaintances all his adult life. He was not proud of his roots and constantly suffered from the many harsh realities they represented. "How could you possibly know that?"

"I can tell you every dream you have ever had, Mr. Dahlton if you are thinking of them in my presence. How is of little consequence. What is, is the fact that it gives me the ability to help you extend your life. I can feel your distrust and the struggle you are having because you want to believe what was just said, even though deep down, you know you shouldn't. I know that what I am telling you is fantastic, more than fantastic. It is unbelievable, but I assure you, what I am telling you is the truth."

"I need to know how." Hal sat up as straight as he could, struggling against the pillows for support.

"Dreams are preparation for the afterlife, Mr. Dahlton. Every fragment of your experiences, good or bad, is filtered and recorded in your subconscious mind nightly during the process of sleep. You only remember fragments of some of the more intense moments. However, when you pass over to the afterlife, your subconscious is released, and your spirit lives in a realm of those experiences."

Not letting him finish, Hal interrupted, "So you don't really die?"

"The way I prefer to describe it is you are no longer active in this world. So, the proper way to phrase this would be that your body perishes, but your experiences live on through eternity."

"How do you know this?"

"Because I am what is traditionally referred to as a ghost. Before you say anything, please let me finish. I know how crazy that sounds. I choose to use the term because it is easily recognized and it is quite apt. I am very much alive by any comparable standard. However, my time has already come and gone, and yet I am still here among *the living. After I passed, for whatever reason, my subconscious mind would not let go. In the spiritual realm, this is a complete impossibility, so I... came back. This has left me anchored to both worlds since it happened so long ago."*

"How long ago?"

Bruce could hear the thoughts of the normally practical businessman, who believed in the existence of no problem that couldn't be solved with his wealth and influence.

He was starting to believe what this stranger was saying. He knew it was dangerous, and the belief was based on his desperation. Like the audience member who wanted to believe the magician could make the pretty assistant disappear, he was a willing participant in what, to his mind, had to be an illusion. "I am three times your senior, sir."

"And during all that time, you have had your... ability?"

"Yes."

"Before you passed, did you have any awareness of your gift?" The room was getting dark. It was a combination of the snowstorm increasing and the approaching night, which came in the early afternoon at this time of year.

"No, none. I was a very average man in every way. I never thought much of the metaphysical or the afterlife, at least no more than the typical person, until the day I passed away."

Hal looked at Walter and said, "You said you have seen Mr. Lloyd perform his duties before?"

"Yes, it was exactly as he said. He performed his services for a former client."

Bruce felt Hal's internal struggle, fighting to ignore the obvious thoughts invading his mind, and tried to stay focused. It was incredibly difficult, as he felt some hope that he could push back the inevitable.

Staring intently at Bruce, Hal said inquisitively, "So, what exactly would you do for me?"

Bruce knew what the reaction would be, but with little choice, answered, "If I am in the room with you at the moment you pass, I can merge with your subconscious mind. When this happens, whatever is in me that allows me to not die protects your spirit as well." Sadness overtook the dying man as he realized how ridiculous all of this was. Bruce patiently waited as Hal, who made his fortune by reading people, could see the guilt on Bruce's face.

Hal, in a near whisper, grunted, "You may leave now Mr. Lloyd." The words were spoken so lightly neither of the other men clearly heard them. It was as if his vocal cords were protecting him from making an error.

Knowing what he was thinking, Bruce quickly said, "Mr. Dahlton, I don't feel guilty because I am lying. I feel guilty because I can see what you are thinking right now. You were about to ask me to tell you something that nobody else could know to prove my ability. I saw the paddle, sir." Bruce felt the rush of embarrassment, as if it was his own, as he saw Hal's first wife in her stockings and garter belt administer her annual birthday gift to him. Every year after the birthday dinner, the powerful man would indulge in a night of masochism. He would put on his wife's panties, and she would take him over her knee and paddle him until he was sexually satisfied. The embarrassment turned to a deep shame now that the moment was shared. Bruce quickly added, "If you want me to leave, I will, but please understand that once I leave, I will not be coming back."

The shame was overwhelming as Bruce tuned out Hal and moved his attention to Walter. The lawyer was wondering if bringing him here had been a mistake and what his actual motivation for doing so had been. Did he really do this for Hal's benefit, or was he using his clients' money to lure the healer back for his own edification? Their last meeting left so many unanswered questions that Walter knew the true answer.

A knock on the door pulled him from his thoughts. Sveltyania entered the room. Approaching the bed, she said, "Gentlemen, if you would excuse me, I have to administer Mr. Dahlton's medicine now."

There was a loud crashing noise, pulling James from his sleep. He sat up quickly and looked at the front of the room. In the reflection of the glass, he thought he could see the outline of the man he just left in the dream. Bruce's face was expressionless, almost looking as if it was floating in midair. As the realization came to James that if he could see the reflection, it clearly meant he was in the room, he fought dizziness and got to the light beam. After he waved his hand frantically, he whispered, "Turn on the front lights." As the room lit up, the face was gone. There was nothing but open space. Feeling like a child evading the bogeyman in the closet, he yelled into the light beam, "Open the front door!"

"Sir, that isn't a possibility."

"Get me a leader!" As he waited for the attendant to come on, he tried to get the images of what he had dreamed out of his head.

<hr>

The next morning, James was in the corridor, sitting on the edge of a planter that held a very dusty artificial plant that seemed out of place in its surroundings. He was watching the door to Shirley's room when the man in the striped pajamas he had seen his first night there came up to him.

"She's a pretty one, eh?"

His accent could have been Scottish but had a hint of something else. James, raising his eyebrows, mumbled, "Pardon?"

"The girl who stays there. She's a pretty one." He took a seat next to James, so close they were touching. "When I saw you with her the other night, I knew you fancied her."

"I would not say that I fancied her."

"Suit yourself, didn't mean to pry. So, how're you enjoying your stay?"

"Haven't been here long enough to say."

"Name's Robert. Robert Roberts. My father had a bit of what one would call a wry sense of humor." His eyebrows lifted, selling his point.

The man never stopped staring at the door. Wondering if he should offer his hand, James kept his arms folded. "I'm James Aickman."

"Well, nice to meet you. Maybe one day, we can eat together. It's about the only thing here worth doing—other than sleeping, that is. Now, don't take that the wrong way. I'm enjoying every minute, but every once in a while, I wouldn't mind a little more action."

Fearing he might be about to start sharing his definition of 'action,' James quickly changed the subject. "How long have you been here now?"

"A little over a month."

"Oh. How's it been?"

"I have enjoyed my time here. But I do think they're a bit odd with all their secrecy. Their path to enlightenment and all that jazz. I know we aren't supposed to talk about these things, but you seem like a good enough fella. When they come to you and start explaining the afterlife, do yourself a favor and keep an open mind. I didn't, and all it did was delay the inevitable. When you are open, you will know, and it's a great feeling." The man cocked his head and rubbed a nose that showed the telltale signs of alcohol abuse. "Come now, don't look at me like something under your shoe. I'm not a fanatic—at least I don't think I am—but I'm here to tell ya, one fella to another, you have great things to look forward to. When you learn, it'll change you."

"I didn't mean to look any way."

"It's all right, I understand. Heck, I was the same way just a few weeks ago." He leaned in close and lowered his voice. "I would like to tell ya more, but I can't."

"And why is that Mr. Roberts?"

"Just call me Robert. You'll soon understand. You don't have long to wait. They usually come after week two. Another ten days ain't long to wait for the knowledge you will gain. Until then, enjoy the quiet fella."

"How do you know how long I have been here?"

"Wasn't eavesdropping. That ain't proper nor polite, but I heard you when you were talking with the young 'un. My apologies for that, but you were talking pretty loud. Easy to do with a looker like that one."

"I understand." James glanced at the man's wrist, remembering how he looked to be pinned to the table last night. Coming down the corridor, he saw Shirley. She wore a red top, making her stand out. "Robert, it was nice meeting you, but I really must go now."

Nodding toward the young girl, he said, "Bet you do, fella, bet you do."

The look in his eye, coupled with the way he said it, made James's stomach turn. He walked away, taking deep breaths of the cold air. They met in front of large double doors identical to all the others surrounding them. "Do you have a few minutes to talk?"

"Well, let's see?" She put her finger to her lips and darted her eyes upward, mimicking a demeanor of deep thought. "Yes, I believe I can fit you into my sitting around and doing nothing until dinner. Would right now be convenient for you?"

"Yes."

"My place is one door down."

After walking a short distance, she placed her hand on the screen, and the door opened. The interior space was nearly identical to James'. It might have been slightly larger, but with little furniture, it was hard to gauge. No longer able to hold in all the anxiety, he quickly blurted out, "Are you having odd dreams while you are here?"

She let out a quick giggle. "Well, you get right to it. No, I wouldn't say that my dreams are any different here. Why?"

"I think something is happening to me." He wanted to say more, but the words would not come. It was as if his mouth was protecting him from opening up until it felt just right.

Shirley absentmindedly placed her hand over her bracelet and spun it slowly. The metal tugged at her skin, making it wrinkle. "It can be very disorienting being isolated here." She stared past him to the plasma screen as if she saw more than was there. "You will find after a few weeks the feelings will be replaced with calmer thoughts."

"I thought you said you had only been here for a few days?"

"No, I don't remember that." She pulled her sleeve down, covering the bracelet. "Relax, James, it's the only way to finding peace."

"Shirley, I distinctly remember what you said."

"We will have to agree to disagree then, won't we? Hey, why don't we go for a walk? That always makes me feel better."

"Please listen to me. I don't know what is happening."

Her face quickly changed, making her look older. Frowning with arched eyebrows, she said, "We aren't supposed to bring visitors into our rooms. Leave now, sorry." She took a few steps to her bed and the glowing light beam. "I will catch up with you later, OK?" Waving her hand over it, the beep filled the room.

"Hello, Shirley. What can I do for you today?"

"Please open the main door."

The door opened. Across the hall, a pair of workers, one male and one female, stood with fixed smiles, wearing their Institute uniforms, each holding a helmet beneath their arms. They stood staring into the room. "James, please go now."

"What happened to you?"

"Nothing." She took a step forward and leaned in, whispering. "Be careful who you talk to." She extended her hand and shook his.

James left the room, staring at the cameras in the corridor that looked as if they had doubled in number since he last noticed them. Feeling very scared, he walked, staring at the glass walls surrounding him, back to his room. The corridor was wide and open, yet James felt as if the glass walls were narrowing as he walked along with his escorts, wordlessly keeping stride with him. When they finally got to his room, he placed his shaking hand on the screen. Neither of the escorts spoke as he entered.

After having a glass of whiskey from the well-stocked bar, James knew he had to leave. He also knew the reality of returning to the outside world would not be easy and that it would cost him. Pondering if he should wait until the morning to decide, he began drifting off to sleep.

Bruce followed Walter down a very narrow hallway into the kitchen. It didn't fit in with the other rooms. In its utilitarian layout, the spacious kitchen had an unassuming design. The counters were clean but cluttered, much like the exposed stainless-steel shelving above. Walter, turning, asked, "Would you like a drink?"

"No, I am fine."

The lawyer ignored him and poured two glasses: four fingers full of whiskey. After inserting ice cubes, he took the glasses to the worn eating nook that the cook used for his meals, which was nestled in the far corner of the room. Walter slid across the red leather bench and took more of a gulp than a sip. The aged spirits stung the back of his throat. Bruce, seated across from Walter, picked up his glass and brought it to his nose. He breathed in the scent of an aging barrel. With his eyes closed, he placed the glass back on the Formica surface. Apparently, the sniff was enough. With the tip of his finger, he slid the heavy glass to the middle of the table. In his same steady tone, Bruce said, "Why did you schedule this meeting without discussing it with your client?"

The liquor was already reducing the intensity of his stare. "You saw his reaction. If you couldn't share those rather intimate details, what chance would I have to convince him?"

"Fair enough."

"If I may offer one bit of advice, you really shouldn't embarrass him."

"I didn't tell him what to think."

"If you do it again, he will kick you out, even if he has spite himself."

"So be it. Let me remind you: you called me. I can leave right now if you would like."

With a deep sigh, Walter looked at the untouched whiskey, took a sip from his own, and said, "Would you prefer coffee or tea? The coffee here is extraordinary."

Bruce shook his head a quarter of an inch.

"How many times have you done this for a client?"

"Once a year since I discovered the ability. The process is extremely taxing. So much so that each time I take months off in between."

Finally realizing Bruce wasn't going to continue, Walter asked, "How's that?"

Understanding the unique relationship with the lawyer, Bruce took advantage of being able to talk to someone who could not reveal what he said. "Each time I share with my client, it brings me closer to my leaving this world."

"How do you know that?"

"I have been alive for a very long time. It has afforded me vast knowledge."

"How long do you have?"

"More than I would like at the rate I am going." He was not willing to share that he would be alive for at least two more centuries, assuming he kept meeting willing clients.

"So, you would prefer to pass on?"

"Frankly, yes."

"How is that possible?"

Bruce was having a hard time concentrating. It was a typical reaction to being in such a large city. Even in the large penthouse, he could feel fragments of the other tenants' emotional states. Their anxieties, fear, and joys all assaulted him in a constant barrage. The *white noise was easy to ignore when he focused on Hal, who was so close to a place Bruce knew intimately. With only Walter as a distraction, it was getting more difficult by the second. Doing his best to ignore their feelings, he breathed deeply. "It is possible, Walter, because in death, there is peace, or at least, there is a greater peace than is known to the living. From the moment you pass on, you are no longer held back by the teachings of this world or your mortality, as mortality is experienced differently in the spiritual world."*

"How?"

"Your time is spent reliving what you did while alive. Once you cross over, the only memories you have are what you have stored over a lifetime of sleeping." Bruce could hear the barrage of thoughts from the man sitting across from him. In response to his unasked questions, he continued, "The memories are as real as if they were actually happening. You look, feel, and act as you did when you were alive. The only difference is everything you do is predestined, although it feels authentic. All who have passed are unaware that they are reliving their earthly life. Each day, they wake to these experiences, and it is as if they are new regardless of how many times they are remembered."

"And that continues infinitely?"

"Yes."

"All of your experiences?"

"Yes, good or bad, nothing is exempt in the afterworld." Bruce could feel the impact of his last comment. Reliving his childhood was one of the worst things Walter could imagine. Bruce added, "It is not as bad as all that. The bad moments do not share the same quality of time. You relive them, but it goes by at a vastly accelerated pace."

The swinging door to the kitchen opened, and the nurse in her perfectly pressed white scrubs entered the room. Bruce sensed Walter's longing as he looked at her in the bright light of the kitchen and, for the first time, noticed how her eyes held a knowing gentleness, adding to his already growing attraction. It was more than just seeing her away from his sick friend and the grimness of the death room that

Hal was bound to. Thinking it had to be the way she carried herself when not on duty that brought out her sexuality, he sipped his drink.

Staring at Walter, she politely said, "Mr. Dahlton is ready to see you." She smiled warmly before walking back to the hallway to her room. The simple gesture gave the middle-aged woman a girlish appearance.

Bruce slid across the leather booth. Walter reached out over the table, firmly grabbing the slender man's arm. "And what about the good moments?"

"They, too, are subject to time. To those who lived well, they go by much slower."

"If the afterlife is as good reality, if not better, why do you help people live longer?"

James felt a hand on his arm. Groggy, he opened his eyes, and the man from his dream was standing before him. Spilling the remnants of his whiskey on his lap, he sat up from the chair. The handsome man stood to the side with a curious look on his face.

"James, can you see me right now?" His head moved slightly to the right as if he was examining a complex puzzle.

"What are you? How did you get into my dream like that?"

He waved his hand in front of James's face. When James flinched, Bruce's eyes opened wide. "You can see me!"

"Why are you here?" Not waiting for a response, he pushed past the dream man, walking toward the glowing signal.

Bruce called out in a voice that was unlike his own, much less dignified. "Pin him!"

James's arm was pulled violently to the table. The bracelet that held him in place felt like a magnet. He pulled with all his strength; the metal band didn't budge an inch. Looking up at the man, he called out in a squeaky voice, "What are you doing?" He yanked again, using his other arm as leverage. With a grunt, he gave up. "Release me immediately."

Bruce sat down on the chair opposite James. Crossing his legs, he straightened the pleat in his pants. "I will, in time."

"How did you do that?" He looked at the light beam, then back at the bracelet, punctuating the question with his eyes.

"I am still sharing Hal's subconscious. When he had this place created, the programmers' built in access to all the functioning systems for him." He looked around the room before adding. "Stop all recordings."

After a beep, the digital voice said, "Recording stopped, sir."

Fighting against the restraints, he said, "You have been observing me?"

"Not me. Your captor has." Bruce stared at James. "You have figured it out, haven't you? That you will not make it out of here. Well, at least not intact."

James gave up on pulling at the metallic band and slumped forward. "What is going on?"

"What you saw in the dream was real."

"How can that be?" The words evaporated into the silence. "All of it?"

"Yes. What you experienced was exactly how the conversation happened over a decade ago. Since then, I have been stuck, lending myself to Hal."

"But in the dr... conversation, you said it would only be for six months."

"Yes, that was the arrangement. At least, it was until Hal hired someone to find me. When they did, I was stuck in a deep sleep, lending myself to him. Since then, they have kept me under sedation, blocking my return with endless disciples. That is why he started this clinic. He brings new people in and lends his subconscious to them for days at a time without their consent or knowledge. During that time, they see glimpses into the future, becoming 'enlightened.'" The normally stoic man let out a grunt of a laugh. "Between joining with others and the sedation, he prevents me from catching up with him. Keeping him alive."

"Why don't you approach him like you're appearing to me?"

"I haven't been able to. I think I can with you because you don't dream. This creates a conduit."

James wanted to still be asleep, but he knew he was awake, giving him little choice but to believe the unbelievable. Ignoring all else, he went back to the dream and remembered what Bruce had said. "So, when you die, your memories live on?"

"Yes. As you experienced me telling Hal, every night when you sleep, they are stored, and once that occurs, that becomes your new reality."

"What if you don't dream?" James didn't want to know the answer, but he couldn't hold it back.

"When you end this life, all will end. I am sorry to have to tell you that."

James could see the pain on Bruce's face. Remembering from the dream that he could see and feel anyone around him, his sadness sunk in, making his chest feel as if it was being stepped on. Each breath took effort as his mind raced out of control. Of all the thoughts that were running through his mind, he could not stop obsessing about why he was there. If he hadn't taken this assignment, none of this would have happened.

In answer to his thought, Bruce said, "Dwelling on the hows and whys will only lead to suffering." Bruce looked at the door. "We haven't much time. It will not take them long to discover that I overrode the recording mechanism." Bruce looked at the glowing light. "I am going to trust you because I know I can. Release him."

There was a beep, and then his arm came free. James rubbed the area around his wrist, feeling as if the metal was still pulling his arm down. Adrenaline caused his legs to shake, yet he knew he wouldn't run. "What did you mean we haven't much time?" Panic surfaced in waves, making his heart feel heavy.

"Will you willingly allow me to take over your subconscious?"

"No! Why?!"

"Because it will end my connection to Hal."

"How do you know that?"

"Right now, I can't feel him, so, yes, it should." Bruce closed his eyes and bunched up his fists. "I don't for sure, but I strongly suspect it will work."

"How long will you take over?"

"That, I don't know."

"Who will be in control?" His mind raced, thinking of the others in the complex and realizing they were all there serving Hal.

"To answer your first question, I will be in control for as long as I need to get clear of Hal. To answer your reason why, I help people to live longer because I have many sins to atone for. Giving others slightly more time to correct their behavior is the best way I can think of to do that. If I didn't, they would face an eternity of experiencing mainly bad moments, never escaping them."

"If we all eventually are reliving our past lives in a continuous loop without awareness, then how does anyone know what is real?" Frantically, he tried to remember anything that happened before he came here, coming up with only brief fragments of thoughts.

"The much more relevant question would be, why would that matter to either of us, James? If you are content on any plane of consciousness, why yearn for more? It is the conceit of man to want everything to be explained instead of just simple acceptance that we exist purely to experience all that is around us. Through this acceptance, you will never have to face the cruelty of apparently finite mortality."

Bruce waited patiently, living inside James's thoughts for a few moments more. It took effort for James not to press for a more concise answer. He knew the judgment it would draw from the youthful-looking, ancient man staring intensely at him. It wasn't pride that stopped him. It was fear. Bruce watched James's face drop as he struggled to decide what reality he was currently experiencing. The weight of the thought accelerated, making him feel as if he aged several years as the seconds ticked by. Every joint ached, and it felt as if electricity was being inserted into his veins.

Bruce responded gently to James's frantic mind. "Some mysteries are best left unanswered, my friend. As the saying goes, happiness comes to he who always lives today as if it is his last."

James thought longingly of Shirley and the closeness he had felt toward her since their first meeting. Suddenly realizing for the first time the complete futility of worrying about what tomorrow would bring, James took a deep, cleansing breath. As he struggled to remember anything other than the last few days, James felt terror that layered him in a cold sweat, unable to shake the feeling that he had done all of this before.

ABOUT THE AUTHOR

Jason Fischer is a horror and crime author specializing in anthologies. His recent works have appeared in over a dozen books and magazines. He lives in the far south Chicago suburbs with his wife Julie.

MORE CHILLS FROM VELOX BOOKS

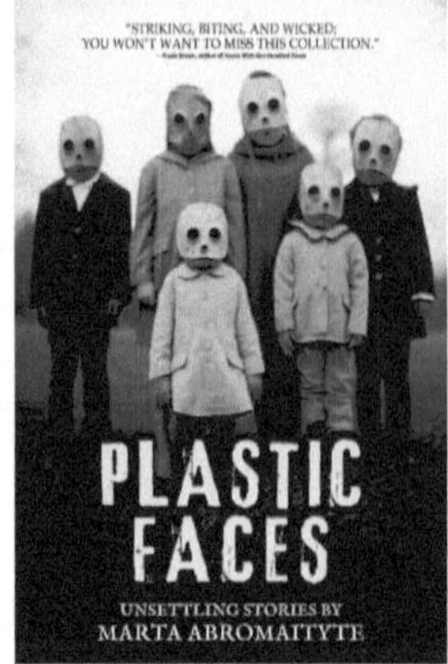

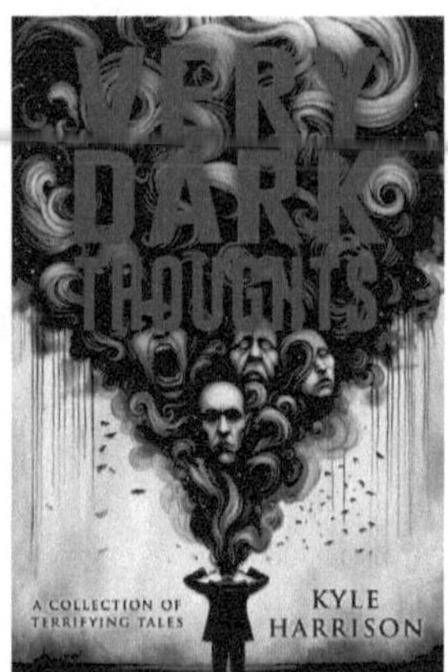

MORE CHILLS FROM VELOX BOOKS

MORE CHILLS FROM VELOX BOOKS